NIGHTS OF THE ROUND TABLE

"We still have to do our job," said Howard Morris. "If the Russians are mounting an operation against us over here we can't hand it to the British. It's our baby and we're paid to look after it."

Mosby looked at Shirley. So that was why two innocent American citizens, who were not at all innocent, were about to sucker an innocent British citizen, who was also not in the least innocent.

"But as to why Dr. Audley will help you," the CIA man changed the subject smoothly, "he will because he simply won't be able to resist it. The historian in him will snap at Badon Hill and King Arthur—and the intelligence man in him will snap at the puzzle. It's as near as dammit a psychological sure thing, knowing the way his mind works."

• • • • •

OUR MAN IN CAMELOT

OUR MAN IN CAMELOT

BY

ANTHONY PRICE

THE MYSTERIOUS PRESS

New York • London • Tokyo

MYSTERIOUS PRESS EDITION

This Mysterious Press Edition is published by arrangement with
the author.

Cover design and illustration by Stanislaw Fernandes

Mysterious Press books are published in association with
Warner Books, Inc.
666 Fifth Avenue
New York, N.Y. 10103
A Warner Communications Company

Printed in the United States of America

First Mysterious Press Printing: May, 1988

10 9 8 7 6 5 4 3 2 1

For John Grassi

PROLOGUE:

*Captain Finsterwald
and
AIC Merriwether*

THE MAILMAN DELIVERED the packet just as Captain Finsterwald and Airman First Class Merriwether had finished searching Major Davies's cottage.

The click of the letterbox flap caught Harry Finsterwald halfway down the stairs. With letter-bombs uppermost in his mind he froze where he was and waited until the delivery had been accomplished. By that time, however, he was reassured about the packet's contents, because with the treatment it had received, if it could ever have exploded it would have done so already. It had been too wide for the aperture, and folded double it was almost too fat, but not quite; with a dry rasp of disintegrating paper it tore its way into the cottage, hung for a moment by a tattered corner, and finally dropped with a dull thump on to the mat.

Merriwether's black face appeared round the sitting room door as the sound of the mailman's footsteps died away in the distance.

"He got some mail?" Merriwether sounded surprised.

Finsterwald looked down at the crumpled packet. "Some

sort of catalogue. Or maybe a circular." He turned it over with his foot. "Nothing interesting."

"That figures. You finished upstairs, Harry?"

Finsterwald nodded. "Uh-huh. He's clean."

"Same here. He's so clean it hurts."

"*Was* so clean. Nothing in the desk? Nobody write to him?"

"If they did he didn't keep their letters. Just bills in the desk, and not many of them. Seems he liked to pay cash."

Finsterwald frowned at him. "You don't reckon so clean is too clean, maybe?"

The big negro shrugged. "Nothing to say it is, and they checked him out good before he did that little job for them in Israel. No next-of-kin, no girlfriends, far as we know, so no one to write him. Like they say, he was a loner. Some pilots, they're like that."

Finsterwald grunted disapprovingly. "Just a goddamn birdwatcher, and birds don't write letters."

"Not his kind, anyway." Merriwether wiped his face with his handkerchief. "There's a pile of his bird books back there . . ." He thumbed over his shoulder, ". . . funny thing though . . ."

"Funny thing?"

"They's all brand new, almost never been opened. You'd have thought, the way he was always looking out for them, they'd have been more—dog-eared, I guess. Like my Air Force Manual."

Finsterwald nodded. It had become a standing joke between them which no longer required even a smile, the Air Force Manual. "Maybe he knew it all too."

"Which is more than we know about *him*." Merriwether looked round uneasily. "Eighteen years in the service, but nobody really knew him. High security rating, flew planes, watched birds. Period."

"He was one damn good pilot. Remember that citation in the file for those Hanoi bridge pictures—like he was a little bird perching on the girders?"

Merriwether looked down at the Busy Lizzie plant on the

window-sill. It was just beginning to droop for lack of water.

He shrugged again. "So he was a good pilot. But not good enough when it came to the crunch."

"We don't know that, Cal." Finsterwald sat down on the stairs.

"That's right. We don't know that. Nice day, not too high, not too fast, no malfunctions, navigator transmitting, radar plot on course—then *pow*! No pilot, no co-pilot, no plane, no *nothing*." He pointed a long brown finger like a stick of milk chocolate at Finsterwald. "And that's what we got—nothing."

"'Like it was a missle'," quoted Finsterwald.

"Except we know it wasn't, because there was nothing in that whole bit of sea to throw it at them."

"Which the British confirm," agreed Finsterwald. "And their radar cover's on the top line in the Irish Sea these days, you can bet." He paused. "So it had to be the plane —okay. So we'll recover the wreckage and then we'll know. Don't get so hot."

"Then we'll still know *nothing*—" the chocolate finger jabbed the air savagely "—because we'll still not know *why*."

"Means they got a man on the base at High Wodden."

Merriwether laughed. "Oh, man—tell me something I don't know. They got a man at Wodden—we got a man at Archangel. Every base with a major nuclear strike capability we got men at, they got men at, sweeping away the snow, tending to the garbage, delivering the goddamn laundry . . . But you tell me, Harry—you just tell me why their man 'ud want to knock down one little old RF-4c on a routine training mission over the Irish Sea."

Harry Finsterwald stared at his feet. "Well, it sure wasn't because they didn't want us to see something, because Davies wasn't on a fixed mission course. They wouldn't know where the hell he was going until too late."

"Right. And if I wanted to keep something under wraps

in that whole area I wouldn't turn it into an air-sea rescue zone." Merriwether shook his head.

"And it wasn't just to screw us up, because they'd have taken out an F-111, not an RF-4c."

"Right again. So it has to be the crew—and the way young Collier checks out all the way down the line he wasn't the one. One will get you ten he was an innocent bystander. And for my money, one will get you a hundred that it was Davies, clearance or no clearance." Merriwether looked round the hallway suspiciously. "I can't put my finger on it, man, but there's something about this place that doesn't feel right. Like there's something I've missed."

"They should never let aircrew live off base," grumbled Finsterwald. "They got every last thing they need there, for God's sake."

"Except birds, maybe."

"They got those too. With feathers and without."

"But he was only interested in the feathered kind. He even used to walk down the runways spotting them."

Their eyes met in perfect disbelief and perfect accord. What was too good to be true could never be safely accepted: it was the vacuity of Major Davies's personal file that was damning. Because like nature, the CIA abhorred a vacuum.

"So we re-check everything," said Finsterwald.

"Every last goddamn thing, man." Merriwether smiled at his partner. "Starting with the mail."

Finsterwald bent down and picked up the packet.

> *Major David Davies, USAF,*
> *c/o Rosemary Cottage,*
> *Middle Green,*
> *Paynsbury, Wiltshire.*

He turned it over.

James Barkham & Son,
New, Second-hand and Antiquarian Bookseller,
7-9, Archdeacon's Row,
Salisbury, Wiltshire.

The buff-coloured, manila envelope was already ripped down one side, revealing the edge of a thin grey booklet. Finsterwald inserted his finger in the tear and completed the job.

He stared in wonder at the booklet. "Oh, brother..." he murmured. "Oh, brother!"

Merriwether frowned. "You got something?"

Finsterwald read the address again.

Major David Davies, USAF...

"Harry, what have you got?" Merriwether said sharply.

"What have I got?" Finsterwald looked up for a moment, then down again. "I've got *The Welsh Latin Chronicles: 'Annales Cambriae' and Related Texts. By Kathleen Hughes. Sir John Rhys Memorial Lecture, British Academy 1973. Price 30p net. From the Proceedings of the British Academy, Volume LIX (1973) London: Oxford University Press*. That's what I've got, Cal."

Merriwether shrugged. "So they sent him the wrong thing. He asked for *Birds of Britain* and they glitched the order. It happens."

Finsterwald opened the pamphlet.

"I guess so.... There's a letter here, anyway—and a bill—so whoever it was—" He stopped suddenly. "Uh-uh, it's for real, because it's addressed to him—*Dear Major, Herewith, as per your esteemed order, a copy of Kathleen Hughes's Rhys Memorial Lecture on the Welsh Latin Chronicles*..." He looked up again to meet Merriwether's frown. "There's no mistake. This is what he wanted and this is what he got. There's a lot of other stuff about it."

"Okay, okay. So read the letter, man, read the letter," said Merriwether.

"Well, there's nothing about birds in it—that's for sure."

"So he'd gone off birds, that makes sense. Read the damn thing or give it me, for God's sake."

"All right. Where was I?" Finsterwald bent over the typescript.

"You were up to Welsh Latin Chronicles."

"I've got it—

. . . Welsh Latin Chronicles. . . . As I foresaw, it contains no information of special interest to you, except perhaps a passing reference to Badon on page 7, at the foot of paragraph one, in which it concedes the importance of the battle as a reason for its inclusion in any British chronicle. You will, of course, note the footnote on that page, with its cross-reference to page 13. I can no doubt obtain for you the paper by T. Jones in the Nottingham Mediaeval Studies and K. Jackson's 'Arthurian Literature in the Middle Ages'; L. Alcock's 'Arthur's Britain', mentioned in the same note, you already possess.

"I have so far been unable to obtain the relevant issues of The Transactions of the Honourable Society of Cymmrodrian, but these are notoriously difficult to track down.

"As to the—"

Finsterwald stopped abruptly, as though his pickup arm had been listed off the record.

"Go on," commanded Merriwether. "Don't stop when you've gotten me hog-tied, man."

Finsterwald cleared his throat.

"As to the Leningrad Bede, I can confirm that this is in the Leningrad Public Library (CLA XI, No. 1621), and that it is a handsome manuscript with fine ornamentation, probably copied from the author's original by four scribes at Wearmouth or Jarrow not later than A.D. 747. A complete facsimile of this was published by Arngart of Copenhagen in 1952. I have written to a colleague of mine in Copenhagen with reference to this, but I do not believe that

it contains more of interest than the Cambridge MS which you have already examined. I must advise you that the cost of obtaining this would be considerable, but I will await your instructions in this regard.

"No information is forthcoming from the Russian Embassy about the Novgorod Bede. The official on the cultural attaché's staff to whom I spoke had never even heard of it, and I frankly do not place much reliance on his promise to enquire further into the matter (For the record, incidentally, the splendid euphony of 'Nizhni Novgorod', where the MS came finally to rest, was replaced after the Revolution by the name 'Gorky', after the celebrated revolutionary of that name, so that we should properly refer to the 'Gorky Bede'. But I cannot bring myself to do this).

"The origins of the Novgorod Bede are certainly mysterious, not to say romantic. Legend has it that the MS travelled eastwards to 'New' Novgorod with the great spread of Russian monasticism after A.D. 1200. Although not as fine as the Leningrad MS it is without doubt very ancient indeed. There is a story, though an unsubstantiated one, that it was damaged by fire, possibly during the Revolution but alternatively during a German air raid in 1941 or 2. Gorky was certainly bombed by the Germans, and it was the objective of a great sweeping drive up the Volga from the South—the drive which took them to Stalingrad (formerly Tsaritsyn and now Volgograd—the Communists have no poetry in their souls).

"But I digress—I'll say he digresses—"

"Go on."

"Okay. *But I digress. A friend of mine in Cambridge tells me that there is a particularly acute essay on Badon by the late Professor Bullitt in the 1935 volume of the Transactions of the Cambrian Archaeological Society. TCAS volumes rarely if ever come on the market, but there are complete sets in the Bodleian Library at Oxford and the Public Library at Cardiff.*

"As per your instructions, I enclose a full account of your purchases, rendered to the above date.
"Wishing you all success in your continuing researches,
Yours very sincerely,
James Barkham"

Merriwether was silent for five seconds. "That's the lot?"

"The lot?" Finsterwald stared at him. "What more d'you want for God's sake? He was in communication with the Russian Embassy—a serving officer on active duty. That's not just breaking the rules, boy. That's the rule book down the toilet."

"Hell, man—he asked some bookseller about a book, he didn't ask them himself. And an old book too. So let's not go into orbit till we know what this Bede-thing is. One in Leningrad and the other in Gorky—you know what it is?"

"Never heard of it. Leningrad and Gorky are both non-strategic targets. They're industrial/population primaries— iron and steel, oil refineries, major generating centres. They'd maybe figure in a second strike."

Merriwether started to giggle, then checked himself quickly. "Harry, Harry—he's talking about history books, not nuclear warfare. Old books and old history."

Finsterwald examined the letter again. "Well, he sure isn't talking about birds, and that's the truth," he admitted grudgingly.

"Now there you've got a point," Merriwether agreed. "It looks like his bird watching was strictly for the birds. Seems he was doing one thing for our benefit and another for his own, and *that* is kind of suspicious. Let me have a look for myself."

Finsterwald watched in silence as his partner read the letter.

"'Wishing you all success in your continuing researches'," Merriwether repeated finally. "Whatever he was doing, sounds like he meant business... You ever heard of this battle of—what was it?—Badon?"

Finsterwald shrugged. "Search me. But it'll be easy to look up—unless it's some kind of code-word."

"Uh-uh." The negro shook his head. "If Davies wasn't on the level and this was coded it'd be about birds, not battles."

"Then why the hell the bird cover?"

"We don't know it was a cover. He could have been interested in battles as well as birds. No law says what a man does in his own time."

"And I say it still doesn't add up. It smells from here to—to Novgorod."

"Could be you're right at that..." Merriwether flipped over the typescript to reveal the bill beneath it. For a moment he stared at the list of items casually, then he stiffened. *"Jesus!"*

"What is it, Cal?" His partner's sudden excitement hit Finsterwald like a shock-wave. "Pay dirt?"

"Pay dirt?" Merriwether's lips curled. "Man—I've been slow. I've been one stupid black son-of-a-bitch."

"How?"

Merriwether held out the bill. "Look at it—just look at it."

Harry Finsterwald looked at the list.

The Observer's Book of Birds.

A Guide to the Birds of Britain.

The Bird-Watcher's ABC.

"So he did bird-watch," said Finsterwald.

"He bought a pile of bird books," corrected Merriwether. "That was four months ago—see the date?"

Edward Grey: The Charm of Birds.

British Birds in Colour.

Gildas. De Excidio et Conquestu Britanniae. Trans.

Nennius: Historia Britonum. Trans.

Malory: Le Morte d'Arthur. Trans.

Bede: Historia Ecclesiastica. Trans.

"Bede." Finsterwald looked up sharply.

"Keep going, man."

Geoffrey of Monmouth: Historia Regum Britanniae. Trans.

Alcock: Arthur's Britain.

Morris: The Age of Arthur.

Chambers: Arthur of Britain.

Bullitt: Britain in the Dark Ages (Two vols.).

O'Donnell Lectures: Angles and Britons.

Stenton: Anglo-Saxon Britain.

Finsterwald's eye ran on down the page—

Continued overleaf

"For God's sake—it goes on forever," he protested. "He must have spent a goddamn fortune!"

"Not a fortune. About £200—say about 500 bucks."

"But just on books."

Merriwether grinned. "In four months? On his pay that was just the loose change. If it was women or horses you wouldn't think twice about it."

"But these are—hell, they're weird." Finsterwald slapped the list as though it offended him. *"The Archaeology of Post-Roman Britain. . . . A Gazeteer of Early Anglo-Saxon Burial Sites.* Just those two set him back—nearly 25 dollars. Cash money."

"Cash money." Merriwether echoed the words happily.

"Sure. It says 'cash' down here." Finsterwald consulted the list "As of this moment he owes just 38 pence—30 for the pamphlet and 8 for the postage."

"Exactly right, man. He paid cash money for everything he bought—that's what his cheque counterfoils say. And from the dates on that bill he must have called at that bookshop almost every week to pick up what he'd ordered. Only the last time he must have asked for a full list of what he'd bought—'as per your instructions' it says. And when he didn't turn up last week the bookseller just popped the latest thing in the same envelope and brought him up to date with the news."

Finsterwald nodded. "Okay—so what?"

"Harry—" Merriwether spread his hands "—so this is probably the first letter Barkham ever wrote to him. If he called in every week, and paid cash for what he bought, there wouldn't be any need to write to each other. And the guys who cleaned this place out must have known that. They just didn't know there was a letter in the post."

Finsterwald opened his mouth, then closed it.

"The guys who—? What guys?"

Merriwether waved his hand, for the moment ignoring him. "I knew there was something wrong with this place —it's got a wrong feel to it, like 'who's been sleeping in my bed, man?' Only I was dumb, and I just had to go looking for something that 'ud tell me I had the right feeling."

"For Pete's sake—what guys?" Finsterwald pleaded.

"Who knows what guys? The ones who stopped Davies's mouth. The guys from Nijni Novgorod, maybe, I don't know. But for sure someone's been here before us."

"How do you know?"

Merriwether pointed. "That piece of paper you're holding tells me how. Because there's not one of the books on that list in this house but those five bird books—" He thrust four chocolate fingers and a chocolate thumb at Finsterwald. "So where those books go? They didn't fly away like birds, man. 'And good luck with your continuing researches'—what researches? There's not one scrap of paper in his desk says he was researching anything, nothing . . . And you can't tell me someone who buys all those books doesn't make a single note 'bout what he's working on."

Finsterwald stared at the list.

Keller: The Conquest of Wessex.

"There must be forty—fifty—books here," he said finally.

"Not here now, there aren't. Just five—on bird-watching." Merriwether's derision was unconcealed. "And we nearly bought it, Harry. We came looking for a pilot who watched birds, and that's what we got, and that's what we were meant to get. Until the mailman delivered the mail."

"But for God's sake—" Finsterwald lifted the list "—what would anybody want with *this* lot? It's crazy."

"Not to somebody, it isn't. Looks like the Major researched into the wrong piece of history."

The Tale of Sir Mosby
and
King Arthur

– I –

I<small>T WAS LIKE</small> they said: the seventh wave was often the biggest one.

The last big one had slopped over into the castle moat, smoothing its sharp edges. Then there had been six weaker ones which had all fallen short. And now came the fatal seventh.

Mosby had watched it gathering itself out in the bay. At first it hadn't looked much, more a deep swell than a conventional wave like it's white-capped predecessors. But where they had broken too early and wasted their strength in froth, the seventh had seemed to grow more powerful, effortlessly engulfing the first fifty yards of the line of saw-toothed rocks to the left and only revealing its true nature when it burst explosively over one tall pinnacle which until now had remained unconquered.

As the pinnacle disappeared in a cloud of spray the castlebuilder looked up from his work. For a second he stood still, the sand dropping from his hands, staring at the oncoming wave. Then he swung round and lifted up the toddler beside him and deposited her within the innermost walls of the castle.

Mosby took in the scene with regret. It wasn't just that the big Englishman had been working like a beaver for upwards of an hour getting the castle just the way he wanted it, but also that the end-product was a work of art the like of which Mosby had never seen.

It wasn't just a pile of sand, but a real castle, with inner and outer walls and regularly-spaced towers, each capped with a conical fairy-tale roof, rising to a massive central keep. There was a moat and a drawbridge complete with a barbican and a defensive outwork, all of which had been constructed to a carefully drawn ground plan which had been marked out in the smooth sand before construction had started.

In fact it wasn't only a real castle, but obviously an actual one—he had watched the man count off the towers one by one as though checking them in his memory, finally nodding in agreement with himself that he'd got it right. It was a good bet that somewhere, maybe not far from here, on some hill above some sleepy English town, he'd find a great grey stone pile, dog-eared by centuries of neglect, matching those walls and towers. And maybe once upon a time some highly paid craftsman had built just such a model to show the King of England what he was getting for his cash.

The child's squeal of excitement broke his flash of historical inspiration. Defeat on the natural breakwaters of the rocky headlands on either side of the bay seemed to have concentrated the wave's power: it swallowed the last retreating remnants of the sixth wave and surged forward up the beach towards the castle.

The outer walls and towers were instantly overwhelmed, dissolved and swept away irresistibly as the rushing water encircled the castle, meeting in its rear in a triumphant collision on the site of the drawbridge.

For two seconds the child stood surrounded by the towers of the inner keep. Then, as the wave began to retreat, these last defences cracked and toppled outwards to be swept away with the rest. The ruin of the castle was complete. It was a goddamn pity.

As far as the child was concerned, nevertheless, the breaking of father's masterpiece was the making of the occasion, and presumably that was the nature of the deal between the two because he showed no sign of irritation as she danced in triumph on the wreckage.

"Ozzie, Daddy—say Ozzie," squealed the child.

Shirley lifted her head from the towel on which she lay sunbathing beside Mosby. He saw the little two-way radio tucked under a folded edge and, in the same glance, couldn't avoid also seeing the shapely breasts which had been freed from the bikini top.

"Harry says he's fixed the car," she murmured. "He's getting out now."

"Great." Mosby's eyes felt like chapel hat-pegs.

"And stop peeking, Mose honey. Watch the birdie, not the boobs."

"Say Ozzie, Daddy—Ozzie-mandy!"

Mosby smiled a warm, husbandly smile. "Shirley Sheldon is a shameless slut," he hissed.

"Shirley Sheldon is trying to revive her long-lost tan." She lowered herself back on to the towel. "You just mind the store like a good boy—just keep your mind on our business."

Mosby shook his head in despair and turned back to observe the big Englishman.

"Ozzie-mandy, please, Daddy."

"All right, all right."

The Englishman looked around him, first to his left, then his right and finally behind him. Mosby lolled in his deck-chair as one half-asleep, his arms hanging loosely. There was no one else at all on the tiny beach; either it was not well-known or (which was more likely) Harry had devised some way of temporarily closing the track which led to it.

Secure behind his dark glasses Mosby watched himself being scrutinised. He sensed that there would be no ozziemandying unless he could give the impression of being dead to the world, so as a final piece of encouragement he drew a deep breath and returned it by way of what he judged to be a realistic snore.

The Englishman struck an attitude.

"I met a traveller from an antique land—" he intoned in a deep voice.

"Who said: Two vast and trunkless legs of stone
Stand in the desert . . ."

He accompanied the words with gestures in the style of some great nineteenth century tragedian, the child watching him with her mouth hanging open, obviously understanding nothing, but enjoying everything.

> *"Near them, on the sand,*
> *Half sunk, a shattered visage lies, whose frown,*
> *And wrinkled lip, and sneer of cold command—"*

He paused in order to frown, twist his lips hideously and finally sneer horribly. The child gave two little excited jumps, but made not a sound even when her hands came together.

> *"Which yet survive, stamped on those lifeless things,*
> *The hand that mocked them, and the heart that fed:"*

Mosby was overwhelmed by a feeling of unreality. He knew there couldn't be any mistake, the identification was utterly positive.

> *"And on the pedestal these words appear:*
> *'My name is Ozymandias, king of kings:*
> *Look on my works, ye Mighty, and despair!' "*

Shirley raised her head again, this time clasping herself to herself more modestly. "What the hell's going on?" she grated.

The sound of her voice couldn't possibly have carried

over the crash of the waves; it must have been his own involuntary movement which the man caught out of the corner of his eye.

"Nothing beside remains—" he faltered. Mosby shifted his position, sinking further into somnolence, and snored again obligingly as a warning to Shirley and an encouragement to Ozymandias.

> *"Nothing beside remains. Round the decay*
> *Of that colossal wreck, boundless and bare*
> *The lone and level sands stretch far away."*

Ozymandias bowed to his daughter and the child applauded him. Mosby himself concentrated on adjusting his preconceptions about the British.

But now there was a movement in the corner of his own eye. The man's wife had risen from the tartan rug on which she had been lying and was strolling down towards the sea's edge, a tall willowy ash blonde with that haughty don't-give-a-damn British aristocratic expression which repelled and attracted him at the same time, at least when he encountered it in the female of the species. He smiled inwardly as he remembered arguing with Doc McCaslin over that look, as to whether it was bred or bought, with Doc finally convincing him that if caught young enough any little sow's ear from the East End of London—or Brooklyn—could be converted into this sort of silk purse by English private education. All one needed was forty thousand spare dollars, give or take a few thousand, over ten or twelve years.

The woman stopped at her husband's shoulder. "If the king of kings is ready it's high time we were going. Cathy's had quite enough sun for one day and the tide's coming in fast. And we're late for tea already."

A nice voice, less refined than the expression, with affection taking all the sting out of the marching order. That heart was present, and in working order. Lucky Ozymandias.

Mosby felt envious, but also benevolent. Whatever happened afterwards, he didn't want to spoil this moment of family togetherness: the least—and the most—he could do was to give them a last bit of privacy. He snored again.

"Come on then, love," said Ozymandias, taking the little girl's hand and turning his back on the sea. As he did so another seventh wave swirled round their feet. When it receded the castle site was no more than a dimpled irregularity in the sand. The woman was right, the tide was coming in fast now. Another five minutes and it would be around his own feet, which would account nicely for their own movement from the beach—as he had intended it should.

He waited until the Englishman and his family had reached the cliff path before touching Shirley's shoulder.

"You nearly spoilt it," he explained.

"Uh?" She wrinkled her nose. "Spoilt what?"

"The poetry. He was reciting poetry for his daughter. Shelley I think, or maybe Keats. I guess I'm a bit rusty."

She looked up at him curiously. "Shelley or Keats?"

"One or the other. Shelley for choice."

"Well, well! I sure never would have tagged you as a poetry buff. Sex maniac—yes. Poetry buff—no. Or him, come to that." She stared at the cliff path. "He doesn't look like a civil servant either, come to that—more like a retired quarter-back."

"Don't underrate him." Mosby left the "or me" unsaid. "Remember what Harry said: his IQ goes off the top of the graph."

"If that child of his is already sold on Shelley and Keats then it runs in the family."

Mosby shook his head. "I think she just likes the performance." He stood up, still staring down at her. Sixty-six inches and one hundred and sixteen pounds, all nicely tanned and landscaped. And every inch, every pound, inaccessible. "But now it's time for our performance, Mrs. Sheldon. And we'd better be good."

She rose effortlessly to her knees, fixing the bikini top as she did so. On mature consideration Mosby decided that she was as disturbing with it as without it.

She met his eyes. "You've got that hungry look again, honey. Like you could eat me. It's getting kind of wearisome."

Mosby turned away to gather up the towels. Hungry was right: it was a fact that starvation had to be less bearable when you travelled in permanent company with a three-star Michelin dinner, but it was a fact she would never concede. He was suddenly very glad that they were actually starting work at last.

As they topped the cliff path he saw at once that Harry had done his work well. There were still only two cars in the dusty little parking place, and the Englishman already had his head stuck under the raised bonnet of his.

As he watched, the man straightened up, scratching his head in a gesture eloquent of bewilderment. Very soon, when he realised that the trouble had no simple diagnosis, that bewilderment would turn into the despair of a holiday father marooned with his family five miles from the nearest telephone.

He raised the trunk of the Chevrolet and began to pack their gear. Just a little time now. Shirley was already establishing their curiosity by staring in a frankly American fashion.

Finally she came round the wing of the car.

"Say, Mose honey—" her voice carried clear as a bell in the stillness following the despondent whine of the Englishman's self-starter "—that poor man's having awful trouble with his car."

Mosby straightened up. "Huh?"

"Why don't you go and help him?" There was much more of the Old South in Shirley's voice than usual—it was only half a mint julep away from the Southern belle's "You-all".

Mosby looked quickly at the other car, noted that the Englishman's wife had heard—she could hardly avoid hearing—and was looking at them, and ducked round the side of the car.

"You want me to go and help?" he said loudly.

"I think you ought to, honey." The order was wrapped in velvet pleading. "It'ud be neighbourly."

"I'm no goddamn mechanic. Besides, if he wants help he'll ask for it."

"Honey, *they* don't ask—don't be mean. Go on." The velvet wrap was off and he could hear the Fort Dobson psychologist's final admonition: *the British expect American wives to wear the pants—true or false, they expect it. When Shirley wears them, that's better than waving a marriage certificate.*

"Okay, okay. So I'll be a samaritan if it makes you feel good," he waved his hand in submission before pivoting away from her towards the Englishman's car.

For a moment the Englishman pretended not to see him, then he lifted his head.

"Got some trouble?" Mosby began tentatively.

Understatement of a summer's day. Trouble with a car here and now, and all sorts of trouble to come one way or another if everything goes according to plan.

The pale blue eyes blinked behind the spectacles. "The bloody thing won't start, that's the trouble."

"Could you use a second opinion?"

The Englishman grinned ruefully. "To be honest—I could use a first opinion. It's probably something ridiculously simple, but . . . I'm afraid I'm just not mechanically-minded."

That was what Harry had said, but it was nice to have confirmation straight from the horse's mouth: it made for confidence in other directions.

"Gas okay?" Mosby lent over and sniffed. "Yes, you're getting gas all right. . . . And she turns over, so the battery's fine."

"Doesn't fire . . ." Mosby busied himself doing nothing very much. "No spark—the plugs are okay too—I guess it could be the ignition. And odd things happen with ignition parts, they go faulty for no reason. If there's something wrong with the coil—or maybe the distributor—then you're going to need a garage job . . ."

Shirley was advancing across the open space between the cars, heading towards the wife.

"Have you got far to travel?" she asked.

"Far to go?" The woman was slightly taken aback at the directness of the approach, her natural reserve battling with an equally natural inclination to be courteous with a friendly and helpful foreigner. "No, not very far—six or seven miles. We've got a cottage at Bucklandworthy."

"Bucklandworthy? Say, that's where we are. We're renting the white house on the headland—St. Veryan's."

"Down the road to the lighthouse?"

"That's right." Shirley nodded eagerly. "You know it?"

"Our cottage is on the corner—the Old Chapel—"

"With the thatched roof? Why, that makes us almost neighbours."

Mosby finished his examination of the distributor. "I can't see anything wrong, but that doesn't mean a thing . . ." He shook his head doubtfully.

Shirley craned her neck over his shoulder. "Have you fixed it, honey?"

"'Fraid not." Mosby wiped his oily hands together. "I just don't get it—I guess it must be electrical."

"Is that bad?"

"Well, it looks like a garage job." Mosby looked at the Englishman apologetically. "Like you say, it's probably nothing much, but . . ." He shrugged, frowning again at the engine. At least there was no need for play-acting: whatever Harry had done was bound to be undetectable as well as ingeniously simple.

"Well, not to worry," said Shirley cheerfully. "Because these good people have that thatched cottage just two steps up the road from us at Bucklandworthy—they're our neighbours, honey."

"Huh?" Mosby looked up from the engine. "What did you say?"

Shirley gave her new friend a despairing look. "Once he gets his head in an engine—" her voice sharpened "—they live just next door to us almost, in that cute thatched cottage up the road from St Veryan's."

Mosby allowed the light to dawn. "Is that so?"

"We don't actually live there," the wife explained. "We're renting it for two months."

"Two *months*!" Shirley looked around her. "It really is beautiful down here, but I don't think I could last that long."

Mosby gave a derisive grunt. "Just because we have to pump the water from the well—honey, you just haven't any of the old pioneering spirit. You're a two-bath-a-day girl, that's the trouble."

"I've got plenty of pioneering spirit. I just happen to prefer civilisation and company," Shirley snapped. "But never mind that—" her tone softened "—if you can't get that engine going, just quit playing with it. We can take these good people right home to their door with no trouble at all."

The wife looked uncertainly at her husband, then at her daughter. The child was hanging out of the car window staring round-eyed at Shirley. As well she might, thought Mosby: Ozymandias himself had nothing on Shirley, with the sculptor not born who could read those passions and the ice-cold heart that fed them.

Mosby grabbed the moment of uncertainty. "We surely can—nothing easier. It'ud be a pleasure." He swung towards the man. "Besides, if I know anything about the local garage they're not going to have anyone to send down here straightaway, it'll be more like tomorrow morning. And you sure as hell don't have to worry about leaving the car down here, because no one's going to drive it away."

"Well . . ." The man paused diffidently " . . . it's most awfully kind of you—"

"—it really is," echoed the wife gratefully. "I don't know what we should have done."

"Not at all. There's plenty of room, and like my wife says, it's right there on our way. No trouble at all." The fish was hooked: now was the moment to make sure it didn't escape. He grinned at them both, playing out his assigned rôle to the last syllable. "Come to that, I reckon you'd be doing us a good turn. We haven't said a word to anyone since we've been down here but 'good morning' and "thank you' and we're beginning to feel kind of cut off from society."

"Isn't that the truth!" exclaimed Shirley. "It's been almost as bad as when we got stuck in that village in the middle of nowhere in Spain, and there wasn't one single breathing person who spoke one word of English. I got so tired of my single Spanish phrase—*Hay alguien que hable ingles?*— and the answer was always *No,* which is the same in Spanish as it is in English. *Muchas gracias* and *adios,* that's how I felt."

Mosby gave the man a meaningful look, almost a pleading one, and received a guarded flicker of sympathy in return. So Harry's psychology had been right on the button: the moment of gratitude was also the most vulnerable one. *Remember what the Good Samaritan probably said to the guy as he rolled on the bandages: "Going down to Jericho, eh? Say, maybe you could give me an introduction to the Chamber of Commerce there?"*

"I'm afraid we do tend to be rather stand-offish as a people," admitted the wife apologetically, in an attempt to fill the awkward silence. "It's a national defect, you know."

"I think the language has a lot to answer for," Mosby grinned at her. "I'll never forget Shirley's face when the milkman said he was going to knock her up on Sunday morning. And all he wanted to do was settle the week's bill, but she thought—"

"That'll do, honey," Shirley cut in quickly, frowning at him. "I'm sure these good people would rather be on their way home than hear about how I pay the milkman—"

Mosby caught the Englishman's eye again, saw that the double-entendre had registered, and burst out laughing. "Oh, God, honey—how you pay the milkman—!"

Shirley sighed helplessly as she turned back to the English couple. "You have to forgive my husband . . . There are times when he's just not fit for decent company."

This time the Englishwoman laughed. "I have just the same trouble with my husband. It's the nature of the male animal—'Slugs and snails and—'"

"'Puppy-dogs' tails'," supplemented her daughter. "'That's what boys is made of.'"

"That's right!" Shirley's good humour returned with the discovery of well-informed allies. "And you are made of sugar and spice and all things nice, I can see that right away. And what's your name, honey?"

"Cathy." The little girl extended a small, dirty hand.

"Cathy. Why, that's a lovely name—aren't you lucky!" Shirley shook the hand formally before turning again to the mother. "And I'm Shirley—Shirley Sheldon. And this is my husband, Mose."

"Mosby," corrected Mosby quickly, bitter for the ten millionth time that he had never been able to escape the hideous diminutive.

"Mosby," echoed Shirley, flashing him a malicious smile. "Mosby Singleton Sheldon the Third—he doesn't like anyone to get the idea that 'Mose' is short for 'Moses' but he still answers to it if I smile nicely."

The Englishwoman smiled. "Well, I'm Faith Audley, and this is my husband David."

"Hi, David," said Shirley.

"Hullo." Audley nodded to Mosby. "It's very kind of you to come to our rescue, Mr Sheldon."

Smiles all round, ice broken, small talk in the afternoon sunshine: Hi, David—call me Shirley . . . Hi, Faith—call me Mosby.

Meet your friendly neighbours from the CIA

* * *

They rode in silence for a few moments, while Mosby manoeuvred the big car round the worst of the pot-holes to reach the beginning of the track. But silence was okay at this point; the hook was well and truly fixed, only the fish was a big one and needed careful handling still or it might break the line and get clear away. This was the time to let a sense of obligation and good manners combine to override that self-confessed national defect and force one of them to make the running.

"Mosby?" Naturally it was Faith who spoke first. "That's an unusual christian name—obviously a family name."

"Yes, ma'am. At least, it's become one."

Shirley gave a short laugh, half derisive and half affectionate. "Actually it's a piece of genuine American history. But you'll never have heard of the original Mosby, I'll bet."

She was good, she was real good, thought Mosby with admiration. Good and quick to turn an opportunity into an opening the subject would find irresistible. Even that last 'I'll bet' was a shrewd piece of psychology aimed at the target.

"American history?" The challenge roused Audley.

"Uh-huh, American history," she led him on lightly.

"Mosby . . . Mosby . . ." Audley repeated the name, frowning. "I seem to remember there was a Mosby—in fact a John S. Mosby. If that 'S' stood for 'Singleton' that would be the one, I take it?"

"Why, you're absolutely right!" Shirley clapped her hands in admiration. "Well, fancy your having heard of him. Isn't that something, Mose? You're famous even over here."

Faith Audley turned towards her husband. "And who was John Mosby, darling?"

"Colonel John S. Mosby." Audley looked at Mosby with obvious interest. "American Civil War. He was a celebrated Confederate guerrilla leader. Played merry hell with General Grant's lines of communication. That right, Mr. Sheldon?"

Mosby grimaced. "Well, not a guerrilla leader—that's damn Yankee propaganda. He was a regular horse soldier, 1st Virginia Cavalry, and then a scout to old Jeb Stuart himself. And what the Yankees called guerrillas were Mosby's Rangers—43rd Battalion of the Virginia Cavalry."

"I do beg your pardon." Audley's eyes lit with pleasure. "And the 43rd's pardon too."

"Aw, honey, they *were* guerrillas," exclaimed Shirley, coming to Audley's rescue. "Why, the Yankees even hanged some of them. And they put a price on Mosby's head too—what was it, $5,000?" She grinned at Audley. "So he wasn't all that expensive."

"Honey, five thousand bucks was good money in those days," Mosby disagreed. "Come to that, I could use five thousand bucks now . . . But that doesn't make him a guerrilla, anyway—it's like David said: he played hell with Yankee communications. Burnt their bridges, blew up their trains, grabbed their payrolls—"

"Huh!" Shirley goaded him, entering the spirit of the game with more than a suggestion of sincerity.

"—which he sent back to Richmond, every last dollar accounted for," Mosby overrode her scorn. "And no one ever collected on him either, I can tell you. Not one dollar."

"And he was your ancestor?" Faith Audley inquired quickly, as though trying to nip a new historical-marital discord in the bud.

"Well, not exactly. My great-grandfather rode with him, and later on he married a Singleton from Virginia. So he called his son Mosby Singleton in their honour. And after that it got to be a habit."

Faith nodded. "And you're the third. How fascinating—don't you think so, David?"

"I do. The Confederacy produced some remarkable cav-

alry commanders. J.E.B. Stuart and Nathan Bedford Forrest were in the Murat class. And there was Morgan and
the Lees, and Wade Hampton and Joe Wheeler." He bowed
towards Mosby. "And John Singleton Mosby, of course."

Shirley gave him her most dazzling Scarlett O'Hara
smile. "Well, I sure have lost my bet, and that's a fact. I
can see you're a real expert, David—and I can see your
heart's in the right place too."

"With the South, you mean?" Audley took the implied
question seriously, ignoring the charm. "I wouldn't say my
heart was involved on either side, to be honest. But it was
an extremely interesting war certainly."

"You mean you don't have sympathy for Dixie? But I
thought Britishers always favoured the underdog, no matter
what."

Audley looked at her over his spectacles, aware at last
that he was being gently needled. Then he smiled slowly.
"Madam, anyone who had to contend with generals like
Robert E. Lee and Stonewall Jackson, not to mention
Stuart and Forrest—and with someone like John S. Mosby
at his back—cannot have felt very much like an overdog.
My sympathies are distributed evenly, if not my admira-
tion."

They were both playing parts now.

"But you just have to admit the South was more romantic. Everybody admits that, even the Yankees do now."

Audley considered the proposition gravely. "Ye-ess. I'll
give you romantic. Wrong, but romantic—and the North
was right, but repulsive. . . . It's just like our own civil war,
Mrs Sheldon. The Cavaliers were romantic and the Parlia-
mentarians were right. Our Prince Rupert would have
made an absolutely splendid Confederate. And if Oliver
Cromwell would have disapproved of Grant's drinking
habits he would certainly have respected Abraham Lincoln,
no doubt about it. . . . Though if he resembles anyone in
your war—Cromwell, that is—I rather think it would be
Stonewall Jackson." He pursed his lips and nodded at Shirley.

"Gee!" Shirley breathed out admiringly, allowing her mouth to drop open rather as the child's had done earlier. "Now I know why I lost my bet. You've just got to be a professor of history. I'll bet that instead."

Audley smiled his slow smile again, obviously rather taken with her despite himself.

"What are you betting?"

"David!" Faith Audley chided him. "You—"

"I'll bet—" Shirley overrode the warning heatedly. "I'll bet drinks and dinner at our house tonight against drinks and dinner at your house. That's what I'll bet."

"David." Faith repeated urgently. "You are the limit, really." She turned to Shirley helplessly. "He isn't a professor of history, Mrs Sheldon."

"He isn't?" Shirley laughed happily, obviously in no way put out by losing her bet again.

"I'm sorry to disappoint you, Mrs Sheldon," said Audley.

"Shirley's the name, please—and you don't disappoint me at all. You interest me. You know all about John S. Mosby—and Oliver Cromwell—but you're not a professor . . . and you sure don't look like a schoolteacher."

"I don't?" Audley's eye flickered. "And what does a schoolteacher look like?"

"Kind of mild, at least deep down. You don't look mild."

True, thought Mosby. It was like being on the foothills of a mountain range: things still grew and blossomed there, but you only had to scrape away the thin covering of soil to reach the same hard rock as that which towered into the clouds ahead. There was a line there where civilisation and savagery overlapped, a no-man's-land. And that, for all his fine culture, was this man's land.

"Indeed?" Audley's amusement was evident. "Then what do I look like?"

"A professional confidence trickster," said Faith drily, "who is this time not going to be allowed to escape with his ill-gotten gains. If anyone's dining with anyone tonight, then you must both come to us."

Mission accomplished.

"Shucks, no!" Shirley protested. "I lost."

"Not at all," replied Faith firmly. "My husband isn't a history professor. As a matter of fact, he works for the Government. But he is a historian too."

"I didn't say I wasn't."

"And you weren't going to say you were." She shook her head in despair at Shirley. "We're actually down here so that he can put the finishing touches to a book."

"A book?" Shirley echoed the words reverently. "A history book?"

She was out-running the script, but with things going so well it was the right thing to do.

Audley grunted modestly.

"On Oliver Cromwell, maybe?"

"No. Someone a bit earlier."

"Who would that be—if you don't mind me asking?"

"Not at all. I'm writing a biography of William Marshall, Earl of Pembroke. But I don't expect you've ever heard of him."

"I'm afraid not. I guess he was before Sir Walter Raleigh and John Smith founded Virginia, huh?"

Mosby recognised his feed-line and acknowledged it with a snort of derision. The corner where the road to St Veryan's branched to the left was just ahead now, so he had just enough time to whet Audley's appetite.

"Some, honey, some. Four hundred years, give or take a few." He glanced sidelong over his shoulder at Audley. "Right?"

There was a moment's pause, during which Audley was no doubt wondering whether he'd hit the button by guess or by God.

"That's right," said Audley, with the merest touch of surprise in his voice.

"'The best knight that ever was'," quoted Mosby. "It was Archbishop Langton who said that, wasn't it?"

The pause was a fraction longer this time, while Audley tried for the first time to place Mosby in anything narrower than the 'Tourist, male, American' classification. And with reason, because the odds against casually meeting an American familiar with twelfth-century William Marshall were about as long as those against meeting an Englishman who'd ever heard of John Singleton Mosby.

"That's right, it was Langton." Audley controlled his third-degree surprise well. "Are you a mediaevalist, then?"

"Heck—no. But I was reading about him just a few days ago . . . Well, actually I was reading up Eleanor of Aquitaine and her daughter—and Chrétien de Troyes . . ." He trailed off.

"Chrétien—?" Audley had difficulty in keeping the disbelief out of his voice. "And you're not a mediaevalist?"

Mosby was relieved to see the thatch of the old cottage just ahead. The narrow English country roads, meandering between high banks, required just too much concentration for comfort.

"Far from it." He laughed.

"Say—" Shirley leant forward excitedly "—is this William Marshall one of your Round Table guys?"

"It was Wace added the Round Table, honey—I told you," he replied patiently. "Chrétien de Troyes added Lancelot. But I guess William Marshall could have doubled for Lancelot okay any time."

He braked to a standstill under a roaring jungle of honeysuckle alongside the cottage. Sandcastles and honeysuckle and thatched cottages; Confederate colonels and mediaeval heroes—and now even Sir Lancelot du Lac himself.

For a moment he saw Mosby and Lancelot galloping down the runway at Wodden, plumes flying in the wind, Navy Colt and lance against the SRAMs of General Ellsworth's F-111s. And if that was mind-boggling it was hardly more so than some of his recent reading; if the Agency accountants ever studied the slush fund in detail they might have difficulty swallowing Gilda's *De Excidio Britanniae* and the Venerable Bede's *History of the English Church and People*.

Faith Audley shook the sleeping child in her arms gently. "Come on, sleepy head—wake up." She smiled at Mosby. "No problem about bedtime this evening . . . I'm sorry Mr Sheldon—"

"Mosby. It may sound odd, but it's easy to remember."

"Mosby—I don't think it's odd. My husband's second christian name is Longsdon, anyway—" Good manners struggled with her desire to break up the conversation and get the tired child out of the car. "But I'm beginning to lose track of the conversation. You're not a historian—?"

"No," cut in Audley decisively. "An Arthurian."

The change in inflexion was small, almost unnoticeable. But it was there and it was significant, Mosby sensed instantly. And it reminded him of something which momentarily eluded him: with most Britishers you had to multiply any sign of emotion by ten to get the real message, even among friends. Among strangers the factor was considerably higher, so that minute distinction could mean—

He had it.

Scorn, contempt and disdain—in an American that *Arthurian* would have been a sneer of unconcealed derision: to Audley *Arthurians* were flat-earthers, UFO watchers, Bible Belt ignoramuses, kooks and weirdos of no account.

"Tintagel," said Audley coolly. "That's why you're here —to see Tintagel."

Yes, that had to be it, thought Mosby, remembering Tintagel's clear dedication to the separation of money from the crowds perspiring tourists who had come to pay homage to King Arthur—but a King Arthur who obviously owed more to Walt Disney and *Camelot* than to history.

"Gee, how did you guess?" For once Shirley had missed the warning signs, but Mosby could see a Grand Canyon opening up between them. In another moment Audley would be remembering a previous engagement for tonight, and all their good work would have gone down for nothing.

"Tintagel—yuk!" He flogged his brain to separate the legends from the facts. The trouble was that in forty-eight hours of concentrated study he had encountered damn few facts, far too few with which to cross swords with an expert.

"I didn't dig Tintagel too much," he observed cautiously, playing for time.

"Too many tea shops and souvenirs?" Faith nodded understandingly. "David positively refuses to go there. But then he doesn't believe in King Arthur anyway, do you darling?"

Final confirmation beyond all doubt—and God bless you, Mrs Audley, ma'am.

Audley gave a scornful grunt. But as things stood that might well include Mr and Mrs Mosby Singleton Sheldon as well as King Arthur, so the sooner that short-lived alliance was broken, the better.

"Me neither," said Mosby quickly. When it came to facts there was only one he was reasonably sure of, and although it had been planned to keep it for the second phase he judged now that it was the only bait that might recapture Audley. "But I do believe in Badon Hill."

"Badon?" Audley's tone was different at once, edged not with disdain but with curiosity.

The child on Faith's lap stirred, stretched and opened her eyes.

"What about Badon?" repeated Audley.

Mosby met his stare steadily. "It'ud be one hell of a thing to find it—for sure."

"It would be interesting, certainly . . . But impossible now, short of a miracle."

Little Cathy looked around her, momentarily unsure of where she was until her mother's arms tightened around her.

"Mummy, I'm hungry," she said loudly.

Mosby grinned at her, then back at her father. "Come on up to our place tonight for drinks and I'll show you something."

"What?"

"A miracle, maybe."

– II –

A YEAR OF proximity had sharpened Mosby's awareness of Shirley's meteorology; even before the front door had closed on Audley he sensed the fall in her barometer.

"So now we don't believe in King Arthur, huh?" she challenged him.

He glanced at her quickly before reaching for the gear shift, confirming the storm warning. But for once he felt no inclination to come out of the weather. "Yep. As of now, he stinks."

"Just because Audley doesn't believe in him?"

He let the car roll forward slowly. "You got it in one, Shirl honey."

"Great. And what if he believes the moon is made of green cheese?"

"Then I should give the proposition very serious consideration. You want I should tell him he's crazy?"

"Is he crazy?"

"What do you mean 'is he crazy?' So he recites poetry to his daughter and builds sandcastles and writes books on mediaeval history—" Mosby broke off as he remembered

36

the Englishman's eyes behind the spectacle lenses. Cold eyes not easily to be forgotten. "You ask me, I think he's a whole lot tougher than he talks. Which you pretty well told him to his face, I seem to recall."

"I don't mean that..." She trailed off uncertainly as they broke through the last belt of woodland at the head of the valley which stretched down to the sea. He caught a glimpse of the grey-white facade of St Veryan's halfway up the righthand shoulder of the valley and beyond it the terrible black lines of jagged shark's tooth rocks which stretched out into the ocean as continuations of the headland. Far beyond them, though deceptively close, Lundy Island stood up high out of the white-topped rollers.

Lundy high, sigh of dry

What was frightening about this beautiful coastline was its contrast: on one side the little green fields snug behind their high banks, and on the other the hungry sea rolling endlessly against the land.

"I don't mean that," Shirley repeated herself. "I know I'm supposed to be the dumb one, and you've read the books—"

So that was it, of course. He ought to have allowed for that uncongenial rôle playing the devil with her temper.

"—But at least I can read the titles. And I don't see how people can write whole books about someone who doesn't exist—according to Audley."

Mosby shook his head. "It isn't as simple as that. And besides, we're after Badon, not Arthur."

"But Harry Finsterwald said Badon was Arthur's greatest victory. Now Audley says there was no such person—and you behave as though we're still in business."

"You're damn right, we're still in business. You saw the way he sat up the moment I mentioned Badon?" Mosby looked at her quickly. "Harry Finsterwald may not know as much as he thinks he does, but someone's got Audley figured right, that's for sure. They supply the box of tricks to play the next act with, like they promised, and I think we can get him moving the way they want us to."

"But I still don't see—" She checked as the house came into full view; there was a large grey utility van parked beside Finsterwald's little British Ford. "We have company."

Mosby relaxed as he read the 'TV and Radio Repairs' legend on the utility. "It's okay. That's Harry's partner—he said to watch for the TV repairman, remember?"

Shirley stared at the utility. "I wonder which one of them he is," she murmured.

Mosby grinned at her wryly. They had intermittently shared a private game of trying to spot the other members of the Special Operations Unit at Wodden, but they had been dead wrong about Harry Finsterwald so there was little chance that they'd be right about his partner.

"Just so it's not General Ellsworth himself, I couldn't take that," he murmured back. "He hates my non-combatant guts."

"So does Harry. Let's face it, honey: you're just not popular."

"Harry's a creep—so's General Ellsworth. They don't sweat, neither of them. And you can't trust a man who doesn't sweat." He reached for the door handle. "So long as they don't like me I can't be all bad."

He smiled to himself. She was right about Finsterwald taking an instant dislike to him, but it was an endearing blank spot in her understanding that she was quite unable to grasp the reason for it. And one of life's smaller ironies, too: that to a man who fancied his looks and talents as much as Harry did it was not only an error but also an injustice which had turned her into Mrs Sheldon, and not Mrs Finsterwald.

But it was a total stranger, or at least someone he could not instantly recognise from High Wodden, who greeted them in the hall of St Veryan's.

"Captain Sheldon—Mrs Sheldon. Good to meet you." The stranger offered his hand to each of them in turn, Shirley first.

Civilian manners. And hair longer than General Ellsworth permitted, military or civilian. But hair cut as expertly as the British tweed suit, and neither the hair nor the suit fitted the face: hair black and shiny as a raven's wing and face swarthy as a Mexican bandit's.

"Howard Morris. UK Operations Control." The voice was wrong too—anglicised mid-Atlantic, if not Ivy League. The man was a mass of contradictions.

"Hi, Doc." Harry Finsterwald appeared in the sitting room doorway. "How d'you make out then?"

Mosby sickened as Finsterwald gave him a comradely smile for Control's benefit, revealing some spectacular crown and bridge work as he did so. Typical fancy West Coast dentistry—the smile of a man who was willing to pay for his smile.

"According to Mose we're in business," said Shirley.

Morris looked at her. "But you're not so sure?"

She gave him back the look with interest. "I don't know. But then I don't know what the hell's happening anyway."

"So what's the problem?"

"Just Audley doesn't believe in the existence of King Arthur."

"The devil he doesn't!" Morris turned towards Mosby. "Is that so?"

Something stirred in Mosby's subconscious as he met the man's direct stare, but he had no time to identify it. "You want Audley to look for Badon, like Major Davies was looking, not for King Arthur—that's what Finsterwald here briefed us to set up. If that's what you still want—and if you've brought the stuff Harry promised—then I reckon we're in with a chance. But Shirley's right, the way she feels: it's time someone explained why we're doing what we're doing."

Finsterwald emitted a derisive sound, half laugh, half snarl. "Oh, come on, Doc, be your age. You don't expect the reason why to be part of the deal, do you? You different from the rest of us or something?"

"Uh-huh. Not me, Harry. I'm not different." Mosby kept

his eyes on Howard Morris. "But this deal is different. And for my money so is Audley."

"I go along with that," said Shirley. "I don't know about King Arthur, but there's something not quite right about Audley."

"You think he's suspicious of you?" Morris frowned.

"No, I wouldn't say that." She shook her head slowly. "I think he's bought us so far . . . It was just—I don't know— just the way he looked at each of us when Mose offered to help him fix the car. Like he was trying to recognise us . . . It wasn't he was suspicious. He was more like kind of watchful."

Morris stared from one to the other in silence for a moment, as though trying to gauge the accuracy of their joint impression. "But you're quite sure he wasn't suspicious?"

"Why the heck should he be?" said Mosby. "What's a Home Office statistical analyst got to be suspicious about when a couple of Americans give him a lift?"

Morris's lips parted. "Always supposing he is a Home Office statistical analyst. Which he isn't."

Mosby glanced angrily at Finsterwald, but before he could speak Morris intervened. "Don't blame Captain Finsterwald. The Captain only did what he was told to do."

"Oh, just great." Only Shirley could get so much scorn in three little words. "So now you're going to tell us what he is?"

"At the moment he's exactly what he says he is: a man writing a history book on—" Morris looked at Finsterwald questioningly, "—on who was it?"

Finsterwald swallowed. "William Marshall, Earl of Pembroke. Born about 1146, died 1219," he said grudgingly, as though he didn't like hearing himself admit any knowledge of such esoteric information. "Doc has the rundown sheet on him."

"On the level?" Shirley balanced the question delicately between insolence and genuine request for confirmation.

"William Marshall, that's right." Morris ignored her. "Audley started getting interested in Marshall when he was in the Middle East ten years back, studying crusader castles. He's been working on him off and on ever since—couple of years ago when he was a visiting professor in Arabic studies at Cumbria University."

Mosby remembered the sandcastle, its meticulous layout, the careful counting off of the towers. . . . William Marshall had been a crusader, and later on one of Richard the Lionhearted's top advisers, so the biographical sheet had stated. And the whole thing was crazy, except that he was beginning to lose the capacity of being surprised by anything.

"And now he has a six-month furlough to complete his book." Morris paused to nod at Shirley. "On the level."

"Uh-huh." Her voice was almost neutral this time. "So he's a real-life historian pretending to be a statistical analyst. And I was beginning to think he was King Arthur in disguise, maybe."

"Not quite King Arthur, Mrs Sheldon. But perhaps Merlin the Magician, that's what we're hoping." Morris smiled at her, tolerantly, still unprovoked.

"He'll darn well need to be a magician," said Mosby quickly, "if you want him to find Mount Badon for us."

"You think so?"

Mosby weakened under the intensity of the dark eyes. "I'm not an expert on Arthurian history."

"But you've read the books on Davies's list, Captain."

"Not all of them." Mosby rallied. "You don't become an expert on the Dark Ages in forty-eight hours by reading a few books, anyway. It'd need more like forty-eight months."

"Unfortunately we don't have forty-eight months."

"How long do we have?"

Morris shrugged. "That we don't know. Perhaps no time at all. Certainly very little time."

"To do what?" asked Shirley. "To find this—Badon Hill place? Which Mose doesn't think can be found at all?"

"Is that what you think, Captain?" Morris paused. "That it cannot be found?"

"Nobody's found it yet. There's no Badon on the map."

"But I understand people have suggested where it might be."

"Oh, sure—half a dozen places. But there's no way of proving any of them . . . after fifteen hundred years."

"Except Major Davies thought differently."

"But Major Davies is no longer with us."

"Exactly. Which we are assuming is a case of cause and effect. All evidence that he was searching for Badon Hill was most expertly removed from his lodgings, and simultaneously he was also removed—equally expertly."

Finsterwald stiffened. "We found the plane?"

"A portion of it."

"It was on the radio we'd given up the search," said Mosby.

"That was for public consumption. For the British—and others." Morris's voice hardened a fraction. "We got a piece Friday afternoon."

"Only a piece?"

"The major debris is probably several miles to the west, in deeper water. The section we have was detached because of a violent internal explosion."

"So the bastards fixed him," muttered Finsterwald. "And right on the goddamn base, too."

"They did. But that's no concern of ours—Air Force Intelligence will deal with that when we give them the word, and not before. At the moment it's an accident, with the normal accident procedures. Because the longer they believe they've pulled off the double, the longer we have to catch up on what they're really doing."

They.

What *they* are really doing.

"And just who is 'they'?" asked Mosby.

Finsterwald gave a snort. "Now who d'you think has the know-how—and the gall—to knock down one of our planes in a NATO backyard? Harold Wilson?"

Mosby gave him a half-smile. If UK Operations Control

could take a bitching from Shirley in his stride, then he could take a squadron of Harry Finsterwalds with no trouble. "Yeah, well now you've mentioned him, Harry, I'd say he's got the gall and MI6 has the know-how. Only I just can't work out the connection between either of them and Badon Hill. But then the same applies to the KGB— Second Directorate, Clandestine Operations Division, that would be the one, I guess. Unless they've gotten themselves an Ancient British History Division, that is." He looked back at Morris again. "But if you can't answer that one—"

"Or won't," murmured Shirley.

"Or won't—I'll settle for an easier answer first."

"Which is—?" Morris regarded him with interest.

"Which is—which side is Audley on? British or Russian?"

"What makes you think he's on either?"

"You've practically said as much. So did Shirley—'the way he looked at us' she said. I don't know about 'watchful', but whatever it was you remind me of him every time you look at me."

"Hah!" Morris beamed at him. "So you have an instinct —that's very good . . . Not reliable, but still useful, an instinct. But it doesn't tell you which side, eh?"

Mosby decided to rise to the challenge. "British, for choice."

"More instinct?"

"Uh-huh. Logic this time. The guys who took out Major Davies will be waiting for us to come knocking on their door. But you want them to go on hoping they've succeeded for as long as possible. Which means Audley isn't on their team. And as Harry doesn't fancy Mr Wilson as the villain of the piece that means he must be working for the British—Audley, I mean. Okay?"

"Logical certainly."

"You want more?"

"Whatever you've got."

"Okay. Theory this time. Shir—Mrs Sheldon and I represent a substantial outlay in Agency planning and resources. We've been over here four months just being ourselves, which is nice, but not very cost effective. And Captain Finsterwald arrived about the same time, and for a bet he's been doing even less in Base Publicity. *And* he's got a partner tucked away somewhere, so there are at least four of us—which sounds like a special Operations Unit."

Morris nodded cautiously. "Could be."

"That's only Theory One. My Primary Operational Field is counter-intelligence—Mrs Sheldon's too, for another guess. And Harry's for a third." He looked quickly at Finsterwald. "Though I wouldn't be certain about that, maybe he's just a strong arm boy."

Before Finsterwald could react Morris said: "Go on."

"That makes us a counter-intelligence SOU, which the book says is a reaction pattern to early warning of a KGB clandestine action. And what little you've actually admitted so far confirms that—plus what you haven't actually denied. If this was Latin America or Africa it'd most likely be straight insurgency or urban terror, but over here the law enforcement is sophisticated and the people are—"

"You're beginning to lecture us, Captain."

Mosby grinned sheepishly. "Sorry. I was getting carried away."

"By your own brilliance." Finsterwald yawned.

"Which is better than getting bogged down in his own stupidity," observed Morris mildly. "Theory two: A KGB clandestine action is about to start. You don't have a theory of how King Arthur comes into it by any chance?"

"According to Audley he doesn't come in at all," said Shirley. "He never existed, remember?"

"And what do you say to that, Captain?"

"Oh, I can account for that okay. It's really pretty simple. But do I rate another question first?"

"I guess you've earned it. So go ahead."

"The way Harry briefed us, we're not liaising with Audley—right?"

"Correct."

"Then we're going it alone—and the British don't know?"

"That's two questions."

"I'll just take the last one, then. They don't know what's going on?"

"So far as we know, they don't. Theory Three?"

Mosby drew a deep breath. "No more theories. Just I don't like this deal any more."

"Reasons, then."

"Reasons? My God, aren't they obvious? A KGB operation in Britain—we don't know what, but we know there is one—and we're not going to warn the British? Instead we're going to try and sucker one of their agents to work for us without knowing it. You want I should like the job?" He stared at Morris in genuine surprise. "No way, Mr. Morris, no way."

"He isn't exactly an agent. Not in the formal sense, anyway."

"In what sense, then?" asked Shirley.

Morris smiled. "Your . . . husband's instinct flattered me, Mrs Sheldon. He's a senior executive adviser to their Joint Intelligence Co-ordinating Committee. Our last assessment ranked him Number Four to Sir Frederick Clinton."

"The Joint—" She bit the word off.

Jesus, thought Mosby with a swirl of bewilderment: Morris had quite calmly made everything ten times as bad. They were now messing with the topmost brass in the British Intelligence hierarchy, on the fringes of their equivalent of the 40 Committee, if not the National Security Council itself. Ozymandias was just two levels down in direct responsibility from the Queen of England, separated from her only by Sir Frederick Clinton and the Prime Minister.

Ozymandias, with his ordinary family and his ordinary family car . . . and his sandcastles . . .

"It isn't quite as crazy as it may sound, Captain," said Morris.

"It isn't?" The very severity of the shock-wave had the effect of steadying Mosby. Because they couldn't be that crazy they had to be stone-cold sane. Nothing in between would do.

"For a start, this operation isn't directed against the British. The USAF is the target."

"You mean we do know something about it?" said Shirley.

"We certainly do. In fact we had the first authentic word of it out of Moscow Control nearly five months back—of an operation against the USAF in Britain. Scheduled, some time July through September. We even know who's running it: Party Secretariat Member Comrade Professor Nikolai Andrievich Panin. One of their top men."

Just great, thought Mosby: two top men and Dr and Mrs Mosby Sheldon III in their appointed rôles as a couple of slices of salami.

"And?" said Shirley hopefully.

"And we have their operational codename." He looked at Mosby. "Which ought to ring a bell with you now. *Operation Bear.*"

"Bear?" Mosby frowned. "It's a pretty common Russian—" He stopped.

"The bell ringing, huh?"

"Uh-huh." Mosby shook his head. "Or only very faintly if I'm thinking what you want me to think. It's pretty goddamn thin reasoning."

"But a start."

"What is?" asked Shirley.

"Bear," said Mosby. " 'Bear' is one of Arthur's nicknames, at least according to those who believe he ever existed. 'Artos the Bear'—it's a sort of play on words, because *artos*, or something like it, means 'bear' in Ancient British. And there's a crack in one of the very early Welsh chronicles about some king being 'the bear's charioteer'. But it's damn obscure—and *artos* can mean a whole bunch of other things too. In fact it's a typical Arthurian puzzle: you can argue it a dozen different ways and it can mean anything or nothing."

"Very good—I'm impressed," said Morris encouragingly. "You've done your homework."

"Well, I'm not impressed," said Mosby. "It's like if the Thai Intelligence mounted an Operation Elephant and we decided it was connected with the Republican Party. It just doesn't mean a thing."

"Not by itself, I agree. But we do have one other fact which also didn't mean a thing by itself. . . . You see, we do try to keep tabs on all the top SovCom personnel, especially the KGB controllers. What they do, where they go, who they visit, and the rest of it—it all goes into the data bank for processing.

"So we just happen to know that Comrade Professor Panin went on a trip about nine months back to Gorky, on the Upper Volga. And we also know that while he was there he borrowed a book from the Public Library—as a matter of fact we have that from two independent sources. And he's never returned it, either."

"He's going to have a big fine to pay, after nine months," said Mosby.

"The biggest. Because it was the oldest book in the library—it was written in the north of England about twelve hundred years ago." Morris smiled. "Does the name Bede ring any bells with you, Captain?"

Unreality again: John Singleton Mosby, William Marshall, Chrétien de Troyes, Arthur of the Britons, David Audley . . . Nikolai Andrievich Panin.

And now Bede. Bede, the monk of the monastery of Saint Paul at Jarrow. Bede the Venerable, just two steps from becoming a saint.

"Sure. He wrote one of the main source-books for the period—*A History of the English Church and People*. I've got a copy in there—" he pointed to the sitting room behind Harry Finsterwald "—it was on Davies's list."

"But not this copy, Captain. This is the Novgorod Bede, one of the oldest Bede manuscripts in existence. That's what Panin has got. And that was what Davies was enquiring about two days before his death."

– III –

MOSBY FOLLOWED HOWARD MORRIS into the sitting room with misgivings churning up inside him.

Audley and Panin were bad enough, since for sure neither had reached his present eminence by the exercise of brotherly love. But at least they were bad enough in a known way: it was like meeting two tigers on his first trip in a foreign jungle where the larger predators usually remained deep in the undergrowth—just plain bad luck.

But Arthur and Badon were something totally different, totally unexpected. The pile of books on the table directly ahead of him was a reminder that up until now he'd managed to rationlise them, so that they had become part of his cover and a way of manipulating Audley, fundamentally no different from any other disguise or deception plan. Yet now, after what Morris had revealed, they were no longer the means to some unknown end; they were somehow part of the end itself.

Morris waved a hand towards the occupants of the room. "Dick Schreiner—State Department. Cal Merriwether—Harry's other half."

"Mrs Sheldon—Captain." Schreiner was too well schooled by his trade to look at Mosby with envy.

But it was Merriwether who caught Mosby's eye. He couldn't place the coloured man at all, not even when he'd mentally replaced the sober grey polo-necked pullover and well-worn blue jeans with uniform.

He frowned with embarrassment. "The BRU configuration crew? I'll place you in a minute—"

Merriwether grinned hugely. "You ought to, Doc. You had me in your chair three-four weeks back."

"I did?" Mosby's embarrassment began to turn to annoyance with himself. "The name's familiar. If I could see inside your mouth there'd be no trouble, I tell you. I never forget a mouth."

"How about this, then?" But instead of opening his mouth Merriwether abruptly changed his expression from one of lively amusement to sullen vacuity. "That help you any, sir?"

"The car pool—you're a driver . . . and I did fillings on your lower left—posterior four and six—right?"

Merriwether signalled success by restoring his face.

"I hope I didn't hurt you," said Mosby.

"I didn't feel a thing, Doc. You've got the magic touch." He bowed towards Shirley. "Mrs Sheldon."

"Looks like we're going to need a magic touch," said Shirley.

"Audley'll need it too—to find Badon Hill," said Mosby.

Schreiner glanced at Morris quickly, then back at Mosby. "It really is impossible?"

"Nothing's impossible—at least, according to General Ellsworth."

"Your base commander at Wodden?"

"That's the one and only." Mosby nodded towards Finsterwald. "You know the Holy of Holies?"

"Huh?"

"Harry, Harry—the General's reception office. Where

he keeps his flags and his model planes—and the desk you could land a B-52 on."

Finsterwald returned the nod unwillingly, as though he'd been too busy smartening his salute in Ellsworth's presence to notice whether the General had a desk or a brass bedstead.

"Well, there's a plaque on the wall right behind his chair —an oak plaque with gold lettering, remember?"

The flicker in Finsterwald's eyes indicated that the plaque had registered. Which figured, because it was fixed just six inches above the General's head, and that was where Finsterwald would have looked. Finsterwald and most everyone else, to be fair; so it was probably the way the General intended.

"*No Mission is Impossible*—remember?"

"Sure, I remember." The nod was more confident. "Matter of fact I go along with the idea."

"Great."

"A man says a thing can't be done he usually means he can't do it."

"Is that a fact? Well, maybe you should be looking for Badon Hill, not Audley." Mosby turned back to Schreiner. "Let's settle for improbable, then."

"But there is such a place—that's definite?"

"There *was*." Mosby ran his eye over the table, and from there to the pile of books beside Shirley's chair. "By your foot, honey—the little dark blue book."

The pages fell open obediently at the marked passage. "This is the earliest thing there is—*On the Destruction of Britain*. Written by a monk named Gildas in the middle of the sixth century. 'Gildas the Wise' they called him, but he's really rather a pain in the ass."

"A history book?" asked Shirley.

"The hell it is! It's about as much a proper history of Britain as the collected *Washington Post* editorials on Richard Nixon are to a history of the United States. Gildas wasn't interested in history—he was in the business of denouncing the rulers of Britain as a bunch of rat-finks who were letting the country go to the dogs. They'd won the war against the Saxons and now they were losing the peace—the old story."

"So where does Badon come in?"

"Ah—it comes in sort of incidentally when he's preaching about the good old days of Ambrosius Aurelianus, 'the last of the Romans'—a sort of George Washington who started the war of liberation against the Saxons. It's like he's reminiscing on the side . . ." He scanned the page for his pencil mark. "Here it is:

> . . . nowadays his descendants in our time have declined from the integrity of their ancestors . . .

—that's typical Gildas—

> . . . From then on the citizens and the enemy were by turns victorious, so that God might test in this people, the modern Israel, whether it loves Him or not; until the year of the siege of Badon Hill, almost the last and not the least slaughter of those bandits, which was forty-four years and one month ago, as I should know for it was also the year of my birth . . .

He was a Badon baby, and he never forgot it."

"So when was he born?" asked Shirley.

"That's the trouble, honey—and it's also absolutely typical of the whole subject: nobody's quite sure. But round about A.D. 500, give or take ten or fifteen years."

"So the Britons had beaten the Saxons—the Anglo-Saxons?" said Schreiner. "I thought it was the other way round."

"So it was—in the end. Gildas was writing in about 550, maybe a year or two earlier. At that time the Britons had been on top for the best part of half a century, since the battle of Badon. The Saxons just had toe-holds on the coast in a few places. But the next really reliable account of what happened dates from two hundred years later." Mosby nodded at Howard Morris. "From a monk named Bede."

He reached across the table for the orange-backed paperback. "*A History of the English Church and People*."

"Bede was like Gildas, then?" asked Shirley.

"He was a monk like Gildas. But that was about the only thing they had in common, honey. Because for a start he was one of the Anglo-Saxon bandits—by then they'd kicked out the Britons from most of the island, like Gildas had said they would. And the Anglo-Saxons had become the English and the Britons had become the Welsh, more or less."

"My God!" said Finsterwald fervently. "And who were the goddamn Scotch?"

"They were mostly Irish, man," said Merriwether helpfully. "And you can tell that because of the whiskey and the bagpipes, which they both got out of the deal."

So Merriwether was the real brains of the Finsterwald/ Merriwether partnership, thought Mosby.

"That's about right, actually." He nodded. "But the big difference is that Bede was a real historian, not a Bible-thumper like Gildas—

. . . Ambrosius Aurelius, a virtuous man of Roman origin, the only survivor of a disaster in which his royal parents were killed . . .

—and so on . . . Let's see. . . . Here we are:

Thenceforth victory went first to one side, then to the other, until the Battle of Badon Hill, when the Britons made a great slaughter of the invaders. This took place forty-four years after their invasion of Britain . . .

You see, he'd obviously got a Gildas manuscript to work from, but not quite the same one. Only he had a lot more material as well, and he knew how to use it. Not only oral tradition and local stuff—he even sent someone to Rome to check on the Papal archives, which must have been a hairy trip in those days. As I say, he was a real historian, all the modern historians agree on that."

"And he doesn't mention Arthur," said Howard Morris. "Neither does—what's his name—Gildas."

"You got it in one." Mosby nodded at him. "Arthur doesn't get a mention for another hundred years nearly— about A.D. 800, at least not one that ties him in with the right things."

"The right things?"

"Yeah. There's some early mention of an Arthur of some sort in the far north—'Artorius' was an old Roman name. But it doesn't look like our guy." He searched through the pile again. "Nennius is what we want now—"

"Another monk?" asked Shirley.

"Bishop of Bangor in North Wales, but it amounts to the same thing. Only the clergy could read and write in those days . . . Here we are: *Historia Britonum*—'History of the Britons'. Except it wasn't a history."

"What was it?"

"Just you wait and see . . ." He opened the book at its marker.

"Then Arthur fought against them with the kings of the Britons, but he was the war leader—

'them' being the Saxons. Then he lists all the battles Arthur fought . . . one at the mouth of the river Glein, four beside the river Dobglas, the sixth beside the river Bassass, the seventh in the forest of Celidon—"

"I've never heard of any of them," said Shirley.

"Nor has anyone else, seems. The next one was at Castle Guinnion—

when Arthur bore the image of the blessed Mary, ever virgin, on his shoulders, and through the strength of Our Lord Jesus Christ and the holy Mary,

his maiden-mother, there was great slaughter of the
heathen and they were put to flight—

—and the ninth was in the City of the Legion. That just
might be either Chester or Caerleon. The tenth beside the
river Tribuit; the eleventh on Agned Hill. And now we
come to it—

The twelth battle was at Badon Hill, where Arthur
slew 960 men in one charge, single-handed. And he
was victor of all these battles."

"Phew! Nine-hundred-and-sixty at one go!" exclaimed
Shirley. "That even beats General Ellsworth."

"Yeah, well let's say it runs him close. But that sums up
Nennius: a lot of folk-history and superstitious hot air, plus
one or two facts. It could be all true and it could be all
hooey."

"Except Badon Hill," said Schreiner from the depths of
the armchair into which he had sunk.

"That's right, exactly right. And Badon also turns up in
the *Annales Cambriae*, which is a sort of calendar of important dates in Welsh history compiled by a bunch of
monks in the eleventh century. It says in that for 'Year 72',
which is somewhere about A.D. 500: *Battle of Badon, in*
which Arthur carried the cross of our Lord Jesus Christ on
his shoulders for three days and three nights and the
Britons were victorious."

"Sounds like they had it mixed up with one of Nennius's
battles," said Shirley.

"Honey, when you start digging into the Dark Ages, and
especially into Arthur, most everyone seems to have everything mixed up. But when you come down to it out of this
lot—" he waved his hand over the table "—apart from the
serious modern history books, the only two worth a damn
are Gildas and Bede. Gildas because he actually lived in
the period, and Bede because he was way ahead of his time
as a historian. All the rest is strictly 'maybe'."

"But what about the Knights of the Round Table and Lancelot—and Camelot?" said Schreiner. "Is that all pure invention then?"

"Not quite pure, but damn nearly, so far as I can make out. I haven't read all the stuff—the further it gets away from the actual historical time, the more there is of it. Seems a lot was made up by a man named Geoffrey of Monmouth in the twelfth century—a lot of the traditional 'King Arthur' bits. It even had a political angle then, because the Kings of England wanted to keep up with the French kings—"

Harry Finsterwald stirred. "For God's sake, we have to have the history of France too?"

Howard Morris started to speak, but Schreiner overrode him. "Until we know the exact specification of Operation Bear—and why Panin took the Novgorod Bede back to Dzerzhinsky Street with him—you're damn right, Captain. The history of France and the history of Britain, and the history of ancient Peru, if need be. Plus how many arch-angels can dance on the point of a needle too."

Mosby hurriedly revised his estimate of Schreiner: not just State Department Intelligence, but pure State Department. And not just State Department holding a watching brief if he was ready to slap down a CIA operative in the presence of UK Control—to do that required National Security Council authorisation for sure.

Another tiger?

Well, maybe he could find that out by giving the beast a gentle prod—

"I don't know, maybe Harry's right," he said doubtfully. "It's getting kind of way out, where we could end up."

Schreiner looked at him sharply. "You let me be the judge of that, Captain Sheldon."

"But—"

Howard Morris raised a finger. "Tell the man, Doc. Just tell him."

That made Schreiner a tiger for sure, right down to the last whisker. And a tiger in a hurry, too.

"Okay. It's like the English Joneses had to keep up with the French Joneses—the French had the Emperor Charlemagne as their royal ancestor. All the English had was a bunch of Norman pirates. But after Geoffrey of Monmouth had got through with Arthur they could trace themselves right back to Troy. And it made such a darn good story—the Arthurian part—that all the story-tellers of the time got into the act. So after that it just snowballed, all the way to Malory in the fifteenth century and Tennyson in the nineteenth—and Walt Disney and Broadway in the 20th. Plus any number of other guys—in fact Milton nearly wrote about King Arthur instead of Paradise Lost."

"All of which was just invented?" persisted Schreiner.

"Well . . . not quite all. This is where the thing gets kind of—strange. Like there's something deep down in it that's *not* invented. A sort of racial folk-memory."

"For example?"

"Okay, an example . . . Yes, well take the Knights of the Round Table, which is a load of crap. One guy added the knights and another added the Table, and they built the whole story up from that. Because mediaeval knights wanted to read about mediaeval knights . . . But if you actually go back to A.D. 500, that's the time when the heavy cavalryman is the big new secret weapon. And just before the Romans got to hell out of Britain they set up a mobile strike command. So if you add those two facts together, you've just maybe got something that isn't a load of crap. No knights rescuing damsels in distress and slaying dragons, but a disciplined cavalry force . . . the Saxons fought on foot, remember, so they'd have been at a disadvantage . . . And no 'King' Arthur, but just a first-rate cavalry commander—"

"A war leader," said Shirley.

For a moment Mosby thought she was making fun of his brand-new academic pretensions. But when he looked into her eyes there was nothing to confirm the suspicion; rather, she seemed on the edge of being interested.

He nodded cautiously. "A war leader, yes."

"Very good," Schreiner made no attempt to hide his approval. "That fits very well."

"Fits very well with what?"

"Never mind. It'll keep. So where does Badon Hill figure in this folk-memory?"

Mosby rubbed his chin, the hastily-acquired facts suddenly blurring in his memory. He was so used to Shirley cutting him down to size that she had diminished him now without even intending to, reducing him to what he knew himself to be: an instant expert whose shallow understanding was impressive only in the company of those more ignorant than himself. Up against Audley it would be very different.

"It doesn't really figure at all," he said finally.

"But you said there was such a a place?"

"Sure I did. There was. In fact if there's one sure fact in the whole thing it's Badon Hill."

"Because Gildas and Bede say so?"

"Gildas and Bede and everyone who matter: somebody gave the Saxons the biggest hiding of their lives about A.D. 500. Even the modern archaeologists check it out, because Saxon burials inland stop dead about that time and don't really start up again for half a century or more—two, maybe three generations. So it must have been a *great* battle."

Merriwether unwound gracefully. "Then how come most people never heard of it, Doc? I read some British history once. Long time ago, but I remember the battles—Hastings, Agincourt, Waterloo, Trafalgar and such. But no Badon Hill."

"Because the Britons threw it away, is why. If they'd carried on the good work they could have finished the Anglo-Saxons for good—the Britons were better organised, the Saxons were just savages. It was like—like if the Red Indians had tried to invade the United States in about 1800. . . . So the Britons had them licked but they squabbled among themselves, like Gildas said, and blew the deal. If they hadn't then there'd have been no England

and no English. It'd all have been Britain, all speaking Welsh or something like it. In fact we'd be speaking Welsh at this moment."

Merriwether laughed. "Man—you've made your point. If it'd got me speaking Welsh it must have been some battle!"

"You're darn right. One of the all-time big ones: Saratoga, Gettysburg, Midway, Waterloo—Badon. But as it is, we don't even know where it is."

Schreiner frowned at him. "No clues at all?"

"No real clues. It was a hill and it was a siege of some sort. So perhaps a hill-fort, or an isolated hill. But nothing for certain. There's a gloss in one Gildas manuscript, where some old monk wrote in extra words—"

"Which manuscript?" asked Schreiner quickly.

"I don't know—not the Novgorod one, anyway." Mosby searched through the books again. "Here we are— it's a footnote in *Arthur of Britain* . . .

usque ad annum obsessionis Badonici montis qui prope Sabrinum hostium habetur . . .

those last five words only appear in the Cambridge manuscript, seems."

"Meaning?"

Harry Finsterwald made a tiny, half-strangled sound.

"I've got it translated here somewhere . . . 'up until the year of the siege of the hosts at Badon Hill which took place near Sabrinum.'"

"And I take it there's no such place as Sabrinum?" said Shirley.

"There's a Sabrina, actually, honey—Roman name for the river Severn. But nobody rates the gloss worth a damn. They usually don't even list it among the possible places. They reckon it dates from later mediaeval times."

He tossed the book back on to the table, watching Schreiner out of the corner of his eye as he did so. It all added up, but then at the foot of the column there was

something wrong with the final figure: ultimately this interest in Arthur and Badon and the Novgorod Bede had to be
simply a cover for something else, for the KGB and the
CIA both. And yet Schreiner's concern for the historical
details was curiously intense, as though it mattered to him
what Mosby himself felt about it . . . the way he'd been
allowed to run off at the mouth about it, when Harry Finsterwald had been slapped down . . .

He shrugged. "All of which means there's no way of
finding Badon. And even if there was you'd have one hell
of a job selling me the idea that the KGB gives a damn
either way."

Schreiner cocked his head belligerently. "But I don't
have to sell you anything, Sheldon. I just have to tell you."

Tiger, tiger! thought Mosby. The State Department
really was calling the shots on this one.

"Okay. So just tell me."

"I intend to. Because there isn't going to be any foul-up
on this operation." Schreiner looked round him coolly.
"This isn't a goddamn banana republic where you can
throw your weight about. So once we know the shape of
things we're going to handle them diplomatically, with no
brawling on the side between you and the KGB. . . . And
you—" he pointed at Mosby "—are going to do just exactly what you're told to do. No matter how crazy you may
think it is."

"Uh-huh?" Mosby yawned. "Like playing pat-a-cake
with David Audley?"

"Or even with King Arthur and the Knights of the Round
Table?" said Shirley.

Schreiner turned towards her. "That just happens to be
exactly right, Mrs Sheldon. As of now you're going to
forget you ever heard of the KGB—because as of now
your cover story is your actual mission. You and your . . .
husband are assigned to locate the map reference of Badon
Hill, England. Just that."

"Just that?" Shirley flicked a glance at Mosby. "Which
according to my . . . husband . . . isn't possible."

Schreiner smiled. "'Improbable' was what he finally settled for, I thought. And with David Audley to help you I'd rate your chances better than even—especially as you have an advantage no one else has ever had before you."

"Which is?"

"Which is that sooner or later—and it had better be sooner—you will pick up Major Davies's trail."

"And where's that going to get us?" said Shirley.

Calvin Merriwether stirred. "Just so you follow it, ma'am—it's going to get you all the way to Badon Hill," he said.

– IV –

Mosby studied Calvin Merriwether's dark, intelligent face for a moment. This time there was no trace of humour in it.

"So he really was on to Badon Hill."

"I told you so, Doc." Harry Finsterwald had lost a little of his stuffing, but his voice still had an edge to it.

"I thought that was just part of the cover story, Harry. I didn't actually buy it."

"Well, you better buy it now, man. Because it's true," Merriwether said. "He thought—"

"Thought?" Mosby pounced on the word. "You don't have any evidence?"

"Evidence? We know what he bought, if that's evidence. All the books you've been reading so carefully. And we got what he said, if that's evidence—"

"Said to whom?"

Merriwether raised a long-fingered hand. "Just wait and let me finish, don't get over-heated, Doc. He talked to his bookseller, the man he got all his books from. Hunted all over for him, the bookseller did—far as the Russian Em-

62

bassy, to find out about the Novgorod Bede. Not that they told him anything, but he sure tried. 'Cause Davies was just about the best customer he had, so it made good sense."

Mosby looked at Howard Morris. "The bookseller's on the level?"

"The bookseller's straight down the line," Merriwether's hand cut through the air. "We've checked him out every way, and he's one hundred per cent pure. 'Part from the fact that if he wasn't he wouldn't have given us so much so easy."

"Right," said Finsterwald. "And apart from the fact that he's 78 years old."

"So what did he give you?"

Merriwether glanced at Howard Morris. "Okay I tell Doc, then?"

Mosby frowned. "What the hell? Shirley and I are supposed to have been friends of Davies, according to the cover story."

"Which 'ud make you about the only friends he had," said Merriwether. "Only person we can trace he ever spoke to was the bookseller. He was a real loner."

Morris nodded. "Go ahead, Cal. Not that there's much of it."

"Well, there is and there isn't according to how you look at it . . . but seems he first went to Barkham's four-five months back—Barkham being the bookseller. Old-fashioned firm. Talk to you about books as soon as sell you one, and rather you bought nothing than something you wouldn't like." Merriwether smiled reminiscently. "Took him quite a time deciding I was a fit and proper customer for him to do business with—I had to sweet-talk him round."

Shirley laughed. "What did you buy?"

"What did I buy?" Merriwether pointed to the table, grinning. "Most of those books your husband's been reading, that's what I bought. I told Barkham I was a friend of

his Major Davies, who'd been posted back to the States
suddenly and I'd come to settle his bill—"

"Yes?"

Merriwether held up a small black tape-recorder. "You
want to hear the real thing?" He glanced towards Morris.
"We got time?"

"When's Audley coming here?" Morris asked Mosby.

"Not till nine. We got all the time in the world."

"But we haven't . . . Keep it short, Cal."

"'Tisn't long anyway. But I'll give you the bit that
counts . . ."

"—thirty-eight pence, Sir. Thank you—"
Sharp 'ting' and slither of cash drawer.
Clink.
"—and sixty-two pence change . . . fifty—"
Clink.
"—and ten and two . . . and your receipt, sir—"

Merriwether cut off the tape. "Not quite far enough. You
don't want to hear about how interested I am in ancient
history. I'll just run it some more."

"He owed only thirty-eight pence?" asked Shirley.

"Always paid cash money except the last time. Which
was lucky for us, we'd never have got on to Barkham otherwise. Here we go—"

"—depends where your particular interest lies, sir.
There is the formal history of the period, as represented by
Collingwood and Myres, and by Stenton for example . . .
and what might be termed the Arthurian history, by—ah
—by those who take his historical existence for
granted . . . which is a literature in itself."
Dry chuckle.

"Some might say more literature than history, a good
deal of if . . . Malory and Spenser, for example, and the
early French writers . . . But I don't think they would be
your taste, sir . . . very specialised. . . . And there's the

modern literature of fiction—Miss Sutcliffe's *Sword at Sunset* and T. H. White's *The Sword in the Stone* are the superior representatives of that, I would say."

"Isn't that a kid's book—*The Sword in the Stone?*"

"Indeed it is, sir. And Miss Sutcliffe's book is also popular with the younger readers. But they are both a great deal more—ah—adult than much of the fiction their elders ask me for—"

"Get that," said Merriwether. "They ask for, but they don't receive, not from old Jim Barkham they don't. He'd sooner sell canned beans than books he doesn't like."

"—may find them rewarding."

"I don't seem to remember Major Davies talking about them."

"Ah, no sir. The Major is strictly inclined towards the history. He is acquainted with the literature . . . indeed, he is remarkably well-acquainted with it. But history is his first love, I would agree."

"Mine too, Mr Barkham. I was thinking of starting with, say, Bede?"

"Bede? Well, that really would be starting at the beginning. . . . I take it you do not read Latin?"

"I'm afraid not. They didn't teach that at my school."

"Nor do they teach it at many of our English schools now, I fear, sir . . . They maintain there is no call for it—a very short-sighted view, but there it is . . . However, there is Mr Sherley-Price's translation in the Penguin Classics, which is both excellent and inexpensive—a rare conjunction these days."

"You don't have a Novgorod Bede by any chance?"

Pause, then the same dry chuckle, this time more prolonged—

"I can see you've been talking to the Major, sir—Mr—?"

"Merriwether, Mr Barkham. I understood you were getting him a copy, huh?"

"Oh, no sir. I think you must have misunderstood him

there, Mr Merriwether. Indeed, I'm now tolerably certain that no translation or facsimile has ever been made of the Novgorod manuscript . . . and I don't expect there ever will be now."

"Why not?"

"Well, frankly, I don't think the Russians are much interested in such things these days. The man at their embassy to whom I spoke—although he was alleged to be concerned with cultural matters—was singularly unforthcoming at first."

Pause.

"At first?" Merriwether's voice was casual. "You mean he came back to you?"

"That is correct. Yesterday in fact, and he was most discouraging . . . though I suppose we should be grateful that he followed up my enquiry in the first place, which I did not expect him to do."

"So what did he say?"

"Yes . . . well, it appears that many of the manuscripts from the old monastery there were severely damaged in a German air raid, and—though now I'm reading between the lines of what he said, as it were—and no attempt was made to repair any of them until quite recently. Which means, of course, that many of them will have been allowed to decay irreparably, because you cannot leave a damaged parchment to its own devices for thirty years and expect it to improve . . . it is unpardonably careless of them, really . . ."

"Uh-huh?" *Merriwether's voice was distant now rather than casual.*

"Well, now it seems they have at last got round to it, and repairs are in progress. Which means, of course, that the manuscript will be totally unavailable for study for months, possibly years. Restoration is a very slow process, Mr Merriwether."

"Yeah, I guess it must be . . . So I'm not going to be able to write the Major that you've had any success, huh? We're never going to know what was in it?"

"Oh, no, Mr Merriwether, that's not quite true. There is Bishop Harper's description of it, don't forget that."

"Bishop Harper?"

Pause.

"There now! I was forgetting that I haven't seen the Major for a fortnight or so . . . And I didn't even learn about the good Bishop until this Monday, after I had written to him."

Pause.

"Uh-huh?"

"He was Suffragan Bishop of Walthamstow in the later 1850s and far ahead of his time in ecumenical matters, so it would seem. At any rate, he was particularly concerned to re-establish relations with the Russian Orthodox Church after the Crimean War . . . the war with the charge of the Light Brigade, Mr Merriwether . . . and he travelled extensively in Russia during the late 1850s and 1860s, visiting many of the monasteries there, including that at Nijni Novgorod. So he was very probably the first Englishman to see the Novgorod Bede since it was sent with the English missionaries to Germany in the eighth century . . . Did you know that the early English Christians played a notable part—one might even say a heroic part, since so many of them were martyred—in the conversion of the heathen Germans?"

Pause.

"Can't say that I did, no." *Merriwether's voice was now not so much distant as hollow.*

"Not many people do know, it's true. Yet it was one of the most glorious periods in our whole history. Bede wasn't unique, he was one of a generation of great English churchmen . . . But there it is: the manuscript probably went to a German monastery like Fulda, and thence to somewhere like Wismar or Stralsund on the Baltic, and from there in a Hanseatic ship to the lands of the Teutonic Knights who were invading Russia in the middle of the Middle Ages—the 'Drang nach Osten', Mr Merriwether:

Russian, Russian,
Wake yourself up!
The German is coming,
The uninvited guest—

"That's not a 20th century poem, it was written in the fourteenth century . . . and so to some German-Lithuanian monastery, at least according to Bishop Harper's theory— somewhere like Dorpat—where it was captured by a Prince of Novgorod. And from Novgorod finally to Nijni Novgorod, five hundred miles further east and fifteen-hundred miles from Jarrow, where it was written. Always travelling with the missionaries of God, English and German and finally Russian—isn't that fascinating, eh? Only to be threatened in the 20th century by another 'Drang nach Osten'—Hitler's bombers! There's the pattern of European history for you—twelve hundred years of it. And now two American gentlemen like the Major and yourself want to find out about it—even more remarkable!"

Pause.

"So what did the Bishop say, then, Mr Barkham?"

"Oh, I don't know yet, sir. I haven't been able to lay my hands on a copy of his collected letters. It was privately printed, you see—I've never even seen a copy, much less sold one. What I've been telling you comes from a colleague of mine in Cambridge, who once had a copy many years ago. But we'll both continue looking for one, if that is your wish, Mr Merriwether."

"Well, I'd sure like to see it—after that story you've told, Mr Barkham."

"Of course, of course . . . But I think you'll be disappointed. Most likely the Novgorod Bede was transcribed from one of our early English copies, possibly from the same one used for the Leningrad Bede. So it is more unlikely to contain any additional material about Mons Badonicus . . . not that that matters now."

Pause.

"No?"

Pause.

"Hah! I can see the Major didn't favour you with his absolute confidence... And I was rather hoping that he had. What a pity!"

Pause.

"You mean about—M—about Badon?"

"Exactly."

"Yeah... well, he was kind of close about it just recently."

"Close?"

"He didn't talk much. He just kind of hinted."

Chuckle.

"Exactly. In fact, I said to him: 'If you think you've found it, then you must prove it.' And all he would say was 'When I'm ready'."

"That's just what he said to me—'When I'm good and ready'. Is that all he said to you, Mr Barkham?"

"Those were his very words. And when I told him if it was true it was a very great discovery he said 'And a very great deal of trouble too'. And not one more word would he say. Which was really rather provoking in the circumstances."

"After all the work you'd done for him, huh?"

"Not so much that, Mr Merriwether... but I was more afraid he might start digging. And he isn't an archaeologist— whatever happens it must be left to them. The only testimony now can be the testimony of the spade, I told him."

Door opening—door closing.

"Absolutely right, Mr Barkham."

"I'm glad you think so, sir. Though my personal view is that his enthusiasm was, shall we say, premature. In fact, if he hadn't been so confident I would have said it was impossible... But you must excuse me while I deal with this customer... If you would care to look over those shelves beyond the desk at the back—on the right—the ones marked 'History'... start at the very top. You'll need the library steps—"

* * *

Merriwether cut off the tape.

"Wow!" exclaimed Shirley.

"He's a great old guy," said Merriwether, smiling. "I had to prise those books out of him one by one, like they were his own flesh and blood."

"He thought you were after Badon too," said Howard Morris.

"That's it, man. I had to promise I wasn't going to start digging up the English countryside."

Mosby looked towards Morris. "The book the Bishop wrote—have we got it?"

"Not yet. But we're looking. And the one thing you mustn't do on any account, Captain, is start asking for the Novgorod Bede. Don't even mention it—leave it to us."

"Okay. But suppose Audley starts asking?"

"He won't."

"Why not?" said Shirley.

"Because he's not an expert on the period."

She frowned. "For God's sake—he's writing a book on it!"

"He's writing a book on a man who lived in the twelfth century—not the sixth."

"But it's all—what's the word—mediaeval."

"So it is. And George Washington and Franklin Roosevelt are all modern. But you wouldn't expect an expert on the Second World War to be an expert on the War of Independence, would you, Mrs Sheldon?" Morris looked at her expectantly for a moment. "He knows what any Cambridge history graduate—any good graduate, that is—ought to know. Which for our purposes is enough, but not too much."

"He knows enough not to believe in King Arthur—isn't that too much?"

Morris turned towards Mosby. "I think you had something to say about that, Captain?"

"Huh?" Mosby tore himself away from the contemplation of the Novgorod Bede. "I—what?"

"You said you knew why Audley doesn't believe in King Arthur."

"Oh, sure. He's just not romantic."

"What do you mean—just not romantic?" snapped Shirley.

"Just exactly that. Remember when you twitted him with the Old South being romantic, and he looked like he'd smelt a nasty smell—like an accountant looking at a bum set of figures? Old Jeb Stuart wasn't a knight in shining armour to him, he was just a 'competent cavalry commander'."

"But that's what you said King Arthur might be, Doc," murmured Merriwether. "In fact it's *exactly* what you said."

Mosby was unabashed. "Sure I did. Only I can show you a photograph of Jeb Stuart, and you can't show me one of King Arthur.

"With Jeb Stuart there's proof and with Arthur there isn't—which is what I've been saying all along. But Audley, he lives by facts, like any good historian *and* any good intelligence man should; lives with them, eats them and sleeps with them. And the facts on Arthur are mighty thin on the ground."

For a moment no one said anything. Then Shirley shook her head.

"So—okay. But then what makes anyone think he's going to help us find Badon Hill?"

"Well, for a start it's a fact." Mosby looked towards Howard Morris.

"But impossible to find, you said."

"I settle for improbable. And it seems Major Davies didn't do so badly."

"But we don't know how he did it," said Shirley.

"That's true," said Morris.

"And the idea of trying to use Audley is crazy anyway. The British are going to be so mad when they find out—"

"*If* they find out. Audley's still got a clear two months of his leave. He's not likely to report back that he's decided to take a day or two looking for a 1,500-year-old battlefield. It doesn't sound like a security risk," said Morris.

Merriwether grinned. "No one's going to argue with you there."

"Except we know better," said Shirley. "So suppose we run into trouble?"

"Then there's a fair chance that Audley's presence will protect you," Schreiner's voice came out of the depths of his armchair. "Even Panin might think twice about making that sort of trouble. It's even possible that Audley's appearance will put them off. Or at least buy us some more time."

Shirley stared at him. "Whereas Mose and I are strictly expendable?"

"Mrs Sheldon—" Schreiner sat up "—we don't even know you. If there is any trouble you are strictly on your own: just an American couple who stumbled into something nasty."

"Oh, great! The British will believe that, I'm sure."

"They'll have to. The chief reason you were both chosen for this is that your cover is perfect. The CIA will never have heard of you—we shall invite M15 to check you both back to the cradle if they want to. You were trained and programmed for just such an operation as this."

"That's reassuring."

"It should be. I said the CIA won't know you. The State Department will fight for you as we would fight for any innocent American citizens in trouble abroad." He nodded. "But what matters is that the CIA remains uninvolved—completely. The situation is too delicate for us to take more scandal."

"You mean the domestic business?" Shirley went bald-headed at him.

Schreiner winced as though he'd bitten on a sore tooth. "Mrs Sheldon, the details don't concern you."

"When it's my neck that's sticking out they do, Mr Schreiner."

Schreiner regarded her balefully. Then he sighed. "Very

well—domestic business, as you put it, plus interference in the affairs of a foreign country."

"We just can't do a thing right," said Merriwether lightly. "No way."

The lighter side of the situation was clearly not evident to Schreiner. "I used the word 'delicate' and I meant it. The CIA has had too much bad publicity, over here as well as in the States. They gave Watergate a lot of coverage . . . and after that the business of the domestic espionage. And they know we keep a big CIA presence over here keeping an eye on their trade unions, too . . . there have been questions about it in the *Post* story about the East German freighter that was rammed and sunk in the Thames a few years back—the Agency was blamed for that, and it didn't help us one bit." His voice became increasingly mournful as the litany continued. "Even the fact that Cord Meyer was a dirty tricks specialist was pretty well driven home by their Press. So we have a new Station Head now—and a new Ambassador at the Court of St James—and we don't want them compromised."

"But we still have to do our job," said Howard Morris. "So if the Russians are mounting an operation against us over here we can't hand it to the British. It's our baby and we're paid to look after it. You understand, both of you?"

Mosby understood, to the uttermost part. Not for the first time, the Agency was between the devil and the deep blue sea. It could not afford to duck the dirtiest jobs, because handling dirty jobs was its designed function and any failure to handle them would be further proof of its incompetence. But if it glitched a dirty job, then that too would be disastrous—and doubly disastrous at this precise time, when its whole function was being questioned. On this one there would be no mercy either in Washington or in London.

"There's a whole bunch of left-wing Members of Parliament—and some of their journalists who admire the Watergate press job—who are just itching to crack the UK

Station wide open," said Schreiner to no one in particular. "That's why you are on your own this time."

Mosby looked at Shirley. So that was why two innocent American citizens, who were not at all innocent, were about to sucker an innocent British citizen, who was also not in the least innocent . . . It was going to be just like riding point for General Custer in his advance to the Little Bighorn.

"But as to why Audley will help you," Morris changed the subject smoothly, "he will because he simply won't be able to resist it. The historian in him will snap at the puzzle. It's as near as dammit a psychological sure thing, knowing the way his mind works."

"Not without tangible evidence," said Shirley.

"Okay. So that's what we're going to give him, Mrs Sheldon. Tangible evidence."

– V –

THEY SAT OPPOSITE each other beside the stone fireplace in the big soft chintz-covered armchairs, he with his massive copy of Keller's *Conquest of Wessex* and she with her *Practical Flower Arrangement*, the first fruits of which blazed on the hearth between them. Room dusted and polished, drinks and titbits on the sideboard, front door on the latch: the very portrait of domestic respectability waiting to dispense friendly hospitality, as painted by the Father of Lies.

Shirley glanced at her watch. "It's nearly nine," she said.

"No sweat." Mosby lowered Keller, trapping the pages with his finger. There was nothing more to be got from him; like Stenton, he was Anglo-Saxon orientated, conceding the existence and importance of Mount Badon, but relegating Arthur to one equivocal footnote. His heroes were not the unknown Britons of the years of resistance, but the invading chieftains, Aelle, Cerdic and Cynric and the all-conquering Ceawlin.

She frowned at him. "You're sure he'll come?"

"He said they would—I think they will. Honey, you

75

know the British don't like arriving on time, they think it's bad-mannered." He smiled into the frown. "I think we've got him figured right—he won't be able to resist Badon. I certainly wouldn't if I was him. It's the 64,000 dollar question of the Dark Ages."

"64,000 dollars?"

"Uh-huh. And if you throw in Arthur I'll make it a million."

"The price of a hill no one can find and a king who maybe never existed." She stared back reflectively. "The Sheldon valuation."

He shrugged. "Just a guess. You can't really put a price on a bit of truth like that—not *that* bit of truth, anyway."

Again she didn't react immediately, but continued to examine him, still with a trace of the original frown.

"What's the matter?" he asked finally. "I got egg on my face or something?"

"No, not egg . . . I was thinking, maybe you're a bit of a weirdo. And that's slightly unnerving."

"Huh? A sex maniac, you mean?"

"Hell, no. Nothing odd about that, it's standard red-blooded chauvinist American male . . . It's this Badon thing—and King Arthur?"

"Don't call him 'King', honey. That's the mark of ignorance. Remember your Nennius: he was the war leader. In those days British kings were fifty cents each and three for a dollar. But there was only one Arthur—if there was one. 'Fact, I wish Audley did believe in him. He's just about the most interesting thing I've ever come across."

"That's what I mean." She leant forward, clasping *Practical Flower Arrangement* to her chest. "I detect a note of enthusiasm you've never shown before, except for other people's teeth and my bed. This thing's really got under your skin."

"Under *my* skin?" Mosby looked at her in surprise. And yet maybe she was right at that, or at least half right. "I don't know about my skin, but it's certainly been bugging the British for a thousand years. You know what they called him? The Once and Future King—like he's going to come back from the dead one day. A man nobody knows anything about, not even for sure if he ever lived. And yet as far as they're concerned he's really kept going. I don't care what Audley thinks. He's really strange, Arthur is."

"It's not Arthur who's strange, it's you getting steamed up about him."

"Not at all, just line of duty research. I'm just Mr Average."

The dark hair swung in disagreement. "Not in this company. Makes me wonder how you got into this business."

From her, after having been kept literally at arm's length for so long, it was an odd question as well as an improper one. "You're not supposed to ask that one, I thought."

"Oh, sure. But now I think I need to know what makes you tick, honey—same as you have to figure how David Audley ticks." She sat back. "Besides . . . sharing a bedroom with a strange man confers some privileges, I guess. Even when it's in the line of duty. Kind of special relationship."

"Special *platonic* relationship."

"That's the way it goes: up to the line of duty, not above and beyond it." She regarded him coolly. "But you don't have to answer, naturally."

It was ironic, not to say annoying, that the first signs of interest she was showing in him beyond the curiosity of a labourer in the same vineyard should coincide with more urgent matters.

"Naturally. But you're right: a man shouldn't have big secrets from the woman in his twin bed. I'm a volunteer, not a draftee, put it like Sam Smith did—

> *My country, 'tis of thee,*
> *Sweet land of liberty,*

—General Ellsworth and I are brothers under the skin. Two old-fashioned patriots."

"I read somewhere that patriotism was the last refuge of a scoundrel."

"Shouldn't believe all you read. I'm a Sam Smith patriot. Now Harry Finsterwald, he's a Stephen Decatur patriot—'My country, right or wrong'. What I call an interchangeable patriot, like those Action Man dolls—dress him up in any uniform, CIA, KGB, M15. Pull his string and he'll say 'buddy' or 'comrade' or 'old boy' for you. But not me."

"You only say 'buddy'?"

The doorbell rang.

"You'll find out when you pull my strings." He stood up. "But you just concentrate on Audley's string for the time being, honey. I'm on your side—remember?"

One trouble with the British was breaking the ice. Or rather, you could break it the first time and get on easy terms, only to find that they were frozen over again the second time and you were back where you'd started.

Mosby had been mildly worried about this, since it was important not to get off on the wrong foot, causing Audley to shy away from the curiosity he must be feeling. With a fellow American it would have been easy, and his approach would have been instinctive. But the average well-bred Britishers of his acquaintance generally twisted themselves into knots to avoid seeming curious about anything; and as for enthusiasm, they treated any manifestation of that as an infectious disease which they could best avoid by keeping their mouths closed.

True, Audley was almost certainly not average—nobody with his job could be that. But he qualified as well-bred, one of Doc McCaslin's "establishment products" until proved otherwise, at least as far as ordinary social intercourse was concerned.

But here, quite unexpectedly, St Veryan's House came to their rescue. Both the Audleys immediately and unashamedly expressed their interest in the building itself, its present layout and the stages of renovation and conversion which had turned it from a spartan farmstead into a comfortable holiday home. Indeed, they poked and pried in such an unEnglish way that Mosby was already halfway to the correct reassessment of their behaviour when Faith presented him with the explanation.

"It's having an old house of our own—we can't resist looking at other old houses," she admitted frankly, having cased the house with the eye of a burglar. "Having an old house is like having a hobby—most people are only too pleased to show it off to a fellow collector."

"But I thought every Englishman's home was his castle," said Shirley. "Drawbridge up—strangers keep out."

"Oh, not any more. Besides, most castles are open to the public nowadays."

Her husband gave a disapproving grunt, as though he deplored the lowering of the drawbridges. "Well, it was 'Keep Out' here in the old days, that's for sure. I'd guess this was a fortified farmhouse once upon a time, complete with loopholes covering the entrance."

"Gee—fortified against what?"

"Uninvited guests." Audley pointed towards the sea.

Mosby stared down the gorse-covered hillside into the combe which cut the cliffs almost down to the little rocky beach below. Suddenly, unaccountably, he remembered the passage he had been reading a few moments before in Keller—the letter written by the Roman bishop bewailing the dreaded barbarian:

Unexpected he comes: if you are prepared he slips away . . . Shipwrecks do not terrify the Saxons: such things are their exercise . . . For since a storm puts us off our guard, the hope of a surprise attack leads them gladly to imperil their lives amid waves and broken rocks . . .

The red-orange glow from the setting sun had seemed to warm the landscape until this moment. But now it was cold, with the promise of darkness to come. And now he felt what the bishop had felt fifteen centuries ago—and what Audley knew too, so well that he instinctively echoed it in an unguarded thought, because they were both in the business of watching for uninvited guests.

"Ugh!" Shirley shivered. "I must remember to lock the door tonight."

Audley looked at her rather vaguely over his spectacles; either he had a low sex-drive or Faith Audley was damn good in bed, Mosby decided. Then he was aware that the pale eyes had moved on to him, and that they were no longer vague. He had the uncomfortable feeling that his thoughts were being read with a remarkable degree of accuracy.

"What my wife means," Audley began, as though the previous remarks had never been made, "is that the possession of old property differs from ownership of new . . . A modern house is in the nature of a consumer durable, like a refrigerator or a mass-produced car. It may have more than one owner, but it has a decidedly finite life-span. But an old house is different: you don't use its life up—it uses up yours. As a historian you should understand that, Mr Sheldon." He smiled suddenly. "But of course you're not a historian, are you. I was forgetting."

Of course he was not forgetting at all: his approach was at once typically British and as transparent as that of a well-mannered but inquisitive twelve-year-old.

Mosby laughed. "Sorry to disappoint you. I'm a dentist."

"A dental surgeon," amended Shirley quickly.

"Same thing. Pull 'em, fill 'em, straighten 'em. A plain honest-to-God dentist." He shook his head. "My wife has this thing about my being a dentist—"

"I do not!"

"Sure you do, honey—admit it, don't fight it. Lots of dentists' wives have it. Hell, lots of dentists have it."

"Have what?" asked Faith politely.

"The feeling that dentists are medical students who couldn't quite make it. Nice guys, but only good enough for pulling teeth . . . And I shouldn't really say 'pulling teeth' either. A lot of dentists, if you mention 'pulling teeth' they get excited and very upset. You got to say 'extract' or they get uptight—they're very formal about what they do because they have to impress you how important they are . . . Me, I don't need that—I'm not a retarded doctor, I'm a dentist."

"And that's important enough," said Audley gently.

"Sure as hell it is. When a kid comes to me and he's knocked out his front teeth—or when a young girl comes to me, and she looks at me and I look at her, and I know she can't get a boyfriend because her teeth are all wrong—then I don't need anyone to tell me I'm important. And what's more, I can put it right, and that's one hell of a lot more than some doctors can do with some of their problems, poor guys."

He grinned all round.

"Mose, honey," Shirley protested, "I don't think any of those things you said."

"You do so. It's just you haven't learned to be a dentist's wife yet, that's all."

Audley coughed. "And you can always cry all the way to the bank," he observed helpfully. "In my brief experience of American dentistry I formed the opinion that it was . . . ah . . . shall we say, well-rewarded?"

Mosby nodded agreement. "You're so right. Beats most doctors any day. And you can be a good dentist and not kill yourself with overwork—you can see your families and have your hobbies. When I get out of this man's air force, you just watch me do it."

Audley frowned at him suddenly. "This man's—? Did you say 'air force'?"

"Sure." Mosby nodded back cheerfully. "I'm over here with the good old USAF—the 7438th Bombardment Wing."

"Stationed over here?"

"USAF Wodden—in Wiltshire."

Audley looked at him thoughtfully. "F-111s, that would be—or is that Upper Heyford?"

"Upper Heyford? Man, they're the *enemy*. In the event

of hostilities we take them out first—Upper Heyford first, then the Russians, that's the word."

"What my husband means," chipped in Shirley, "is that on the base they spend all their time trying to be better than Upper Heyford."

"And Alconbury—don't forget Alconbury. The hell with the Reds—just beat Heyford, beat Alconbury," said Mosby breathlessly. "More sorties, better RBS figures—that's what the General lives on. One day he's going to come to me and he's going to say 'For God's sake, Sheldon, get off your butt and pull more teeth than Heyford'."

Faith Audley laughed. "And what will you say to that?"

"Ma'am, I'll say the only thing wrong with aircrew teeth at Wodden is their molars are too worn—they sit all the time and grind them down worrying about promotion."

Audley gave a small snort. "Not just aircrew teeth..." He gave Mosby an oddly lop-sided smile. "Now, in early mediaeval times molars were also heavily worn, I seem to remember reading somewhere."

"Don't tell me King Arthur's knights were worried about promotion, surely?" said Shirley.

For a moment Mosby was irritated that she had revived the discredited Arthur. But then she was only acting in her assumed character, and—more to the point—she was reacting to what was almost certainly an attempt by Audley to bring the conversation round to the subject which really interested him.

He thought for a moment. "I guess that would have something to do with their diet, eh?"

Audley nodded. "Coarse-ground flour, full of fine grit."

"That would do the trick." He had to make it easy for Audley to come to the point. "That would be your special period—the early mediaeval one, huh?"

"Not really, no. I'm a 1066 man—the Norman Conquest onwards."

"William Marshall," said Shirley. "My husband's been telling me about him. He was quite a guy."

Again Audley smiled, wholly relaxed now. It was like

she had once said: the way to a man's heart wasn't through his stomach, it was through an appreciation of what interested him.

"'Quite a guy'," Audley quoted back at her.

"Sounds like a cross between Winston Churchill, Audie Murphy and Babe Ruth—married to Jackie Kennedy," she led him on.

Audley laughed. "That's right! With a bit of Eisenhower and Henry Kissinger thrown in."

"Who's Babe Ruth?" asked Faith.

"A famous baseball player, love," said Audley. "For us the equivalent might be . . . say Barry John."

"Who's Barry John?" asked Shirley.

"A famous rugger player." Faith raised her eyes to heaven. Then she frowned at her husband. "I didn't know Marshall was a sportsman?"

"Jousting—tournaments, love," replied Audley. "Marshall was the top man on the circuit in his youth. He unhorsed 500 knights in single combat in his lifetime, and even when he was 66 there wasn't one man at King John's court who dared take up his challenge of a trial by battle." He nodded towards Shirley. "Quite a guy."

"Like Sir Lancelot."

"Sir Lancelot . . ." As Audley repeated the name his glance settled on Mosby. ". . . now he would be more in your special field, I take it, Mr Sheldon?"

Mosby had the feeling he was being double-checked for any lingering sign of the Arthurian heresy.

"Not Lancelot, no," he began warily. "He's strictly twelfth century."

"You surprise me. There aren't many non-experts who could pin him down as a twelfth century addition to the legend. For most people he's as important as King Arthur —or even more important."

"For Queen Guinevere certainly," murmured Faith drily.

"That's right. The quest for the Holy Grail is a bit out of fashion; three-quarters of the population's probably never heard of it. But they can recognise a sensational case of

adultery when they see one, they understand that all right."
Audley paused. "But then you said you weren't an admirer
of Arthur's, I remember now."

The very obliqueness of the approach—the conveniently
delayed memory of the final exchange in the car—confirmed Mosby's conviction that the Englishman was
hooked, and more than hooked: he was positively bursting
with curiosity.

"I'm not. It's the period around A.D. 500 I'm interested
in—the real history."

"The real history." Audley repeated the words, and then
fell silent, waiting for Mosby to continue.

"Uh-huh," Mosby agreed unhelpfully. This time Audley
was going to have to work for what he wanted. "It's a
fascinating period."

Pause.

"But poorly documented."

"That's what makes it fascinating."

Again Audley waited—in vain.

"The only new evidence is archaeological nowadays,
and there isn't a lot of that," he said finally, with a hint of
self-doubt in his voice.

"There sure isn't," agreed Mosby. "Our mutual ancestors
weren't exactly well-endowed with the world's goods to
leave behind."

"No consumer durables," said Shirley brightly.

Audley flashed her a microsecond's worth of exaspera-
tion. Then he cracked. "You mentioned the battle of Badon
Hill."

"You mentioned a miracle," said Faith. "That's what interested me. My husband doesn't believe in them—he's
got no romance in his soul, I'm afraid."

Audley raised a finger. "I have never said I don't believe
in miracles, I've simply never seen one myself. But I do
believe in percentages."

"Percentages?" Shirley cocked her head on one side,
questioningly.

"What most people call good luck or bad luck, depending on how it affects them." He stared at Mosby. "I take it that you've had a slice of good luck."

"A slice of good luck and a slice of bad luck... And maybe another slice of good luck now if you can help me."

Audley pursed his lips doubtfully. "I'm not an expert on A.D. 500, if that's what you're hoping."

"Okay—but we'll see, huh?" Mosby shook his head. "You can't be less of an expert than I am. I've read a lot of stuff—" he gestured to the piles of books "—but that just tells me how little I know."

"Well, just show him the stuff, honey," exclaimed Shirley with a hint of weariness. "If it doesn't mean anything to him, he'll say so." She smiled dazzlingly at Audley.

"All in good time, Shirl. Don't rush me." Mosby waved vaguely at her. "Fact is, David, I've always been interested by King Arthur—don't get any ideas, that's just the way it started—ever since I had to do an English course at College."

"You have to do English as well as dentistry?" said Faith.

"This was in pre-dentistry. We don't specialize as early as you British—pre-dentistry's a liberal arts curriculum, because there's a philosophy in the States says you shouldn't go into medicine—or—dentistry—which is very limiting, straight from secondary school. They figure it makes for limited people, so everyone gets a pre-professional education... Me, I got a smattering of French and some biology, and bio-chemistry and elementary physics."

"And English." She nodded. "It's a good idea."

"And English, right. Only our English teacher was a nut—a Tennyson nut," lied Mosby. "We had *In Memoriam* and *The Idylls of the King* until they came out of our ears. And *The Lady of Shalott*—

> *The sun came dazzling thro' the leaves,*
> *And flamed upon the brazen greaves*
> *Of bold Sir Lancelot.*

—not bad for a retarded doctor up to his ankles in other people's teeth, huh?" He grinned at Faith. "Even if it is lousy poetry."

Audley cleared his throat; there was only one thing he wanted, and they seemed to be getting away from it. "And when did the light dawn on you—about Arthur?"

"When I got over here, not until then, to be honest." Easy does it. "There was this pilot in the recon. support squadron, Di Davies. He was a real expert—"

"For heaven's sake, honey—show him the stuff," snapped Shirley. "Let him make his own mind up."

Mosby looked at her for a moment, as though undecided, and then shrugged. "Okay. Maybe you're right at that. Seeing is believing, I guess."

He brought the long shallow wooden box from its resting place on the oak chest by the door and placed it carefully on the coffee table.

Pandora's box.

With his thumbs poised on the metal catches he raised his eyes to meet Audley's. "You just take a look at this."

He lifted the lid and stripped away the glass-fibre covering gingerly. "Glass fibre makes darn good packing, but it itches like hell if you get it on your skin," he explained.

He watched Audley's face intently for signs of the same sense of anti-climax which he in his ignorance had felt at finding Pandora's box full of corroded scrap-metal. But no muscle twitched either with surprise or disappointment as the Englishman peered over his spectacles at the strange collection of objects nestling in their glass-fibre bed.

Then he leaned forward and gently lifted one of them.

"Brooch . . ." He squinted at it more closely. "A bronze brooch . . . Celtic maybe?"

"That's very good." Mosby didn't have to simulate pleasure this time: it was still a relief to find that the assessment of Audley was on the button. "Go on."

"That's as far as I can guess." Audley replaced the brooch as carefully as he'd lifted it. "There's another brooch, much the same as that one." He shook his head.

"Two Celtic brooches," Mosby read from the specification, "one perannular, Plas Emrys type, with enamelled terminals; the other zoomorphic, R.A. Smith's Welsh type. Both late fifth century, early sixth."

He pointed to the next object.

"Obviously a sword, rusted to pieces," said Audley. "Too big for a Roman sword, so I suppose it's Anglo-Saxon."

Mosby shook his head. "No, it is a late Roman sword—a *spatha*. Probably a cavalry sword." He paused. "Try the coins."

Audley pushed his spectacles up on to his forehead and brought his face to within six inches of the box. "I can't really make out much detail—they're very worn. But I guess they're late Roman, except for the four very little ones, which must be sub-Roman."

Mosby nodded at Faith. "He's good, your husband is. They are late Roman: two maybe Theodosius. And the little ones are minims, 'very debased radiate imitations' the book says, only don't ask me what it means. But similar ones have been dated late fifth century, early sixth."

Audley straightened up, gesturing to his wife. "You have a go, love. I think I'd rather stop while I'm winning." He looked down again, and then stiffened suddenly. "Except I know what *that* is." He pointed towards an object in the extreme right-hand corner of the box.

"You do?" Mosby looked at him admiringly. "Now I'm impressed. To me that was the weirdest bit of all, you know."

"It looks like a giant tea-strainer," said Faith.

"Or one half of an Ancient British brassière," contributed Shirley. "Who was that Queen Somebody in the chariot, shaking her spear at Big Ben in London—the statue?"

"Boadicea," said Faith.

"That's the one. It's just what she'd wear—a bronze brassière, C-fitting." She turned to Audley. "But you know what it is, huh?"

"I've seen one before, in a museum up north. It's a piece

of horse-armour, one of a pair that protected the eyes like goggles."

Faith Audley bent over the box as though its contents had suddenly become alive for her. "Yes . . . well, those buckles—they look like horse harness too. They're too big to be belt buckles."

"Dead right. Harness buckles is what they are," said Mosby. "Spot anything else?"

"Nothing horsey. But there's a spearhead, it looks like."

"Spearhead, Saxon, late fifth century."

"Can they date spearheads like that? I thought they were all the same."

"No, ma'am. To the experts one spearhead's as different from another as—as a Navy Colt is from a Peacemaker. And that one's a rare late fifth century specimen, seems . . . But there are some more horse pieces—those little rectangles could be armour of a sort—" he reached inside his coat-pocket for the type-written list "—it says here 'compare fragments of horse-armour found in Dura-Europos excavations'. I don't know where Dura-Europos is, but it sure doesn't sound British."

"I'm sure it isn't," Audley agreed. "It sounds rather East European—Rumania, maybe. That would be Dacia or Sarmatia, where the heavy cavalry came from—" He stopped abruptly, his gaze shifting suddenly from Mosby back to the contents of the box. For a long minute he stared at them, his eyes moving from object to object.

"There are also some bronze pendants, more horse stuff." Mosby consulted his list ostentatiously. "Sort of decorative trappings . . . plus a couple of cuirass-hinges—what they call *lorica segmentata*—"

What would they look at with the same fascination in fifteen hundred years' time? he wondered. What would there be to look at after other great catastrophes and upheavals had convulsed and changed the world, swept it clean and buried its wreckage to be dug up again and argued over?

Fragments of Vulcan rotary cannon, American, late 20th

*century ... blade from axial-flow turbojet, Russian, same
period ... part of starboard flap, unidentified jet fighter,
probably West European, mid-20th century ...*

"But that's infantryman's stuff, Roman. 'Very worn', it
says here," He offered the paper to Audley. "See for yourself."

Audley lowered his spectacles on to his nose again and
studied the list. "'Very worn'," he repeated to himself,
frowning. "Yes, well I suppose it would be ..."

Mosby waited until Audley had checked each of the
things against their more detailed specification. There was
no advantage in pressing him towards a hasty conclusion:
his whole training both as a historian and a counter-intelligence man was weighted against that, and outside his own
particular field he would be doubly cautious.

In the end it was Faith who broke the silence. "What do
you make of it, darling?" she said.

Audley's first reply was a non-committal grunt. "I don't
know that I'm competent to make anything of it, I'd need a
lot more information." He looked at Mosby shrewdly. "Besides, it seems that an expert's already examined it."

Mosby shook his head. "Strictly speaking—no, not one
expert. Different people have seen different pieces, but
you're the first to see this lot all together."

Audley considered the implications of that statement for
no more than five seconds. "Am I to take it that it was all
found together?"

Gently now. "Supposing it was?"

"Then I'd want to know where it came from." Audley's
voice hardened. "Did you find these objects?"

Again Mosby was warned of a pitfall ahead by the
change in tone, but this time he could see no reason for it.

"No, I didn't," he replied cautiously.

It was the right answer as well as the true one: Audley
relaxed visibly, as though he had been saved from an awkward situation. "But you know where it comes from?"

"That's still a sixty-four thousand dollar question—no, I

don't. I told you there was a slice of bad luck, and that's part of it."

"What I don't see is where the slice of good luck comes in," said Shirley. "I mean, it isn't as if there's anything *valuable* there, like maybe gold and jewellery. It isn't even as if there's anything new, either—I've read your old list, and it's all stuff they've found already."

She was playing smoothly now, reacting to Audley's un-willingness to commit himself and feeding him with fresh opportunities for bringing matters to a head. But again it was Faith Audley who rose to the feed line.

She chuckled uncontrollably.

Audley frowned at her. "What on earth's the matter, love?"

The chuckle became a laugh. "I was thinking—" she shook her pale head at Shirley in sympathy "—oh, dear—I can see you're not used to archaeologists, but we know several, and—" she turned towards her husband "—do you remember Tony Handforth-Jones's friend and his valuable coprolites?"

"What's a coprolite?" asked Shirley.

"You may well ask," exclaimed Faith. "A *valuable* cop-rolite—I thought it was a semi-precious stone of some sort."

"Well, what is it?"

"Well, to Tony's friend it was a semi-precious stone," said Audley. "But to the rest of us it was . . . not to put too fine a point on it—and actually you can't put too fine a point on it—it was a piece of fossilised animal excrement. In this instance belonging to a Neolithic dog, I think."

"A piece of—" Shirley stopped.

For an instant Mosby envisaged his final report of this conversation, but then hastily abandoned the vision: that way hysteria lay. CIA headquarters in Langley was not equipped to evaluate dog shit.

"Ah . . . I think what my wife means is that you can't use the word 'valuable' in a conventional way when it comes to artefacts like this, Mrs Sheldon," continued Audley, gesturing towards the box. "All these objects can be identified because they've been found in different places, and in themselves they perhaps aren't especially valuable. But all together in one place—I've never heard of a find like this before, never."

"That's what I told you, honey," said Mosby. "The Roman stuff, all worn out and mended, and the Celtic stuff, and the Saxon stuff—all in one place and not one bit later than A.D. 500. And all the rest of it—"

Audley stiffened. "All the rest of it? You mean this isn't all of it?"

"Hell, no—it isn't the half of it. I only brought the bits that would travel. There are more weapons, all broken—there are two or three Saxon swords, what do they call them—scramasaxes? And more horse stuff. And bones—man, you name it, I've got it."

"Bones?"

"Sure. Human and horse. I've got a skull with the prettiest depressed cranial fracture you ever saw, a classic blunt instrument fatality. And another with what looks mighty like a sword-cut."

"It sounds as though someone's been ransacking a museum," said Faith.

"No, ma'am, not a museum. Most of it's still got the original dirt on it."

"God Almighty! It's far worse than ransacking a museum," Audley burst out angrily. "Someone's ransacked the most important Dark Age discovery since Sutton Hoo."

So that was the key to that earlier hint of anger: he should have guessed from Barkham's reaction that Audley would be as incensed by the possible destruction of an archaeological site as excited by the appearance of the objects from it.

"You're dead right," he agreed. "Badon."

"Badon?" Audley stared at him. "You mean—the date's right . . . and the equipment's right?"

"More than that. I mean the guy who had this stuff reckoned he could prove it."

Before Audley could speak, the phone in the hall pealed out.

"Honey, someone's actually remembered we're alive!" Shirley leapt into her role as the non-pioneer wife. "Go answer it before they change their mind."

Mosby hurried to complement her performance with that of the obedient American husband.

"Sheldon here. Who's that speaking?"

"Gallagher—"

For an instant Mosby was unable to place Gallagher in the ranks of his CIA colleagues, who had been sprouting in the most unlikely places since Davies's death.

"—Is Harry Finsterwald there?"

The sandpaper voice helped him decide: Gallagher's cover as a moronic CAS sergeant, a character straight out of 'The Flintstones', was if anything better even than Finsterwald's.

"Blanche? Hi, Blanche." He held the receiver back from his mouth and called through to the sitting room: "Honey, it's Blanche Castillo."

"Gee, that's great. Does she want to talk to me?"

"You got someone else there, huh?"

"Yes, Blanche, we're both fine. Do you want to speak to Shirley?"

"Okay. Has Harry and that nigger of his gone?"

"Yes, she has . . . No, honey—she's calling about some remedial treatment . . . Yes, Blanche."

"They heading back to base?"

"Yes. Are you worried about it? You sound worried."

"Worried is right. You know an enlisted man named Pennebaker? AIC Pennebaker?"

"Not so as I recall. Should I?"

"If you don't you never will now. He's blown his brains out."

"He—how's that again, Blanche?"

"He's dead. The British police found him in his car about ten miles from the base. Suicide, it looks like, they say."

Shirley came to the doorway. "Has Blanche gotten herself into a tizzy again, honey?"

"Uh-huh . . . I'm sorry to hear that, Blanche."

"Not half as sorry as we are."

"Was he on the short list, then?"

"For the Davies job he was on the short list."

"Is that a fact? I guess that's where the trouble is, you'll find."

"Where it was. He had no right to be off base, so it looks as though he decided to run before anyone caught up with him."

"Certainly looks like that . . . But you don't go along with the local dentist's diagnosis?"

"The local cops? Officially we do. Unofficially we don't."

There was a pause. *"You know where this leaves you, fella? Right in the front line, that's where."*

Mosby could see that all too clearly. If the dead man had been a professional planted on the base it would be near impossible to trace his movements and contacts off it, if he would have exercised professional care. But why had his own side silenced him?

"Just watch yourself, that's all. These bastards aren't playing games."

"I know—and I will, believe me, Blanche. It's nice of you to say so . . . and I won't forget to tell Shirley too. 'Bye."

He turned back towards the sitting room slowly, the force of Gallagher's final warning weighing heavily on him. If Pennebaker had been a KGB plant, and not some poor devil blackmailed into sabotage . . . but the Davies hit had been too cold-blooded for that. So if the man had been a pro, then he wouldn't have been thrown away on some penny-ante operation, but only on something big and nasty which made the loss acceptable if it delayed pursuit.

Shirley smiled at him brightly. "You solved her problem?"

He shook his head. "No. But she's going to have to deal

with it herself." He looked at Audley. "We've got problems of our own, huh?"

Audley nodded. "I think we have, Mr Sheldon."

"Mosby. I know it's one hell of a name, but I've gotten used to it—David."

The Englishman grinned. "I beg your pardon—Mosby. . ." Then the grin vanished. "Before you tell me anything more I think I'd better make one or two things straight."

"Okay. Shoot."

"Well, for one thing, if there's been an unauthorised dig—and from what you've said it looks as though there has been—there could be the very devil of a row about it."

"Does that sort of thing go on?" asked Shirley.

"Not so much now. But there was a lot of unprofessional work with metal detectors not so long ago, and the thing became a bit of a public scandal."

"Is it against the law?"

"It could be—especially if there are precious metals found which could be treasure trove, because they have to be reported to the local coroner. But in any case the land owner has to give permission, you can't just dig where you like."

"Well, supposing he did give permission?"

"There still could be a scandal." Audley pointed to the box.

"And with this stuff there will be scandal, I can promise you that."

"With *that*?" Shirley sounded incredulous.

"I think your husband understands." Audley glanced at Mosby quickly. "Archaeological discoveries can be front page stories in Britain—Fishbourne and Vindolanda were. And if . . . *if* this really did turn out to be the key to Badon —" he shrugged "—I don't believe in the King Arthur legend, but—"

"But one hell of a lot of people do, huh?" Mosby completed the sentence.

"Passionately. Lots of people have never heard of

Badon, but there isn't a single person in this country who hasn't heard of King Arthur."

"It'd be headlines, in fact?"

"The biggest. And there'd be hell to pay—there's going to be hell to pay."

"But—hold on—" Shirley began hotly "—my husband didn't dig this up. He just kind of . . . inherited it, that's all."

"Inherited it?" Audley frowned at Mosby. "From whom?"

"Well, I was going to tell you—I started to. There was this friend of ours, Di Davies—he was a pilot in recon."

Audley caught his wife's eye. "Photographic reconnaissance," he explained.

"That's right. There's been one extra squadron on the base for the last six, seven months—RF-4cs—what you call Phantoms, only these are reconnaissance versions of the ships the RAF flies . . . And Di Davies was a real Arthurian nut, he even called his ship the *Guinevere II*. He came to me for a check-up one day and saw I was reading Keller—Keller's "Conquest of Wessex"—and we got to arguing about Arthur before I even had a chance of getting a look into his mouth. He said Keller was a no-account Kraut-lover and Arthur was the real thing. And what's more he was going to prove it."

"And how did he propose to do that?" asked Faith.

"That's just what I asked him. I said fat chance he'd got of doing it when the British had been trying to do just that for years, and they'd got no place—what'd he got that all the historians and the archaeologists hadn't got?"

"And what had he got?"

Mosby looked at her. "Well, for one thing he said he'd got the exclusive use of one Phantom, with a whole battery of cameras that can do things you wouldn't believe—forward oblique, low and high altitude panoramic, side oblique, vertical, automatic exposure control, image motion compensation, black and white, colour positive or transparency or infra-red, you name it, he'd got it. Plus all the flying time in the world as well as the know-how, he'd got that too."

Faith started to open her mouth, but her husband forestalled her. "So he could take good pictures, I don't doubt it. But if that's his material—" he stabbed a finger at the box "—is it?"

Mosby nodded. "Yeah, I guess so."

"Well, if it is he's come down to ground level." He paused, frowning. "You say you *inherited* it?"

"In a way."

"What way?"

"What way. . ." Mosby sighed. "Last time I saw Di was —well, it'd be about a month back, with one thing and another. I went States-side on a conference, then he had some leave and after that I filled in at Alconbury for a spell when a couple of the guys were sick there. And then he was on exchange duty with the RAF in Germany, at Wildenwrath, for the NATO cross-fertilization programme— it'd be all of two months, wouldn't it, honey?"

"You didn't see him, and I didn't see you," said Shirley. "But I saw him."

"That's the point. Go on, honey—tell it how it was."

She shrugged. "There really isn't a lot to tell. When Mose was away at Alconbury Di came to me and asked if we could store some boxes for him. You see, we've got lots of room and he was in a little cottage off the base where you couldn't swing a cat. He said he just wanted somewhere dry and safe, that was all."

She shrugged again as though she found the repetition faintly boring; and lapsed into silence.

"For God's sake—" Mosby exclaimed with a flash of simulated irritation "—that wasn't all. I told you: just tell it like it was."

"Huh?" The look of incomprehension was pure Billy Holliday.

"The bet, honey, the bet."

"Oh, *that*."

"Oh, that—yes." Mosby gave Audley an apologetic 'I-know-she's-beautiful-but-let's-face-it-she's-also-dumb' lift of the eyebrow.

"You and your silly bet. I can't see why you make such a fuss about it, honestly."

"Because it was for real, that's why."

"Oh—phooey." She scowled at him, and then smiled sweetly at Audley. "Well, naturally I asked Di what was in his precious boxes, had he robbed a bank or something."

Audley nodded at her encouragingly. "Yes?"

"I said if it was a bank job we'd want our cut. And he laughed and said not a bank, but something just as good. And we'd get our cut, only it was going to cost us. Or rather, it was going to cost Mose, because that was the deal—'one bottle of Napoleon Brandy, the finest that money can buy. No more and no less', those were his exact words, and he said I was to make sure and tell Mose that."

"We had this bet—" Mosby started quickly as Audley switched his attention. "We had this argument in the club one night, started when I needled him whether he'd taken any good pictures of King Arthur lately. And he said how would I like a little bet on it—a proper wager entered in the squadron betting book the barman keeps under the bar for guys who are ready to put their money where their mouth is." He nodded at Audley. "And I could see he meant it one hundred per cent."

"So what did you say?"

"Hell, I told him I wouldn't bet on Arthur—because I didn't take candy from babies. Then he said 'Okay, so you won't bet on Arthur—so we'll bet on Badon, I know you believe that exists . . .' And he turned to the barman and he said 'Get the goddamn betting book out, Paddy, and write this down: *Major Davies wagers Captain Sheldon one bottle of Napoleon Brandy, the finest that money can buy, that he will locate the site of Badon Hill during this tour of duty in the UK, his evidence to be assessed by a mutually acceptable third party.*' And he signed it right there on the bar. One bottle of the finest Napoleon Brandy."

There was a moment's silence, then Faith spoke. "You

mean—" she looked from one to the other of them "—but, David, you said that no one knows where Badon Hill was —or is?"

"No one does." Audley continued to stare at Mosby. "Where's Davies?"

"He's at the bottom of the Irish Sea, somewhere between Anglesey and the Isle of Man, with what's left of *Guinevere II*," said Mosby. "But the way I see it, I've still got a bet to settle."

– VI –

THEY'D STARTED OUT at the crack of a grey dawn, following a cross-country route which Audley swore was not only simple and free from traffic bottlenecks, but which also encompassed some of the prettiest West Country and South Midlands scenery. But it rained miserably and one way or another they managed to lose their way four times, twice in a bewildering maze of tiny roads meandering in the middle of nowhere and twice in the middle of towns which they had never intended to visit.

The upshot of these minor disasters was Shirley's frayed temper, the product of her offer to navigate ("Scenery? I'm too busy looking for signposts to see the scenery"), and a time-loss which forced them to snatch a hasty lunch in an Olde Englishe pub so ruthlessly olde Englishe that it could provide no ice to cool the tepid drinks with which they tried to wash down their bread and cheese.

Yet with a perversity that brought Shirtley's temper to fission point, Mosby enjoyed the journey: its sheer unpleasantness, recalling the family trips of his childhood, made him feel more genuinely married to her than he had ever felt before. His innermost and most secret fantasy, that this was really simply Dr and Mrs Sheldon, two innocent American tourists on the track of Arthur, required no special effort of self-deception for a few precious hours. For that brief space of time it was more real than the reality.

And then, with almost startling suddenness, as though the weather itself had caught his mood, the quality of their journey changed. They left the rainy country behind and drove into sunlight, with only a few puffs of high white cloud to set off the blueness of the sky. And when Shirley complained of thirst they stopped for early tea at a little roadside cafe which turned out to be closed but which nevertheless opened specially for them, with the plump little old proprietress fussing about them in a totally uncommercial manner, producing freshly-baked cakes from her oven, hot and delicious.

The change in atmosphere seemed to confuse Shirley.

"I don't know what you did to get that red carpet rolled out for us," she murmured gratefully as they took to the road again.

"All I said was that you were tired and thirsty."

"I guess she thought I was pregnant or something." She looked at herself critically.

"Chance would be a fine thing . . . But it can be arranged if you like the idea."

She gave a discouraging snort.

"Arthur for a boy, Guinevere for a girl." Mosby hastened to hide himself behind a shield of flippancy.

"That'll be the day."

Indeed it would be, thought Mosby wistfully. The millennium.

But now the excitement of journey's end took hold of him. For some time they had been travelling in distinctively Cotswold territory, a rolling landscape of weathered slate roofs and dry-stone walls enclosing small, neat fields —slate and stone which even in its grey old age retained a hint of the pale honey colour of its youth. And as they dropped down off the ridge from the main highway (even the signposts had now become easy to see and simple to follow) he was reminded of Audley's phrase: It's deep in the Cotswolds. *Deep* was right; there was a deepness in this little wooded valley, a sense not so much of secrecy as of privacy, which had somehow survived beneath the tree-tops he'd glimpsed from the turn-off above.

The only indication that the valley was occupied had been the pinnacles of a church tower partially hidden among the leaves, but there was in fact a surprising number of houses clustered around the church, all linked and inter-locked by high stone walls which turned the narrow streets into miniature canyons through which Mosby nosed the big car gingerly, knowing that he'd have to back up if he met any other vehicle larger than a wheelbarrow. But there seemed to be no other vehicles to meet, no other life even; the place was as empty as a Spanish village in the depths of its siesta.

Before he realised it they had cruised right through the place, over a tiny bridge, and on to the hillside beyond.

"Damn it," Mosby muttered, "he said to ask in the village, but there's no one to ask."

"They're probably all having tea," observed Shirley unhelpfully. "Tea and cucumber sandwiches."

With difficulty he backed the car into a farm gateway, and after much manoeuvring between the restricting stone walls managed to get it facing downhill again towards the trees.

This time he knew better what to expect, but there was still no sign of life anywhere until he was almost out of the village again, and then the life wasn't human: his way was blocked by a magnificent Dalmatian sitting right in the middle of the road.

As he slowed to a halt, the Dalmation showing not the least inclination to move, he caught a flash of movement out of the corner of his eye.

"Here's someone now," said Shirley eagerly. "Ask him quickly before he disappears."

The someone was evidently a native of the place, a

swarthy young man with a shock of black hair and devil-slanted eyebrows, by his frayed shirt, stained corduroy trousers and enormous muddy boots most likely a farm labourer. But that at least meant that he'd know the answer to Mosby's question and the expression of amiable curiosity on his face was encouraging.

"Excuse me, sir—" Mosby smiled out of the car at him. "—I'm looking for Forge Close House. Dr Anthony Handforth-Jones."

The farm labourer pointed away towards the dog. "*Inside*, Cerberus—*at once!*" he commanded sharply before turning back to Mosby. The dog rose lazily and ambled to one side of the road.

"Dr Anthony Handforth-Jones," Mosby repeated.

"That's me," said the farm labourer, returning the smile. "You must be Dr Sheldon—I thought I saw you go by just now and I knew you'd be coming back, so I sent Cerberus out to hold you—*get inside, you idiot*—I'm sorry, but I don't want him to think he can have the job full-time, he enjoys it too much already . . . Just back down the road five yards, and the gate's open on your right."

Mosby backed and turned obediently into a gap in the ivy-covered walls which let on to a well-tended circle of gravel bordered on three sides by a house and its outbuildings and on the fourth by a towering beech tree under which several cars were parked. One of them, he recognised at once, was Audley's.

"I guess we're rather late, but we got lost four or five times," explained Mosby apologetically.

"I'm not surprised. You followed one of David's cross-country short-cuts." Handforth-Jones eyed Shirley with approval. "We've learnt by bitter experience never to take the slightest notice of them. Saves a lot of time that way—any way but his way . . . But we suspected you wouldn't know that, so we haven't been expecting you. Besides, he's only just arrived himself."

"Did he try to follow his own short-cut?" asked Shirley.

"Not if Faith was driving." Handforth-Jones chuckled.

"But actually I gather he stopped off on the way at Liddington Hill. Looking for King Arthur, I shouldn't wonder."

Evidently another non-believer, thought Mosby. But what was more interesting was that Audley had taken a quick and rather surreptitious look en route at Winston Churchill's Number One choice for Badon Hill without letting slip his intention. Except—the one thought came quickly after the other—it would be a mistake to assume that he was up to something already, it was far more likely simple proof that he was committed wholeheartedly to the project, even if it wasn't in reality quite the one he believed it to be.

"Don't worry," Handforth-Jones hastened to reassure him, clearly mistaking his expression, "he didn't find anything—there's absolutely nothing to find. It's just an iron age earthwork. A perfectly good iron age hill-fort, but nothing more."

"You don't fancy earthworks?" Mosby remembered what Audley had said about Dr Handforth-Jones: *Not a Dark Ages man, but he'll know who is.* Just what else he might be remained to be seen, but that in itself was the sound of their plan getting into gear.

"Rather depends on whose earthworks. Not yours, I'm afraid."

"Mine?"

"Arthurian—is that the correct term?" On so short an acquaintance Handforth-Jones evidently didn't wish to sound scornful, but the scorn was there beneath the surface all the same.

"David's told you?" Mosby probed.

"Only what he said on the phone." Handforth-Jones raised a bushy eyebrow interrogatively. "Trouble is, term's been over for three or four weeks now and there aren't many people around in the University. In fact, you only just caught us—we're off to North Africa at the end of this week . . . I've done the best I can at such short notice, but whether it'll be good enough is another matter. But then you're something of an expert yourself, David says."

"Me? Hell, no. I'm a seeker after knowledge."

"You are?" This time both eyebrows signalled polite disbelief. "Well, I've got you Sir Thomas Gracey but I wouldn't call him an expert in your field . . . But then I'm afraid you've chosen a period in which the seekers rather outnumber the finders. In fact there are precious few finders—or even no finders at all, that might be more accurate."

Handforth-Jones concluded with a half-grunt, looking towards Shirley as though for confirmation of the obscurity of her husband's obsession. But Shirley was now working hard on her well-rehearsed representation of the Little Flower of Southern Womanhood Drooping for Want of Attention and Refreshment. Mosby wasn't sure whether it was wholly simulated in this instance, or whether the imminent prospect of meeting Sir Somebody Someone was helping to give it authenticity. But he was gratified to see that it worked as quickly on the British male as it did on the American: Handforth-Jones's casual manner at once became solicitous, as though what he had orginally noted as a pleasant piece of decoration he now recognised as a human being, and a guest as well.

"Yes—well . . . well, you'd better come inside and seek some tea first. We can collect your bags later." He pointed vaguely towards the front door. "In fact I think we'd better hurry, or we'll be too late."

Mosby couldn't help looking mystified.

Handforth-Jones intercepted the look. "Not too late for Arthur, they're not going to find *him* just yet. Besides, David refuses to discuss him until you're present. It's just that if we don't get a move on he'll have eaten all the cucumber sandwiches. He was getting through them at a fearful rate when I heard your car the second time—"

It wasn't the moment to catch Shirley's eye, Mosby decided. Not because she might burst into hysterical laughter, but because she might see her own doubts reflected in his

face. Dropped in a steaming Asian jungle full of commu-
nist insurgents he knew exactly what he ought to do, the
Fort Dobson training had seen to that; and she was no
doubt ready at a moment's notice to mingle unobtrusively
with the Saturday housewives of Novosibirsk. But the Fort
Dobson familiarisation instructors had failed signally to
prepare them for cucumber sandwiches in the Cotswolds
with Sir Someone, in pursuit of the Once and Future King.

Which, to be fair to Fort Dobson, was hardly surprising.

They followed Handforth-Jones into the house. Nothing
surprising there, anyway: well-heeled upper middle class
English, still rubbing along in English-style comfort despite swingeing taxes, fast depreciating investments and
the envious eyes of their new Trade Union masters. Rugs,
maybe Persian, on the oak floorboards; pictures, maybe
original, on the walls; delicate china on delicate furniture.

The only thing out of place here was Handforth-Jones
himself, clumping along in his heavy boots with the dog at
his heels, both equally oblivious of their surroundings.

But that only served to remind Mosby of what Audley
had said of the man, half admiringly, half warningly, entirely without rancour: a sharp fellow, Handforth-Jones, a
great raiser of funds for his archaeological projects; a sharp
fellow who, wearying of raising money, had solved his
problems permanently by marrying it ("David, that's a
gross slander! It was true love"—"I didn't say it wasn't my
dear"—"I mean Margaret, not her money"—"And I mean
Margaret *and* her money. The two are not mutually exclusive"); above all, a sharp fellow who could add two and
two and therefore must not be supplied with enough facts
now to make that addition.

They passed through an arched door, down an antique-
timbered passage towards another door, with the tinkle of
teacups beyond . . .

And Sir Somebody beyond, too.

Like the man said, the Fort Dobson man, *the jungle, the*

desert, the sea, you fight 'em and they'll beat you every time. So Lesson One is—you don't fight 'em.

But the Fort Dobson man had never come down in the Cotswolds.

Handforth-Jones held the second door open for them, and over Shirley's shoulder Mosby caught sight of David Audley popping the last fragment of a sandwich into his mouth. There was something about the action—maybe it was the way Audley examined his fingers in search of stray crumbs—that suggested it was also the last sandwich. But then with the relative sizes of Audley and the genteel English sandwich that figured.

Faith Audley rose from the chair beside which her husband stood, relief at their arrival plain on her face.

"You made it!" she exclaimed.

"In the end we did," Shirley admitted.

"Margaret—" Faith turned to a dark-haired replica of herself who had also risen at their entrance "—Captain and Mrs Sheldon—Shirley and Mosby—"

Lesson One in Cotswold survival had to be Good Manners, but it took every last bit of his willpower to keep his eyes on his hostess and not on the mountainous figure standing behind her. It would have been easier if she'd been outstanding in some way, or at least different from his preconceived idea of what this setting ought to produce. But it was like she'd been designed to blend into the scenery.

Shake hands and murmur-murmur.

"I don't believe you've met Sir Thomas Gracey," she said at last.

Blessed relief: he could look at the mountain at last.

"No," said Mosby. That was for sure, because once seen, never forgotten. "I don't believe we have."

"Thomas is the new Master-designate of the King's College at Oxford," said Fairth helpfully.

Of course he was: Mosby held on to reality with the convulsive grip of a drowning man. The ringers here were only Audley and Shirley and himself, the three who looked like what they said they were, but weren't. Or were something else very different first and last. Dr Anthony Hand-forth-Jones only *looked* like a migrant worker, and Sir Thomas Gracey only *looked* like he'd stepped out of the pages of Raymond Chandler.

"Hi," said Shirley, smiling up at an angle of sixty degrees, offering her small hand to be engulfed by Sir Thomas's hairy paw.

It only made things worse: Velma was meeting Moose Mulloy for the first time.

Moose Mulloy shook him by the hand in turn.

"Captain—" the grip was firm and gentle "—or should it be 'doctor'? When I was over in the States at UCLA I had the misfortune to fall into the hands of some of your colleagues, and I recall that American protocol says 'doctor'."

If there was a sting there, then the smile removed it. True, it was rather like being smiled at by a gorilla, and yet it was oddly attractive and as gentle as the handshake.

"Doctor or Captain or mister—but for choice Mosby will do . . . They took you for a bundle, eh?"

"They did very good work." The large head moved in a curious circular motion which was neither positive nor negative, but which was somehow expressive of qualified gratitude.

"They would. They're the best, if you like their sort of thing."

"What sort of thing is that?" asked Margaret Handforth-Jones.

"West Coast dentistry? That's where all the big techniques are—the real high-powered technical gold work, and crown-and-bridge, and precision attachments, it's all done in the West. They think they're the best, and they probably are—technically."

"You don't sound as though you approve," said Sir Thomas.

"Yeah, well . . ." Mosby tailed off. It was a hell of a

wayout thing to be discussing at this stage of the proceedings, and not at all what he'd expected.

"Go on," urged Margaret, "it sounds fascinating."

"It does?" Mosby wondered at such politeness, but
maybe it was the custom here to show an interest in one's
guest's profession, even when it was a gruesome one like
dentistry. "Well, I think maybe I have a prejudice . . . but to
my mind they ignore the underlying physiology and pathol-
ogy. I mean, they take the teeth, which are solid substruc-
tures, and they build complex and beautiful bridge work,
but they ignore the physiology of the living substances
which are supporting these teeth. And I have a feeling—
I've no real evidence, but it seems like common sense to
me—that if you overload the teeth with this sort of very
expensive treatment, then you could be playing tricks on
your mouth and there'll be a price to pay at the end of it."

"You mean the shortened life of the teeth themselves?"
said Sir Thomas.

"You're absolutely right, that's exactly it. And I
think—"

"Honey!" Shirley cut through his enthusiasm warningly.
"You're going to make everyone's teeth ache before you've
finished, you know you are—" She smiled apologetically
at the company. "He has this *thing* about the West Coast—
he'll talk about it obsessively for hours on end if I let him."

Which was true enough, reflected Mosby, aware suddenly that for one happy moment he'd forgotten who and
where he was.

"Then you really are a dentist?" said Handforth-Jones.

Mosby looked at him in surprise. "Is there any reason
why I shouldn't be?"

"No real reason at all. Very useful thing to be . . . much
more useful than an archaeologist, as my wife will no
doubt remind us all." The archaeologist grinned amiably.
"We just didn't believe you were, that's all."

"Why on earth not?" said Shirley.

"Oh, your husband isn't to blame," Sir Thomas hastened
to reassure her. "It's more the company he keeps. We've

learnt to have the gravest doubts about anything David puts his hand to."

"David?" Shirley frowned. "I don't get you."

"Actually, it was King Arthur who made us suspicious, as much as David," explained Handforth-Jones. "The idea of David wanting to help anyone research Arthurian history—we just couldn't swallow that at all."

"Why not?" asked Mosby.

"Not his cup of tea." Handforth-Jones wagged a finger at Audley. "I remember what you said about the South Cadbury excavation, the one that Sunday paper called 'The Camelot Dig' . . . It was in this very room—and you said to call it that almost qualified for prosecution under the Trade Descriptions Act."

Audley shrugged. "A man can always change his mind."

"Not you, David, not you," said Margaret.

"I'm always open to conversion, Maggie. You're not being fair."

"Fair?" Margaret echoed the word derisively. "Why, you're the most unconvertible man I know—the original Doubting Thomas. 'Show me the marks of the nails' ought to be your family motto."

Mosby sensed, rather than actually saw, Sir Thomas stiffen.

"Ye-ess . . . the marks of the nails," Sir Thomas repeated the phrase slowly to himself. "If I taught you anything years ago it was to be sceptical, and that was a lesson you learnt almost too well . . . Which does raise an alternative possibility. And a much more interesting one, don't you think, Tony?"

Handforth-Jones met the glance. "An alternative?" His eye in turn switched first to Audley, then to Mosby, then back to Audley again. It was like watching a chemical reaction. "Yes, I take your point. It could be a case of 'What has it got in its pocketses?' And that would be much more interesting. More logical, too."

"Are we playing some sort of game?" asked Shirley.

"They're always playing games of one sort or another,"

said Margaret. "What sort of game are you playing now, darling?"

"A logic game. David was down in Devon finishing off the great work on William Marshall. Not to be disturbed by his friends—right?"

"Right," agreed Sir Thomas. "And David, as we all know, is likely to be exceedingly scornful of the Arthurian interpretation of early sixth century history—right?"

"And Dr Sheldon is exactly what he says he is."

"So the peace and quiet of Devon is abandoned—"

"And William Marshall is abandoned—"

"And little Cathy is off-loaded on her grandma?" Margaret joined the game tentatively. "Would that be significant?"

"It would," agreed Sir Thomas. "It signifies business, not pleasure. Not—" he looked at Audley narrowly "—official business, because Faith is along for the ride, but business all the same."

"Arthurian business," said Handforth-Jones. "Because—"

"Because Dr Sheldon is what he says he is."

"And a man can always change his mind."

They were both grinning now, increasingly sure of themselves.

"A man who insists on seeing the marks of the nails. Only now he wants to know the latest score on Arthur: who's writing, who's digging." Sir Thomas paused.

"Pure as driven snow," murmured Handforth-Jones.

"Pure indeed . . . What have you got, David?"

Handforth-Jones nodded towards Mosby. "Or what has Dr Sheldon got. Something to change David's mind, perhaps?"

"And that would have to be . . . quite something, I rather think," agreed Sir Thomas. "What have you got, the pair of you? The Holy Grail?"

So the infallible Audley could miscalculate too, thought Mosby, taking a quick nervous look at the man. Or, if he hadn't miscalculated the extent of their powers of addition, he'd underrated their ability to sum him up. The only reassuring sign was that at least he didn't look much disconcerted at the way they played their little games.

"Christ, but we're sharp this afternoon!" Audley acknowledged the look with a nod. "It's exactly as Mr Toad said—'The Clever men at Oxford know all that is to be Knowed'."

"Not all, not quite," admitted Sir Thomas modestly. "But we do know you, David, we do know you. So what have you dug up now?"

" 'Dug up'?"

"Figuratively speaking. I know you don't soil your hands with work in the field."

Mosby breathed an inward sigh of relief.

"Except that it would have to be dug up," said Handforth-Jones. "Nobody's going to turn up an Arthurian text now."

"Are people digging any Arthurian sites?" asked Audley.

"Not that I know of. There's some early Anglo-Saxon work going on, of course. There usually is."

"On an Arthurian site?"

"All depends what you mean by Arthurian."

"What do you mean?"

"God knows." The archaeologist shrugged. "Not my field, as you know jolly well . . . But say, late fifth century, early sixth for argument's sake."

Mosby felt it was time he joined the fray. "Where would you look for an Arthurian site?"

Handforth-Jones regarded him silently for a moment, as though adjusting himself to a damn-fool question within the limitations of good manners. "*If* I did . . ." There were volumes in that *if* ". . . I suppose it'ud be anywhere west of Oxford, south of Gloucester, east of Bath and north of Winchester and Salisbury."

"Why there?"

Handforth-Jones worked some more at the adjustment. "Why there? Well, I suppose that would be the sort of area someone like Arthur would have to defend. The Anglo-

Saxons started off in Kent and East Anglia—and they were already in the Middle Thames, of course. That's where the early burial evidence is. And then they were coming up from the south, from Sussex and Hampshire, in the early sixth century, and north-east from Cambridgeshire."

"But someone stopped them."

Handforth-Jones pursed his lips. "Yes . . . well that's the theory, and there is some evidence, I agree. But when they did finally break through in the second half of the sixth century, this is where they did it—battle of Dyrham, near Bath, in 577. The Britons were finished then: the West Country and Wales were split in two . . . So I see your Arthur as fighting somewhere in these parts, yes."

Audley gave a grunt. "But the Arthurian place-name evidence doesn't exactly fit that, does it."

"It doesn't fit anything. If place-names are anything to go by he must have been a superman. Place-names aren't worth a damn, if you ask me—"

"They have their uses, Tony," said Sir Thomas.

"Not for Arthur, they don't."

"Why not for Arthur?" asked Mosby.

"Because they're too widely spread, for one thing. You can find Arthur's Tombs all over the place, even outside the old boundaries of Britain—where the Picts were, for instance, in Scotland. What he was doing in Pictland, heaven only knows."

"Gee, but I thought he lived in Tintagel," said Shirley breathlessly. "The guide-book *said* so."

"Yes . . . well, that's what guide-books are good at," said Handforth-Jones. "But there isn't a shred of proof—historical proof, that is. Geoffrey of Monmouth invented the Tintagel bit in the twelfth century."

"In the *twelfth*—" Shirley squeaked with outrage, as though for anyone to make up history so far back in history was dirty pool "—he just made it up?"

"Honey, I told you," said Mosby, "Malory and Tennyson and the rest, they all made things up."

"There are half-a-dozen places up and down the country

where he's alleged to be sleeping in a cave, waiting for the call to come and save us all," said Handforth-Jones. "But if the last year or two haven't been bad enough to wake him, I can't imagine what will . . . Manufacturing Arthurian history has been practically a national industry for the last eight hundred years."

"You don't say?" Outrage had given place to disillusion in Shirley's voice.

"I'm afraid so. But you shouldn't find that very surprising, your people have been doing much the same for the Wild West—Billy the Kid and Jesse James and that lot—and that was practically within living memory. It's much the same process at work."

"But they were for real."

"And King Arthur wasn't?" Sir Thomas shook his head slowly at Shirley, smiling a curiously old-maidish smile. "Mrs Sheldon, you must understand the company you are keeping, and then allow for it. These two, in their own twisted ways were once among the very best students it has been my fortune—or misfortune—to teach."

"He was a bright young don once upon a time," said Audley, "though you wouldn't think it to look at him now."

"But over the years David has become a hopeless sceptic," continued Sir Thomas, "and Tony is a professional devil's advocate. They are exactly the wrong persons to be let loose on Arthurian history."

"Oh, come off it, Tom," said Handforth-Jones. "I read an article not long ago—no, it was a book, a perfectly respectable published book, or a respectable publisher anyway—in which some otherwise reputable professor claimed that if you fly over Glastonbury at a great height you can see various mystical signs on the ground—something to do with field-patterns and rivers and suchlike—that prove the existence of Arthur. All quite mad, but it's all regarded very seriously by those who believe in such things. That's the trouble with Arthur: I haven't the faintest idea whether he existed or not, because there isn't any proof. But he does make people who believe in him behave in the most extraordinary way. For all I know he did the Saxons a lot of harm. But I know he's done even more harm to the study of his alleged period. And that's *not* devil's advocacy."

The archaeologist's tone was a degree less bantering now, though as unrancorous as Sir Thomas's had been. Obviously the two men disagreed pretty fundamentally, but not bitterly because this wasn't their particular speciality, so that no professional reputations were involved.

"But you believe in Arthur, Sir Thomas?" Mosby inquired.

"Believe?" The huge seamed face screwed up as though the word was being assessed for flavour. "Perhaps that would be too strong . . . You see, Tony's quite right about the lack of evidence—and the place-names are extremely suspect. Many of them have been made up in comparatively recent times . . . some of the *arth* ones in Wales may simply mean 'bear', which has been distorted in much the same way as the 'wolf' names have been—Woodhill Gate in one of the side valleys off the Whitby Esk, for example . . . the locals pronounce it 'Woodill', which is a corruption from Woodale—it never did have a wood and it's a valley not a hill. And if you turn up a pre-Ordnance Survey map, there it is: *Wolfe-dale*." He paused and then shrugged. "Or again, they may be related to shrine-names for the Celtic goddess Artio—"

High above and far away, the distant sound of aircraft engines rumbled. Not Pratt and Whitneys of the F-111 or the Phantom's General Electrics, Mosby's well-tuned ear told him, but the turbo-props of a big transport. Hercules, maybe . . .

Arth-names and the Celtic goddess Artio . . . Christ! What was he doing here among English professors and Arth-names and monks dead fifteen-hundred years? What, conceivably, could they tell him about Major Davies's Phantom shattered into obscene scrap metal in the emptiness high over the Irish Sea?

He closed his eyes, fighting to distinguish the real from the unreal, as the engine-rumble faded into silence.

"—and Chambers quoted the Rhys theory that Arthur and Mordred were Airem and Mider in the ancient Irish fairy tale."

Goddamn. Enough was enough, surely.

"Sure. But—"

"—But you think there's something in it, all the same?" Audley bulldozed over him quickly.

"Yes, frankly I do. The trouble with Tony—at least when he's not digging up his Roman villas—is that he sees half the truth very clearly and the other half not at all . . . That analogy with the old Wild West, for instance—it's a good one as far as it goes. The old West, the Golden West where men were men and there was land for the taking. Where everything was simpler and more free."

Shirley laughed. "I don't think the West was really like that, Sir Thomas. I think it was pretty uncomfortable."

"Oh, I'm sure it was. Freezing in winter and boiling in summer. Dysentery and smallpox. Starvation and Red Indians—I'm sure it was unpleasant. But there were no payments on the new car or worries about the children taking drugs . . . and it's a natural human feeling to yearn for the good old days, *le temps perdu.* So the Welsh looked back to the days when they were the British—when they had the whole island, not a scroggy corner of it. And later on the English take over the legend—and even people on the continent. In fact the first Arthurian story-cycles are Breton and French; he inspires most of the orders of chivalry on the continent. And here there was Edward III's Order of the Garter, and his Round Table at Winchester—his French Wars were essentially Arthurian Wars."

"All of which proves absolutely nothing about Arthur," said Handforth-Jones.

"Ah—but there you're wrong. So much of it started with Geoffrey of Monmouth, and of course no one believed him—I didn't for one. But then, you see, when Atkinson excavated Stonehenge in '52 and sent off stone chips from the blue sarsens there to the Geological Museum in Kensington they pinpointed the place the stones came from to within half a mile: a hundred and fifty miles as the crow flies, and on the other side of the Bristol Channel. That was the first thoroughly scientific study of Stonehenge, to my mind. And it just *happens* to fit in with another of Geoffrey of Monmouth's stories—which no one had believed either."

"You mean he was on the level?" said Mosby, caught again by the fascination of the Arthurian labyrinth despite himself.

"On the level?" Sir Thomas considered the Americanism with judicial gravity. "No, I wouldn't go so far as that. I think Geoffrey was a literary man of his time, which means that he didn't apply modern critical methods and that lack of evidence simply stimulated his imagination."

"He made things up too, huh?" Shirley's continuing disillusion with things British and English was still evident.

"I'm sure he did. And he was probably less scrupulous than most—he was looking for a good patron and a nice soft job somewhere so he wrote what the right people wanted to hear."

"The right people?"

"Whoever was boss, same as today," said Audley. "And there are still plenty of experts in that gentle art."

"But that doesn't mean everything he wrote was fiction," Sir Thomas went on calmly. "He was a sort of early don, but he was brought up on the Welsh Marches. And he always claimed that he'd had access to what he called 'a very ancient book in the British tongue', remember."

Mosby didn't remember, but nodded wisely.

"Huh!" Handforth-Jones snorted. "Typical spurious mediaeval claim—doesn't prove a thing. Evidence is what you want, and you simply haven't got it."

Audley laughed suddenly, as though it pleased him to see them strike sparks off one another. "But you do believe in Arthur, evidence or no evidence, don't you, Tom?"

Sir Thomas faced him. "Well, quite frankly, I do. Or I

believe that there was somebody—call him Arthur or not, and Nennius did call him Arthur a long time before Geoffrey of Monmouth—someone who came up with a stunning victory for the Britons, big enough to check the Anglo-Saxons for the whole of the first half of the sixth century—" he gestured towards Handforth-Jones "—even Tony has to agree with that, it's what the archaeologists say."

"Ahah!" Audley pounced on the point. "Now you've got to watch yourself, Tony. The Devil's quoting scripture at you."

"I'm not arguing with facts," Handforth-Jones shook his head, "I'm only arguing with conjecture. Damn it, you should understand that, David."

Audley looked to Sir Thomas without answering that one.

"Do you dispute Mons Badonicus?" said Sir Thomas.

"No. That's Gildas, which is fair evidence as far as it goes."

"And where would you place it?"

"Nobody knows."

Mosby understood at last why Audley had kept the debate moving as he had, and why his own flash of irritation had been so quickly capped. First he had ducked the question *What have you got?* by turning the debate on to Arthur; then he had let them argue their own way round to Badon, knowing that sooner or later they must come to it. So in the end they had seemed to come to it without his prompting.

"Nobody knows. But if you had to start looking, where would you look?" Sir Thomas waited for a reply, but Handforth-Jones wasn't to be caught that easily. He shook his head and grinned knowingly at Mosby as if to indicate that he recognised the familiar signs of ambush, even though he didn't know what form it would take.

"It's a pointless question."

"Oh, no. It's a question with two points, and the first is that you don't want to answer it." Sir Thomas stabbed a finger at the archaeologist accusingly. "He doesn't want to answer. And I'll tell you for why." The switch from the first to third person indicated that the next observation was for everyone's benefit—and that the trap had been sprung. "Because he's already given the answer, only it was to a different question. That's why."

"Huh?" Shirley looked suitably mystified.

"'West of Oxford, south of Gloucester, north of Winchester-Salisbury, east of Bath'," quoted Audley. "Tom means you'd look for Badon in the same area as you'd look for Arthur. Give or take a few miles either way."

Give or take—? Mosby struggled with his English geography. He had actually been to most of the towns mentioned, because none was more than an hour or two's drive from USAF Wodden and all were tourist attractions, well supplied with cathedrals and colleges and other ancient buildings. But in retrospect he found it difficult to differentiate one from the other, beyond the vaguest impressions: tall spire for Salisbury, colleges for Oxford, Roman bath for Bath . . .

"Exactly." Sir Thomas nodded emphatically. "If you plotted the possible Badon sites—Bedwyn in the Kennet valley and Liddington Hill near Baydon, and the rest of them . . . none of them need to be the one, but all the ones that fulfil the basic criteria—they all fall within the area Tony said someone like Arthur would have to defend."

Mosby's first elation at having an area drawn for the Badon hunt began to cool. It must measure anything from fifty to seventy miles a side—maybe as much as five thousand square miles.

Sir Thomas continued: "So what Tony is saying is that Badon was fought just where Arthur would have fought it, and just when Arthur would have fought it, only Arthur never existed, so someone else fought it . . . And all I'm saying is *why not Arthur*?"

He looked at Mosby expectantly.

"'It's true, or it ought to be; and more and better besides'," quoted Mosby. The phrase had stuck in his mind.

"Ah, now that would be dear old Winston Churchill. A romantic, of course, but he could very often smell what he couldn't see."

"And not the only romantic," murmured Handforth-Jones.

"Meaning me?" Sir Thomas looked at him sidelong. "Well, at my age I can afford to take that as a compliment. And there are times when my sense of smell sharpens too." He smiled at Mosby. "So why not come out with a straight question, Dr Sheldon?"

The attack caught Mosby by surprise. "Sir?"

"A straight question. Something David is temperamentally incapable of asking. Or answering."

Mosby frowned. "I don't get you, Sir Thomas."

"Tck, tck." Sir Thomas clicked his tongue. "Now it's you who is playing games."

"I am?" Mosby looked at Audley for support. "Are we?"

"I didn't say David was playing games," said Sir Thomas quickly. "Indeed, that's what makes this so interesting now: David may have his fun, but he doesn't really play games any more."

"Except the 'great game', of course," Handforth-Jones amended. "But King Arthur's a bit long in the tooth for that, thank heavens."

Mosby couldn't place the allusion accurately, but it didn't take a genius to guess its meaning as Sir Thomas nodded his agreement: they knew damn well how Audley was employed.

"True, very true." Sir Thomas eyed Audley speculatively for a moment before coming back to Mosby. "And it's that which makes it the more interesting, I'm thinking."

If only you knew, buster, thought Mosby, some of his awe evaporating. The clever men at Oxford didn't know quite all that was to be knowed after all.

"I still don't get you," he said.

"No? Well, perhaps we're doing you an injustice again ... but it does rather look as though David is about to poach on our scholarly preserves. And that does make us a little cautious, because the last time he did that there was a certain amount of trouble and strife as a consequence."

Mosby remembered what Schreiner had said: Audley had had an intelligence assignment in some northern university two or three years before.

"Huh?" Mosby fought for time behind his well-tried look of bewilderment: he was just an American dentist doing his time in the Service, knowing nothing of any of this—just an American dentist with an interest in Arthurian history.

But the knowledge within him was cold as a sliver of ice in his heart. He had been less than fair to the clever men who couldn't imagine Badon Hill as a security risk: to imagine anything else would be crazy, not clever.

Except it wasn't crazy at all. The reality wasn't this gracious well-polished room with its gracious well-polished people in their quiet little Cotswold valley: it was a body drifting in the Irish Sea.

He looked at Audley questioningly.

Audley returned the look calmly. "I told you they were sharp this afternoon."

"Well, I wish to hell I was. All I want to know is—"

"Mons Badonicus," said Audley.

Mosby blinked at him in surprise, silenced by such a major script-change.

"Ye-ess," Sir Thomas nodded slowly, "yes, I think maybe Badon would fit the bill if anything did."

"Badon?" Margaret Handforth-Jones stirred. "What bill? What do you mean, Tom?"

Sir Thomas pointed at Audley. "David's bill. Dr Sheldon there has caught him—seduced him, if you like, away from poor William Marshall. And he couldn't do that with Arthur."

"Why not?"

"My dear—because he's just like your husband. Not a sentimentalist . . . Arthur, Camelot, Excalibur, the Round Table, the Holy Grail—he'd laugh at them. They aren't facts. But Badon—Mons Badonicus, Mons Badonis, call it what you will—Badon is different."

Mosby's awe returned, tinged with worry. Sharp was right: the guy was too goddamn sharp for comfort—altogether too damn explicit in putting his finger on what it had taken the psych. experts a whole day to come up with.

"Put it this way," continued Sir Thomas smoothly, "this is the so-called Dark Ages we're talking about, and the darkest hundred years or so of that. And what do we actually know about them—know as historians know, I mean?

"We know about very few solid facts. We know the beginning and the end of it—in the year 466 the Britons appealed to the last great Roman commander in the West, Aetius, and there were British Christians at the Council of Arles in 443. But Aetius turned them down and there weren't any Britons at the next council in 484.

"That's one end of it. And at the other is Tony's battle of Dyrham, near Bath, in 577, the decisive Saxon victory—their Gettysburg, if you like." He nodded towards Mosby. "Myself, I'd say the battle of Bedcanford, which is probably Bedford, in 571 was equally decisive, but that's neither here nor there. One way or another the Britons were finished by then. They'd lost the initiative for good.

"And the middle fact—the truly fascinating one—lies between those two dates: the greatest lost battle in British history."

"Badon," said Margaret.

"Badon. We don't know where, we don't know how, and we don't know who." He swung round suddenly to stare directly at Mosby. "Or do we?"

"We don't," Audley cut in sharply.

"But you've got a strong clue." There was an edge to Sir Thomas's voice which had not been there before.

There was the risk which Audley had understood when he had insisted on not coming straight out with the question, Mosby realised: to get the information they needed they had to go to the experts, but in their own field the experts were jealous of interlopers. That reference to 'poaching on our scholarly preserves', no matter how gently delivered, had been intended as a warning to the interlopers.

"Maybe."

"No 'maybe'. I know you, David."

Goddamn it, there was more than scholarly suspicion here. They had been sitting self-confidently on their box of goodies, sure that they knew something no one else did. But maybe they'd been a little too confident at that.

"We think somebody had a clue." Audley wasn't going to reveal his ace in the hole that easily.

"Had?" Sir Thomas frowned.

"He's dead."

"Dead?" Sir Thomas switched his frown towards Hand-forth-Jones.

"If he is then it's news to me," said the archaeologist. "And it would've been in the papers for sure."

"Who?" Now Audley sounded puzzled. "Who's this 'he'?"

"You tell us, David."

Audley turned towards Mosby. "It rather looks as though we've got two somebodies, Sheldon."

"Sure as hell does." Mosby's mind had reached the same junction. "'Tisn't likely they've got ours, anyway."

"No . . ." Audley thought for a moment before nodding his head towards Sir Thomas again. "And your man's got a clue to Badon, has he, Tom?"

"Not so far as I'm aware. But he's been looking for one, I do know that."

"An historian?"

"I wouldn't call him that. At least, not in the accepted meaning of the term."

"An archaeologist, then?"

"Certainly not," snapped Handforth-Jones. "Not in any meaning of the term."

"He was an airman, actually," said Sir Thomas.

"*An airman.*" Mosby was dumbfounded.

"An ex-airman, to be precise. Now he considers he's been called to even higher things."

"He was a very good pilot, so I'm told," Handforth-Jones addressed Sir Thomas conversationally. "I met a chap not long ago—he was excavating a site up in the Persian Gulf—he met him when he was leading a counter-insurgency squadron for some obscure sultan down the coast there. He was quite impressed with him."

"I don't doubt it at all," Sir Thomas agreed readily. "But good military commanders are very often deplorable politicians. The Duke of Wellington is a case in point." He nodded at Mosby. "And your Ulysses S. Grant is another. I don't believe that—"

"*Billy Bullitt,*" said Audley.

"Billy Bullitt, of course. Do you know him?"

"I've heard of him, but never met him."

"A treat in store, no doubt. Because he's the man you want to see if it's Badon you're after. Complete with that famous red shirt of his."

"Who's—" Mosby began, only to be instantly over-ridden by Audley.

"But what the devil has he got to do with Badon?"

"Pursuing his patriotic duty, apparently. He was up here for a week last term looking for Geoffrey of Monmouth's 'very ancient book in the British tongue'. He didn't find it, not surprisingly, but he badgered the life out of the people in the Bodleian Library, so I've been told."

"IIah!" Handforth-Jones sniffed. "And he wouldn't leave poor old Fletcher Holland alone at the Institute of Archaeology either—Fletcher's an authority on early English history."

Mosby drew breath to try his question again.

"But—"

"But he was after Mount Badon, was he?" cut in Audley.

"Oh, sure. It was Badon all the time, with Arthur thrown in. In the end Fletcher got so exasperated that he insisted Arthur was actually a Scottish prince of Dalriada, or somewhere, and Badon was Vardin Hill up there—you often get transpositions of *v* for *b*. At which Billy Bullitt went off in a huff."

"Not that you can blame Bullitt for that. If you are an authority, or if you are running a library, you must expect to be bothered by people who want to know things—that's what you are there for." Sir Thomas gave a thin smile. Then the smile faded. "But he also accepted an invitation to speak at the Oxford Union—what was the debate, Tony?"

"Oh, 'This House believe that Britons never will be slaves', or some such rot."

"That's right."

"It's a line from the chorus of *Rule Britannia*," explained Audley to Mosby.

"Well, actually it isn't—as Billy Bullitt was at pains to explain," said Sir Thomas heavily. "It's a line from an eighteenth century masque on King Alfred—not to be confused with King Arthur—according to him. And his point was that in Alfred's time the majority of the Britons were slaves—to the Anglo-Saxons. But at least that was slavery by conquest in war, whereas now nobody had the guts to fight for our country—now we were all slaves, and that was all we deserved to be. We'd lost our honour, apparently."

"Good rousing stuff," murmured Handforth-Jones.

"Rousing is the word. There was practically a riot after the debate and seven undergraduates were arrested for causing a breach of the peace—"

"Thus disproving Bill Bullitt's thesis that they hadn't the guts to fight," said Handforth-Jones.

"Ah, but it was no joke, Tony." Sir Thomas said seriously. "They turned a car over."

"Yes—they thought it was his car, but of course it turned out to belong to some perfectly innocent person. And then—"

"Now hold on a minute." Shirley tossed back her hair and stuck her chest out into the dialogue. "Will someone kindly tell me who this Billy Bullitt is?"

The chest instantly succeeded where Mosby had twice failed, though for a second or so it brought admiring silence rather than explanation.

Then Audley cleared his throat. "I'm sorry. Group Captain William Bullitt, DSO, DFC, RAF retired. Or resigned might be more accurate."

"Group Captain?"

"Colonel would be the equivalent in your air force."

"Uh-huh . . . And we should have heard of him, huh?" She pivoted towards Mosby. "You heard of him, honey?"

"Can't say I have, no." Mosby frowned.

"No reason why you should have. He was a nine-days' wonder ten years ago when he resigned from the RAF, and then he made the headlines a year or two back when he came home from the Middle East. But he's hardly an international figure. More a colourful one—the Press loves the red shirt and the combat hat he always wears."

"Why did he quit your air force?" asked Mosby.

"It was over the TSR-2, wasn't it?" said Sir Thomas.

Audley nodded. "That's right. The RAF's wonder plane of the sixties and seventies that never was."

"Never got off the drawing-board, huh?"

"Oh, it got off the drawing-board. And off the ground too."

"But it was no good, you mean?"

"On the contrary," Audley shook his head ruefully, "by all accounts it was very good—way ahead of its time. But unfortunately also way ahead of its budget too. So the Labour Government scrapped it and ordered your F-111 instead. Which they also cancelled—in the end we bought Phantoms from you."

"Uh-huh . . . and I guess Billy Bullitt had a few things to say about that too."

"A few."

"I get the picture. Your Billy Bullitt equals our Billy Mitchell—"

"Now, honey," Shirley waved him down frantically, "don't go making things worse. They won't know who

Billy Mitchell was any more than we knew this Billy Bullitt."

"Wasn't he the one who bombed the battleship?" said Handforth-Jones.

Mosby clapped his hands. "That's right. Back in 1921 —he said planes could sink battleships. So they gave him an old German one, and when he'd proved his point they said 'Get lost, you bum—and don't show your face round here until after December 7, 1941'."

Shirley sighed theatrically. "You have to forgive my husband. Outside of teeth and King Arthur he's got a butterfly mind."

"Not at all," said Mosby. "If Billy Bullitt's anything like Mitchell then he must be quite a guy."

"More like quite a fascist, according to some people," said Faith Audley with a sudden flash of vehemence.

"A fascist?"

"Now hold on there, love," protested Audley. "He may have been a pain in the neck for some of your Labour friends, but now your schoolgirl prejudices are showing. He's never had any known political connection, left, right or centre."

No known political affiliation: the phrase welled up in Mosby's mind. He had seen it recorded on a dozen files, it was one of the first checks in any security profile.

And now, on Audley's tongue, it meant one thing only: the British had run such a profile on Billy Bullitt.

But just maybe not well enough.

– VII –

NOBODY SEEMED TO mind Mosby's going off by himself on foot after breakfast, ostensibly to explore the village, even though he had used the same excuse to do the same thing after dinner the evening before. In fact everyone seemed pleasantly relaxed, bent on doing their own things along the several lines they had agreed during the evening meal, with no second thoughts and consequently no need for further discussion.

"Make sure you see inside the church this time," admonished Margaret, as she heaped potatoes into a bowl. "It's really quite a good one, and there are some super views from the top of the tower."

"It isn't locked, then?" Mosby repeated his explanation for the previous expeditions's omissions. "The church, I mean?"

"Good heavens, no. Why should anyone want to lock it? There isn't anything of value there unless you count the Mothers' Union banner . . . which incidentally I've promised to repair. It's got the moths in it, or something." She smiled at him over the potato peelings. "You wouldn't be a

dear and collect it on the way back, would you? It's waiting for collection inside the vestry. . ."

As he made his way down the hill between the now
familiar (and, as usual, empty) canyons of Cotswold stone-
work, Mosby reflected that for once General Ellsworth
would be proud of him.

The General was a keen advocate of Good Relations between his officers and what he termed 'the Indigenous
Community'. As a result, while enlisted men were encour-
aged by every means to stay on base (since the only relations they could be relied on to establish with the natives
were sexual), certain mature and reliable officers were
practically ordered to do their bit in the cause of Anglo-
American friendship. Mosby had hitherto not qualified for
this unpopular duty, because the General clearly didn't regard him as a suitable representative of the American way
of life. But now, with a tale of the Mothers' Union banner
which would lose nothing in the telling, he had the means
of changing all that.

The General would also be proud, if not surprised, at the
way he had handled himself yesterday, too, he decided. It
wasn't simply that he'd mentioned Billy Mitchell, one of
the General's heroes, but also that he'd implemented two
of the highest Ellsworth precepts, Co-ordinated Effort and
Delegation of Authority, as to the manner born: Audley,
Shirley and Sir Thomas Gracey were for the time being
doing all the work, while he busied himself with a little
gentle Data Monitoring and Operations Analysis. Which
was exactly what he should be concerned with at the Infor-
mational Phase of his Implementation Structure Programme.

What was strange, almost disturbing, was the comfort he
now derived from his virtuous condition. In his late-night
debates with Doc Hollister on the essential nature of the
Service mind, and in particular the devious mind of General Ellsworth, they had always ended by agreeing that it
was high in crap and low in credibility; or as Doc McCas-

lin put it, 'Man cannot live by jargon alone.' Yet here he was, on assignment at last, instinctively playing it by the General's book.

Self-analytically, he decided that it was his involvement with Shirley that was to blame. Or, to be fair, it was the personnel controller who had united Agent Sheldon with Agent Morgan in simulated wedlock in the belief that nothing was liable to develop between them except maybe a little casual sex, which wouldn't inhibit their efficiency.

That would have been the calculation, and it could hardly have been wider of the mark: Agent Morgan—and that probably wasn't even her real name, he thought with a curious twinge of sadness—had kept her legs tightly together, and Agent Sheldon had graduated through thwarted desire to romantic and protective daydreams . . . Which were ridiculous—he'd even been comforted this early morning by the knowledge that she'd be safe enough in the joint company of Audley and Sir Thomas.

Or perhaps not so ridiculous, because danger there must sooner or later be, that was for sure. Not yet, this tranquil English summer's day, and not here, on the quiet lane to the church. But sooner or later the safe gathering of information among civilised men would end and they would catch up with the killers of Major Davies and Airman Pennebaker, who weren't playing scholarly games . . . Which cold bit of logic must sharpen his wits now, because Information Minimises Risk.

Ellsworth again, for God's sake.

He would have to do something about ditching Shirley. But since Shirley was unaware of his feelings that might not be so easy . . .

Either the village had once been a lot bigger or the old Englishmen who had lived there had reckoned on impressing the Almighty with their enthusiasm, because the Church of St Swithun and All Angels was out of proportion with the rest of the place: it was on the way to being a miniature cathedral.

The element of surprise was increased by its seclusion; it was so completely surrounded by tall elms that it was only possible to get glimpses of it—even from the road on the ridge above the village only the pinnacles had been visible through the trees—and because he hadn't realised the steepness of the valley and the height of the elms Mosby had been expecting a much smaller building.

And yet, surprisingly again, it was neither overshadowed nor overawed by its trees, but stood in the midst of a sunlit churchyard full of ancient tombstones which sprouted from the well-cut grass.

That first impression of loving-care was confirmed by a notice pinned on the board beside the gateway: "This Churchyard received a Special Commendation in the Churchyard Section of the 1974 Best Kept Village Competition. Visitors are asked not to disturb the south-east corner, which has been left in its natural state for the purpose of ecological study."

Mosby pushed the wooden gate gingerly, fearing to disturb the false ecological tranquility of a scene under cover of which millions of insects and small creatures were doubtless busily eating and being eaten. The hinges had been well-oiled, however—as one would expect of a Specially Commended churchyard—and it was not until the latch clicked shut again that he startled a group of glossy young blackbirds from their breakfast among the graves. Even then they flew only a few yards, to settle as though by common consent on another favourite feeding ground, full of confidence and greed. No doubt graveyard worms were especially succulent, even though man's rôle in the food chain of this older part of the churchyard, where the stones were grey-weathered, had long been exhausted.

The crunch of the gravel under his feet was unnaturally loud, so he forsook the path for the grass, pausing to read those stones which still had legible inscriptions.

William Higgs, Esquire/Born May 21 1672/Died March

*17 1743 . . . Benjamin Hunt, Esquire/Born April 3 1690/
Died January 6 1757 . . .* a healthy place, this; or maybe
only the better-off could afford stones in the prime loca-
tions and the poor, dying young, went into unmarked
graves . . .

*Geo. Pratley/Departed This Life/February 12 1752/Aged
72 Years/I know that My Redeemer liveth/And his wife
Sarah/March 3 1752/Aged 70 Years.*

A life-long love story there, maybe, with Sarah hasten-
ing to follow her George. Or maybe just a hard winter
balancing the ecological books.

But it would be nice to think of another stone some day,
somewhere: *Mosby S. Sheldon/Departed This Life*—say—
February 12 2025—that wasn't too greedy—*And his lov-
ing wife/Shirley Aged*—

Nice, but goddamn ridiculous. He didn't even know her
real date of birth any more than he knew her real name.

He still had a full half-hour in hand before Harry Finsterwald arrived, enough time for him to see all the things
Margaret Handforth-Jones would expect him to have seen.

But first things first. The chuch was unlocked and the
door of the vestry was open, as Margaret had said it would
be, and the Mothers' Union banner was there waiting for
him, neatly furled alongside a crisp white line of choir-
boys' surplices and what looked like the vicar's second-
best jacket and emergency dog-collar.

Reassured, he went back into the main part of the
church; the banner could wait until after he'd met Finsterwald. It was one thing to beat General Ellsworth with it, at
a time and place of his own choosing, but quite another to
present Finsterwald with so choice a tit-bit.

Next, the tower—he must be able to enthuse about the
'super views', even if the other finer points of church ar-
chitecture would have to be dismissed on the 'we've-got-
nothing-like-that-back-home' level.

The tower door was concealed behind a heavy curtain

and although it was also unlocked it was secured with a
massive iron bolt, so stiff and set so high up that it would
have discouraged the more adventurous of the local small
fry. And the route thereafter was well-calculated to put off
most other explorers: at first a steep stair climbed awkwardly in the thickness of the stone wall to another high-
bolted door which opened on to a bell-ringing level
festooned with ropes which disappeared into holes in a
ceiling far above; faded biblical exhortations "O Lord,
open Thou our lips" and "Our mouths shall show forth Thy
praise", painted on the walls in large letters, gave place to
a curtly printed card "KEEP THIS TRAP SHUT" thumb-tacked
on a trapdoor at the head of a rickety wooden staircase.
After that there was a level empty except for the continuing
bell-ropes and a naked ladder climbing to another trapdoor
bearing a similar notice; then, at last, the bells themselves,
huge and still in the confined space . . . one of Ellsworth's
ambassadors, an officer of no known religious persuasion,
had become an enthusiastic bell-ringer (and a devotee of
warm English beer into the bargain)—he had even tried to
infect Mosby with his strange mathematical passion for
change ringing, but to no avail . . . and then another ladder
to another trapdoor.

Then blessed sunlight and fresh air, and the cooing of
pigeons turning into the flapping of heavy wings as the trap
banged open.

Mosby caught his breath and steadied himself on one of
the tall stone pinnacles which had looked so delicate from
ground level, but which now had comforting stability. It
was humiliating to have such a poor head for heights, and
especially this particular height, the uneasy treetop zone
belonging neither to earth nor heaven, too high for safety
and too low for detachment. The slight queasiness in his
stomach and the prickle of sweat on his face were the familiar symptoms of the fear he always experienced at the
moment of take-off and landing.

The difference was that here they were totally irrational,
he told himself angrily: the tower of St Swithun's Church

had stood firm for half a thousand years and was probably good for the next thousand. If there was any place where he could get to grips with his weakness it was here.

Looking down was worst, so he would look down first—

In the stillness of the churchyard the movement at the gate caught his eye instantly. And even if there had been no movement the bright blue and yellow of Harry Finsterwald's check shirt would have shouted at him.

He cursed under his breath and looked at his watch. Just when he'd found the guts to experiment with his fear the stupid jerk had to jump the gun by a full twenty-five minutes, breaking the rule (which admittedly he had also broken, but with better reason) that rendezvous times should be kept exactly unless—

Unless.

The sudden thought shrank Mosby into the cover of the pinnacle. Then, very slowly, he raised his head into the right angle where the stone upright joined the parapet and peeked down again.

The confirmation of his fear was immediate. Finsterwald hadn't walked boldly up to the church porch, as he ought to have done, but had slipped to his right behind the cover of one of the trees which flanked the gate. And now he was reaching under his shirt for something in his right hip-pocket.

Mosby stared down incredulously, hypnotised both by the unfolding scene below and by the thought of the sequence of events which must have produced it.

Finsterwald had been tailed off the base, but hadn't spotted his tail and had believed until too late that he was in the clear.

Which wasn't altogether reassuring, because if Harry Finsterwald was no intellectual giant the mechanical things like spotting and shaking inconvenient tails would be right up his alley. Which in turn meant a whole lot of even less reassuring things, like for a start that the tail was smarter

than Finsterwald—and also that Finsterwald would be
goddamn mad at having been outsmarted at his own game.

Mosby's pulse quickened. There was only one thing
Harry could do, having screwed things up so beautifully, to
unscrew them, which was to take out the tail before the tail
could report back. That was what he was now preparing to
do, and he, Mosby, had a grandstand seat for the performance. And there was nothing he could do about it except
pray that Harry had the sense and skill to take the man
alive.

Except, of course, it could be just Harry's imagination.
Or merely Harry's prudent double-check against the remote
possibility that someone had played it cleverer than he had.
Lord, let it be pure imagination or prudence.

Trouble was that the Lord must know, since Mosby already knew, that Harry Finsterwald was short on imagination and long on arrogance. So—Lord, let him not foul it
up right here in front of me. Just let him do it right.

For a minute nothing moved below him. The churchyard
was as still as a churchyard ought to be. Even the blackbirds seemed to have decamped. Above the shielding trees
he could hear the hum of the traffic away on the main road
three-quarters of a mile away on the ridge, but down there
it would be dead quiet, giving Harry the edge.

The minute lengthened. A pigeon—presumably the one
he had disturbed—flapped heavily out of one of the elms
towards the tower, saw Mosby crouching against the pinnacle, and banked off steeply to head away over the valley,
following the meandering stream.

Hope flickered within Mosby. It was going to be all right
after all. Or maybe it wasn't all right; maybe he ought to
wish that there had been a tail on Harry Finsterwald, someone they could catch and interrogate. Someone who could
give them any sort of lead more solid and believable than
the incomprehensible one he'd been following these last
few days.

Then both conflicting hopes were extinguished in a brief
glimpse of movement between the tree trunks outside the

churchyard wall to his right. For the next two or three yards an inconvenient branch obscured the view, then he caught the movement again. Someone was moving warily—too warily for anyone on his lawful occasion—along the line of trees towards the gate.

Where Harry was ideally placed to take him.

Mosby felt a pang of sympathy for the tail, remembering how he'd flunked three tests of this game hopelessly in training. On an unsuspecting, untrained, innocent subject it was easy, but no one had yet found a practical reason for following unsuspecting, untrained innocents, and against a properly trained pro with a bad conscience it was damn near impossible.

He remembered his instructor shaking his head at him phlegmatically, a squint-eyed, honey-faced ex-cop who'd done it all and seen it all.

"You gotta tail you don't make till too late, you gotta be blind. You do the thing right, and you make him—he does the thing right, you still make him. Just ain't no way he can get the edge on you except—"

Holy damn! The memory of the next words punched Mosby's panic button sickeningly. Forty minutes' drive from the base, it could hardly be less, and Harry still hadn't spotted his follower until too late to try anything except this. But no matter he was a fool, there was nothing wrong with his eyesight.

"Just ain't no way he can get the edge on you less he's got a partner doubling with him—"

A partner?

Now he couldn't even see the first man, let alone a second one. Just Harry waiting to jump—and be jumped.

Because that was what was going to happen, sure as fate. If the sole object was to watch Harry to see what he was doing and who he was contacting they wouldn't make the first move. But the moment they realised he was on to them—and, Christ, maybe they already suspected it—it would be the Davies-Pennebaker treatment.

He felt the seconds draining away, and seconds were all he had to figure the angles.

Too few seconds, too many angles.

He could shout a warning—nothing easier. Maybe scare the bastards off; they sure as hell wouldn't know the nearest thing he had to a weapon was a Mothers' Union banner down in the vestry—

But maybe they wouldn't scare that easy—

And maybe throw Harry's attention the wrong way at the wrong moment—

And, either way, blow his cover—

And screw the mission.

The man said: *When in doubt, do it by the book.*

The book said: *When the success of a mission conflicts with the survival of an operative, no operative shall abort a mission without first having evaluated comparatively its importance against the value of the said operative—*

Just great, that was. Evaluate comparatively the value of Harry Finsterwald against the importance of Mons Badonicus—how the shit did he do that?

Maybe he should do like King Arthur—take up the banner and charge—

Then Sir Mosby bore on his shoulder the banner of the Mothers' Union in St Swithun's Churchyard, and through the strength of St Swithun and the Mothers' Union there was great slaughter of the heathens and they were put to flight—

Well—hell—they might die of surprise, at that. But they sure wouldn't mistake him for the local vicar, so—

But why not?

Why not?

By the time he reached the vestry, every trapdoor left gaping behind him, every door swinging, he was almost as breathless as he'd been after the climb up to the tower. The soft life on the base keeping the world safe for democracy had taken its toll.

But the vicar's spare dog-collar was no bad fit, he decided gratefully as he fumbled for its button at the back— if it had been too tight God only knew what he could have done, for there was no time left for more ingenuity.

The grey linen jacket wasn't too bad either; a shade too long in the sleeve and a couple of inches too wide at the middle, but when buttoned up not too loose to hold down the black square of material which hung from the collar. Not a shred of his unecclesiastical—and unBritish—T-shirt was now visible, and that was what mattered.

There was nothing he could do about his blue flared trousers, so that risk had to be taken. At least he was all-vicar—all authentic vicar from the hip-line up.

A hat of some sort would have been a bonus, but one glance round the vestry revealed no hat. He could only hope that they didn't know him by sight already.

Then, as he reached for the banner, he felt a hard object move in the side-pocket of the jacket. A spectacle case, complete with spectacles. The bonus after all.

He perched them on his nose and the vestry blurred hopelessly: the vicar had long arms, but short sight—the only way he could bring things back into focus was by lowering his chin and peering over the frames. But maybe that was no bad thing after all; it might add a vague, even scholarly, look appropriate to his stolen trappings.

But there was no more time. Even now he might be too late.

He seized the furled banner and ran.

At the door at the porch he forced himself to pause. This was the last moment for second thoughts. If they knew him by sight it might be last thoughts once he was outside. But he mustn't think of that. Instead he must rely at the worst on a few seconds of doubt. For who, after all, was the most natural person in the world to encounter in a churchyard on a fine summer's morning?

The vicar.

He grasped the banner firmly with one hand, drew a final deep breath, and threw open the door.

* * *

Light, colour, noise and warmth enveloped him simultaneously, making him blink. The interior of the church had
been cool and shadowy, filled with centuries of peace and
quiet; in the bright sunshine outside everything was a dazzling green and the sounds of the birds and insects seemed
deafening.

Then all these impressions vanished as his senses concentrated on the three figures under the trees near the
churchyard gate.

With a fierce effort of will-power he allowed himself
only the briefest glimpse of them before turning back to
fasten the door behind him. He couldn't stop his calf muscles tightening at the knowledge that his fear had become a
certainty, but he could force his body to move with the
calm deliberation of innocence. He was just a clergyman
closing the door to his church.

Two of them.

And they'd taken Harry alive and kicking, without noise
or fuss, which marked them as professionals for sure. Their
mission had gone sour on them but they were making the
best of a bad job: they had Harry and they could still hope
for his contact.

Unwillingly, he turned away from the door and started
slowly along the gravel pathway towards the gate. Only
now he didn't have to try to slow his pace, that was the
way his legs wanted it. From ground level things looked a
lot more hairy than they had from up above.

Two professionals, one tall and lean and the other me-
dium and thickset, he had gotten no more than that from
the glance except to note that they'd backed Harry up
against one of the trees. His appearance would have disconcerted them, but they certainly wouldn't be in a hurry
to complicate matters with violence if it could be avoided,
particularly to a priest in the shadow of his own church.
The British police wouldn't like that at all—and the British
newspapers would like it a whole lot.

There was a shred of comfort in that; it would confuse

them, even slow them a fraction, and that might just give him the edge he needed—

Then Sir Mosby bore on his shoulder the banner of the Mothers' Union in St Swithun's Churchyard—

He pretended to be wrapped in his own ecclesiastical thoughts as he walked down the path, delaying noticing them until the last moment. He must get the words as well as the accent right, which according to Doc McCaslin's formula for speaking British English meant that he had to speak from the front of his mouth in fragmented sentences.

"Luverly mornin'." He beamed at them over his spectacles.

No reply. Tall and Thin wore a neat grey suit, Thickset the rumpled overalls of a working man. Harry Finsterwald showed no sign of recognition. Range, maybe eight or nine yards.

"Church is open to visitors," he said.

Thickset was holding his right hand rather awkwardly behind his back.

Tall and Thin nodded, returning his smile. "Thank you. But we're just looking around."

Mosby cupped his ear with his free hand and stepped off the path towards them. "Beg your pardon?"

"I said 'we're just looking around'," repeated Tall and Thin clearly.

"Looking round?" Mosby echoed the words vaguely. Thickset swayed nervously, but held his ground, one eye firmly fixed on Harry. "Looking round...I see..." He bobbed his head at Tall and Thin, half turning his back on Thickset and Harry as though he had written them off as sources of conversation. "Must see the interiah of the church, then—can show you round if you wish." He slid the banner from his shoulder as he spoke, letting the shaft rest on the grass. "Stained glass very fine."

Tall and Thin looked at him for a moment with just the beginning of a frown creasing his brow. It could be he'd exaggerated the accent too much, or it could be simple annoyance at his inconvenient appearance. The next few seconds would show which.

"That's very good of you, sir." There was a slightly guttural quality to the 'g' which reassured Mosby more than the words themselves; a foreigner would be far less likely than a native Englishman to question his authenticity. "But we must be on our way very soon, I am afraid."

Mosby smiled and shrugged. "Of course, of course... quite understand...some other time, perhaps...Well, good day to you, then." He nodded to the man, lifting the banner with both hands as he did so as if about to set it back on his shoulder. At the same time he began to turn slowly towards Thickset and Harry.

"And good day to you—" he continued, still smiling.

Thickset's attention was still divided by the need to watch Harry, and as if he understood Mosby's intentions Harry chose that precise instant to take a larger share of it by shifting his feet.

As Thickset's eyes left him momentarily, Mosby sprang towards him, swinging the banner off his shoulder in a great sweeping arc. For one terrible fraction of a second, as the man's reflexes triggered him backwards, it looked to Mosby as though the swing would miss by inches—and as he moved, Thickset's gun hand came into view, swinging from behind his back on the opposite course.

But fast though he was, Thickset couldn't quite make up for that lost moment: the gun was still short of its target when the accelerating banner struck him just above the ear. Mosby had put every last ounce of strength into the sweep for the sake of speed as much as force; he felt the shaft bend and then snap like a rotten branch. The pistol flew out of Thickset's hand and Harry Finsterwald dived for it like an Olympic swimmer. Tall and Thin came back into view, clawing inside his waistband as Mosby reversed his momentum. He ducked as Mosby hurled the broken stump of banner at him and got his gun clear just as Harry squeezed off his first shot. The bullet spun Tall and Thin round and threw him against a tombstone in a tangle of windmilling arms and legs. For a moment the stone supported him, then he rolled off it on to the grass.

Mosby turned back towards Thickset, but saw no sign of movement. He felt suddenly drained of energy, and more frightened than he had been even during the walk down the gravel pathway from the church. Now that it was over he could see the risk he had taken: he had allowed his better judgment of the odds to be overturned by a sudden hare-brained idea which had seemed smart, but which had been plain madness. And he had been delivered from the consequences of his folly by good luck and Harry Finsterwald's snap-shooting.

He watched Harry examine the ruin of Tall and Thin.

Finally Harry straightened up and turned towards him.

"This guy's had it," he called across. That was no surprise to Mosby. There had been something about the way Tall and Thin's body had behaved after the bullet had struck which had suggested a puppet with all the strings irrevocably cut. The only surprise was that Harry's voice was cracked and shaky.

He was glad that he'd had the banner instead of the gun.

Not that Thickset wasn't going to have one hell of a headache, he decided as he walked towards the recumbent figure. The blow had spun him halfway back to the path, so that he'd come to rest face down almost in the shadow of Geo. Pratley's tombstone, and he was still out cold.

He knelt beside the body with a sigh. An unconscious prisoner was also going to be a headache for them too, much more so than a conscious, self-propelled one—

Oh God!

He stared in horror at the one eye he could see, an eye that was open and staring.

The man couldn't be dead, he couldn't be. The blow had been hard, but the tightly-furled banner itself ought to have cushioned the shock, and the snapping of the shaft ought to have taken the killing force out of it. He couldn't be dead.

Harry came up beside him.

"What's the matter, Doc?"

Mosby swallowed the sickness in his throat. "I think he's dead too."

Harry knelt down on the far side of the body and gently felt the neck pulse. Mosby heard him breathe out.

They stared at each other.

"That's about as dead as you can get," admitted Harry huskily.

"He can't be."

"I guess you don't know your own strength, Doc. You caved in the side of his skull like an eggshell."

Mosby gave an uncontrollable shiver.

"Come on, Doc," said Harry Finsterwald gently, "we couldn't help ourselves, you know that. These guys, they weren't going to just kick my ass and send me home—remember how Davies got it. You hadn't shown up, I'd 'uv gotten a piece of the same, you better believe it. So we just evened the score, is all." He paused and looked around him, frowning. "But what we have to do now is get them out of sight, and quick."

Mosby came back to immediate reality abruptly. This was neither the time nor the setting for conscience pangs: no matter it was a graveyard, it was no place to be caught squatting beside the brand-new corpses of their victims. Any moment now the vicar—or maybe the entire Mothers' Union—might come trotting up the path to the church, and then they'd have a fully-grown international incident on their hands as well as a glitched mission.

He stood up quickly, ripping the dog-collar from his neck and stuffing it into his coat pocket together with the spectacles. Apart from the bodies and the broken banner midway between them the scene was as peaceful as before; the insects still buzzed and even the blackbirds were back, squabbling among themselves near the overgrown southeast corner. Their outrageous luck was still holding.

"I can get the car up here and stash them in the trunk," said Finsterwald. "Once I've gotten them back on base I can handle them. But we got to get them out of sight first."

Mosby was aware that he was being jollied out of shock

and into action. Maybe Harry Finsterwald wasn't so bad after all when it came to the crunch—maybe he was starting to repay the debt he owed Mosby for the preservation of his skin. Or perhaps he himself was naturally trying to see the best side of the skin he'd saved.

None of which mattered, compared with the need to tidy up St Swithun's Churchyard.

He pointed towards the south-east corner, where ecology had produced a fine crop of shoulder high nettles.

"Over there," he said. The 'Do not disturb' request on the notice should keep the dead men private for long enough, and if ecology implied survival of the fittest as well as the natural chain of living and dying they wouldn't be too out of place there anyway.

Finsterwald nodded. "Okay. You take the feet, Doc."

– VIII –

SHIRLEY LOOKED ONLY briefly at Mosby before dumping her bag and pile of parcels on her bed.

"Take your dirty shoes off the quilt, honey—you're not at home now."

Mosby eased his shoes off with his toes and raised himself slightly in order to get a better view of things to come.

"Harry give you a bad time?" She stripped off her dress and seated herself at the dressing table.

"Harry's not so bad."

"He's not?" She examined her face in the mirror. "You mean he came up with something on Bullitt?"

"One or two things."

"Uh-huh?" She examined her face carefully in the mirror. "So you had an easy time...Well, I didn't...That town sure doesn't welcome the motorist. It may be beautiful, but it's an awful place to park a car in, and that's the truth. We had to walk miles."

"You get to see it better that way."

"Which wasn't exactly the object of the operation...I look a wreck."

Not from where I'm lying, thought Mosby, marvelling at the sexiness of her back. He had seen it a good many times before, since the strip-off and make-up routine was her standard procedure, and it wasn't the first female back he had ever seen. But there was something about Shirley's back, even down to the slight bulges of flesh which the bra straps pressed up when she lent forward, that never ceased to arouse him. It was just one hell of a sexy back.

And now he was enormously relieved to find that it still aroused him. It signified that he was back to normal again; it was like flexing the fingers on an injured hand and knowing from their movement that no permanent damage had been done. He had killed a man, but Shirley still had a sexy back.

Crouching beside the two bodies among the nettles, waiting for Harry to bring his car up alongside the nearby wall, he had had one long moment of doubt about that. The feeling of shock had passed surprisingly quickly, and Harry's common sense had given panic no time to develop. Plus the certain knowledge that he hadn't *meant* to hit so hard—even that maybe he *hadn't* hit so hard. It had been the brass knob on the end of the shaft which had done the mischief, he had found it on the broken end with the tell-tale blood bright on it. If Thickset hadn't taken that fatal step back—

And then the little pale yellow butterfly had settled on Thickset's open palm—the nettles were alive with pale yellow butterflies—and he had realised that all his explanations were mere excuses. Old wives' tales said that butterflies lived just one single day, but the little butterfly was better off than Thickset. Intention, or accident, or plain bad luck didn't make a damn of difference: the man was dead and he had killed him.

Shirley had stopped looking at herself in the mirror and was looking at him in it.

"You feeling okay, Mose?"

"I'm feeling fine."

"You look rather pale."

"I tell you I'm feeling great. But you could make me feel a lot better very easily, you know."

Now why the hell did I say that? he thought bitterly as he saw the change in her expression. It was like scratching an itch that was already raw with stupid scratching.

"Don't kid yourself. It's me I'm worried about, honey, not you," said Shirley.

"Well, that's a start. And you're beautiful when you're mad—did anyone ever tell you that?"

Even quarrelling with her was better than nothing.

"Only guys who didn't get the message first time. But I need you on the top line at the moment."

"Message received. 'Is Captain Sheldon combat-ready?' as General Ellsworth would say . . . Answer: affirmative. Don't fret, honey. I'm a real killer today."

"You'd better be. You're having tea with Group Captain Bullitt this afternoon."

"Uh-huh? More cucumber sandwiches?"

She stared at his reflection. "Aren't you surprised?"

"Not a lot."

"Or even interested how we got the invite?"

"Not particularly. Audley's a great fixer, otherwise he wouldn't be where he is. So he fixed it."

She examined herself again. "Actually it was Sir Thomas. A friend of his turned out to be a friend of Bullitt's."

"Same thing. Audley knows someone who knows someone who knows Bullitt. Just a mathematical progression, like back at home. That's part of the reason why we got him on our team—he knows the right people."

"Always supposing Billy Bullitt is the right people."

Mosby stared up at the ceiling. The blank white expanse of plaster challenged him, like a screen waiting for its pictures.

"He's the right people."

"Harry tell you something, then?"

"Some . . . but not that."

"But you're very sure of yourself." She appeared to concentrate on her eyelashes.

"Uh-huh."

"Even though it's like hitting the jackpot first pull?"

The screen was still blank. "Could be the machine's been fixed that way, honey."

"You mean they haven't told us everything?"

Mosby sneered at the ceiling. "Remember what Harry Finsterwald said: I have to be my age . . . But in the meantime, knowing how Billy Bullitt ticks could be half the battle."

"And has Harry helped you there? It sounds a tall order —one English air force colonel. You only gave him a few hours to take him to pieces and put him together again."

"Uh-huh . . . But I told you last night: if the British had a special file on him—one that Audley remembered—then there was a chance we had one too. We got a lot of files on a lot of people."

"Mmm . . ." She brushed at the sooty-black lashes. "Which means we do have one?"

No praise and no apology.

"He flew with the USAF in Korea."

"*With* the USAF?"

"There were some RAF pilots attached to our F-86 squadrons for combat experience. The British didn't have anything could stand up to the MiG-15."

"So he had a security clearance, obviously."

"Straight 'A' right down the line. World War Two veteran, and what was better, he had a record of fighting the Communists afterwards—British Military Mission to Greece '45-'48, Malayan emergency '48-'50."

"Sounds our sort of guy." She was no longer fixing her face, her hands were resting on her lap. "And Korea after that . . . He really must have been hooked on fighting by then . . . It makes you think."

"Think what?"

She swung round towards him. "You know he was a

student at Oxford in 1939—what do they call them—an undergraduate?"

"Think what?"

She shook her head slowly. "I didn't spend all the morning in dress shops with Faith, Mose honey. David took us straight off to this college, Sir Thomas's one—and he asked us if we'd had breakfast, for God's sake, would you believe that?"

"Just an old Anglo-Saxon custom, maybe?"

"And then he took us to this other college—that was what he said, but they all look the same to me—and up these staircases, like a rabbit-warren. And there was this room full of old books and papers and dust, and this old, old man. Dr Morton—Dr Oliver Morton. He looked like he was a hundred years old, and he was dusty like the books. And he asked us if we'd have breakfast too."

"Beats hell out of cucumber sandwiches."

"It was spooky, honestly. I saw into the bedroom through the open door, and it was full of books too—in piles, on the carpet. Sir Thomas said afterwards that they get to clean his room maybe once or twice a year, and then they have to put everything back exactly where it was, otherwise he complains that people have been messing about with his things—he knows where everything is, right down to the last cobweb."

"And he also knows Billy Bullitt, huh?"

"That's right. In fact Billy came to see him just recently, when there was all the trouble."

"Is he an expert on Badon Hill, then?"

"No, he's an English literature professor—eighteenth century or something. But that was what Billy studied all those years ago, just for a year. Then he quit and joined the RAF to fight the Germans . . . and he just never came back . . . Not to study, anyway, but he did come back to see Dr Morton whenever he was in England, which wasn't often . . . Did you know he was an orphan?"

"He was brought up by his grandfather, Harry says."

"That's right. Professor William Walter Bullitt—and get

this, Mose—who was professor of Mediaeval History at Wessex University in the 1930s and a leading authority on Dark Age Britain."

"Meaning King Arthur."

"Right. He even wrote a book on him. And the 'L' in Billy's christian names actually stands for 'Lancelot'. He inherited a whole library of Arthurian books from the old guy, so it really runs in the family."

"So?"

"Don't be dim, honey. If anybody's got that book on the Novgorod Bede by Bishop What's-'is-name it'll be Billy Bullitt. The old professor's library was the best of its kind in the country, Dr Morton said."

He had been afraid for the preceding half-minute that she would be drawing that intelligent conclusion, because there was no humane way of softening the blow he must then deliver. Better to get it over quickly—

"No good, Shirl. There's nothing in it."

"What d'you mean?"

"Howard Morris's people traced a copy already."

"Where?"

"The obvious place. In the library of the present Bishop of Walthamstow, where you'd expect it to be. The Novgorod Bede is just an inferior copy of the Leningrad Bede, made about the same time—at least, according to Bishop Harper, and he saw them both. Sorry, honey . . . but did the old man have anything to say about Billy Bullitt—what he was like?"

Her shoulders drooped in disappointment. She shrugged. "He said he was a nice boy."

"Boy? At fifty-something?"

"Maybe he's young for his age." She turned back to the dressing table mirror. "If you're a hundred I suppose fifty-something seems boyish, I don't know . . . What other good news did Harry Finsterwald bring with him?"

Mosby looked up to the ceiling again. "He had one quite interesting story about the nice boy—"

Picture.

"What was that?"

It was an airfield. Not the immense Americanised strip at Wodden, with its ever-increasing new runway extensions disappearing into the far distance, but Wodden as it must have been after the war: empty hangars and derelict huts with broken windows, and weeds spreading along the runway joints.

"What was that?" Shirley repeated.

Movement now: men wandering across the tarmac, scratching their heads over the patches of new oil and the bruise-marks in the grass . . .

"Bullitt had this long furlough coming to him in '48, after he came back from Greece and before he was posted to Malaya . . . Said he was going for a walking holiday in the Scottish Highlands. Only he didn't."

"Didn't what?"

"Go walking . . . There was this film company planned to make a movie about the Battle of Britain. Got plenty of cash on hand, dollars and pounds and Swiss francs. Hired themselves an old RAF field up in the north somewhere . . . bought themselves some war surplus planes, Mosquitoes and Beau-fighters mostly. Which should have worried someone, but it didn't . . ."

She turned. "Mose, you're losing me."

"Wrong planes. Battle of Britain was strictly Spitfires and Hurricanes. These were twin-engined jobs—long-range fighter-bombers, low-level strike, that sort of thing. . . . Be like Hollywood making a picture about Pearl Harbour with P-38s and P-51s."

"So they got the details wrong."

"They had the details absolutely the way they wanted. Because when the film crew arrived on location to start shooting—no planes . . . They'd gone shooting somewhere else. Like, for instance, the Sinai Desert."

"The Sinai?"

Mosby nodded. "1948, Shirl. Lots of Jewish money in motion pictures, always has been. But in 1948 they had other things to spend their money on—things money couldn't buy so easily, though. Not with a world embargo on Middle East arms."

She stared at him. "You don't mean Bullitt flew for the Israelis?"

"Uh-huh. Beats walking in the Highlands by a mile, ferrying hot planes across Europe. Plus maybe a bit of combat at the other end."

"What the hell did the RAF say to that?"

"They didn't say anything—because they didn't know. The British had to hush the thing up, because of the trouble it'd make for them in the Middle East, letting the Israelis pick up the planes under their noses. So they didn't dare dig too deep. And the Israelis weren't talking, naturally."

"So how did we find out?"

"Oh, that's just part of our good old double-crossing history, honey. Because we were slipping the Israelis the odd B-17—just like the Russians were shipping them old Me-109s crated in Czechoslovakia—so we had some of our boys out there to watch how they made out . . . And one of them spotted our Billy and his Mosquito."

"But we didn't snitch on him?"

"None of our business. Just filed it away for a rainy day, like now." He smiled at the ceiling. "But he took one hell of a risk, that's for sure."

"Why?"

"That's the big question. He had enough money, because his grandfather left him loaded in '45."

"Any Jewish blood?"

"Not a drop—pure 100 per cent WASP right down the line. And up until that moment pure British patriot too."

Shirley frowned. "I don't see where patriotism comes in. The British weren't fighting the Jews, not after they quit Palestine, anyway."

"But they sure weren't fighting *for* them, honey. In fact the Jewish terrorist groups—the Stern Gang and the Irgun —they were just like the IRA, sniping British soldiers in the back and blowing up hotels, and all that crap. I tell you, there was no love lost between the Israelis and the British in '48."

"Maybe he just liked fighting."

"So he risked getting kicked out of the RAF for one lousy flight and a week's combat?" Mosby shook his head. "That horse won't run, Shirl. If he liked fighting then he was set nicely to get all he wanted staying just where he was, the way things were shaping in '48. It has to be something else."

"Such as?"

"I'm not sure. It proves he's not a Stephen Decatur patriot, anyway. No 'My country, right or wrong' nonsense."

"Could be he just liked the idea of helping David against Goliath. The Jews had it pretty rough."

"Could be he was living up to his name: William *Lancelot* Bullitt."

"A one-off ride to the rescue and then back to the arms of good Queen Guinevere?" She shook her head in turn. "Uh-huh. If he was anyone at the court of King Arthur it'd be Sir Galahad, not Sir Lancelot—it was Galahad who went after the Holy Grail, wasn't it?"

Mosby sat up. "It was. But how do you know?"

"Oh, I know my King Arthur, even if I never heard of Bede."

"I don't mean that. I mean how d'you know Billy Bullitt is a Sir Galahad?"

"Well, he was once, according to old Dr Morton. Not only a nice boy, but also a very serious one. Much more serious than the usual run of pre-war students at Oxford. In fact he very nearly threw it all up—going to college—to fight in the Spanish Civil War."

Mosby stared at her. "Now that's very interesting. We never picked that up on him—Harry never mentioned it."

"I guess we wouldn't have. Because he went for a holiday in France in the summer of '38—he was going to Oxford in the fall of '38—and while he was there he just slipped across the border to Barcelona, where the Reds were holding out."

"Hell—this is dynamite, honey."

"I don't think it is."

"Why not? We never had one thing up to now connected him with the Communists. He's always been on the other side."

"That's the point. Seems he didn't like what he saw there. He didn't like the Fascists and he didn't like the Communists either, Dr Morton said . . . Like he'd looked for the Grail, and decided it wasn't to be found in Spain any more. But when he came back he joined the University Air Squadron straight off—which is their version of AFROTC. And then when the war broke out in 1939 he went straight into the RAF."

Mosby closed his eyes for a moment, adding these new facts to those in the dossier Harry Finsterwald had shown him in the car two hours earlier. He had thirty-seven years of William Lancelot Bullitt's adult life spread out before him.

He remembered James Barkham's thin, dry old voice: *There's European history for you—twelve hundred years of it. And now two American gentlemen want to find out about it.*

And now the history of Billy Bullitt, the thirty-seven year saga not only of the man himself, but his times: the great war, Britain's 'Finest Hour', the Anglo-American alliance, the hollow victory and the Cold War, the decline and fall of the British Empire, the decline of Britain herself . . .

And Badon Hill overshadowing the legendary King Arthur and the fabled towers of Camelot.

Plus somewhere, somehow, Comrade Professor Nikolai Andrievich Panin . . .

"This isn't the time to go fast asleep, Mose," said Shirley. "Any moment now you're going to have to tell everyone how much you admired St Who's-it's Church."

St Swithun's Church.

St Swithun's *Churchyard*.

"I'm not sleeping. I'm just trying to work out Billy Bul-litt's pattern."

"How he ticks, you mean? Oh, that's easy—every once in a while he breaks out and rocks the boat some just to satisfy his sense of honour."

Mosby opened his eyes suddenly. Shirley had turned back to her mirror to make the final adjustments to her face.

Sexy back, thought Mosby. But sharp, sharp little mind.

Eighteen uneventful British schoolboy years, to be crowned with the accolade of Oxford.

Then a trip to Spain, and his whole career at risk for a moment.

Nine years of distinguished war service, Britain, North Africa, Europe, Greece—medals, promotion and a career.

Then a trip to Israel, and the whole career at risk again for a moment.

More distinguished years. Malaya, Korea, Malaya again, Aden and the Persian Gulf, Cyprus, Germany . . . and finally work on the guidance systems of the TSR-2, the wonder plane.

And then, when the politicians decided to scrap the wonder plane the old pattern re-asserting itself: the outspo-ken letter to *The Times*—and this time the career shattered. 'A nine days' wonder,' Audley had said.

So exile in Arabia, running a counter-insurgency squad-ron for an obscure sultan. But running it brilliantly and returning to Britain in 1971 in a small blaze of glory, and his famous red shirt, like a latter-day Lawrence of Arabia, with a new political career his for the taking—

'He made the headlines,' Audley had said.

Offered Parliamentary seats by three Constituency par-ties, two Conservative, one Liberal, the dossier had said.

Offers rejected. Instead, the pattern again in a bitter tele-vision interview in which he had slashed as fiercely at the political right as at the left, and at management as much as at the unions.

Four silent years in rural Wiltshire, in the midst of

Grandfather Bullitt's Arthurian library and 'No known political affiliation'.

Then the Oxford riot—

Pattern: first the activity, second the outburst. And each time the period of activity had been shorter and the outburst more violent.

"Are you ready, Mose honey." Shirley was wriggling into her best and most spectacular afternoon dress.

Delectable.

"As ready as I'll ever be."

So Billy Bullitt was about to rock the boat again. Only this time it looked like various people hoped—and feared —that he was going to overturn it.

Audley was standing at the foot of the stairs, waiting for them with a shuttered look on his face and two strangers at his back.

"Hi, David," said Shirley.

Audley stood to one side for her.

"Captain Sheldon?" One of the strangers took a pace towards him.

"That's me."

The stranger took a folder from his pocket.

"Special Branch, sir," he said.

– IX –

THERE WERE TWO sorts of loneliness, thought Mosby: that of the forgotten man, the Robinson Crusoe loneliness; and that of the man in the condemned cell, solitary but unforgotten. And at this precise moment he would have given a great deal for the sound of the waves on Crusoe's beach.

Instead he listened to the sound of the big power-mower on the lawn outside. Once upon a time, in another life, he had always liked that Saturday morning clatter, the noise of the beginning of the weekend. But it would never be like that again, just as little pale yellow butterflies would never be just butterflies again.

The bastards had done it smoothly, he had to give them that; they had even done it with a touch of old-fashioned good manners. There had been no uniforms, except that was to be expected of the British and it would probably have been much the same back home. What had bugged him had been the 'pleases' and the 'thank-yous', and the genteel opening of doors, all designed to create the fiction that there was no real compulsion yet at the same time establishing the hopelessness of any resistance beyond argument.

"Special Branch?" He had registered bewilderment rather than surprise.

"Special Branch?" Shirley echoed him. "What's that?"

"Police, honey—sort of FBI-type police." He frowned at the first man. "What can I do for you? Has something happened on the base?"

"We have reason to believe that you may be able to help us with certain inquiries, sir." The Special Branch man pronounced the formula without emphasising any single word in it.

"What inquiries?" asked Mosby.

"Police!" squeaked Shirley, as though Mosby's explanation had been a delayed-action bomb.

"It's all right, honey," said Mosby reassuringly. "What inquiries?"

"I'm afraid I'm not in a position to say, sir. But if you and your wife would be so good as to come with us then I'm sure my superior will be able to tell you."

"Me *and* my wife?" Mosby allowed the first hint of outrage to colour this bewilderment. He looked towards Audley. "What the hell is this, David?"

Shirley squared up in front of the SB. "For heaven's sake, what is my husband supposed to have done?"

"I haven't done anything, honey," Mosby snapped irritably, picking up her line instinctively once more.

"Well, they obviously think you have." She continued to stare up angrily at the SB. "Now, you—"

"Shut up, Shirley," said Mosby.

"I will most certainly *not* shut up. Not until someone tells me what's going on."

The SB man weakened. "We'd like you to answer some questions, madam. That's all."

"What questions? About what?"

"That I can't say, madam. The questions will be put to you by a superior officer."

"Honey—" Mosby began desperately.

"Don't 'honey' me. Where's this superior officer of yours, then?"

"If you would be so good as to come with us, madam, please, then we'll take you to him."

"Why can't he come to us? We haven't done anything."

The SB shook his head. "I'm sorry, madam."

"Oh, great! You're sorry. You want us to help you with —inquiries of some sort. But you don't know what. And you want us to answer questions. But you don't know the questions. So you just go on back to your superior and tell him to send someone who does know. Or better still, he can darn well come himself." She folded her arms defiantly.

Audley cleared his throat. "I think you'd better go with them, Mrs Sheldon." He looked meaningfully at Mosby.

Shirley goggled incredulously at Audley. "What d'you mean 'go with them', David? Whose side are you on?"

"No side. Apparently they only want you to help them with their inquiries—"

"But we all know what *that* means," cut in Shirley scornfully. "We've heard that on your TV dozens of times —and read it in the papers: 'A man is helping the police with their inquiries'—'helping', huh? Why, they're arresting us, that's what they're doing, David."

"That's not correct, madam," protested the SB man, deadpan.

"Then we have a choice? We can say 'Go fly your kite —we don't want to help you with your inquiries?' " said Shirley quickly. "We can say that, huh?"

The second SB man stirred. "We very much hope you won't say that, madam. We have a car here and we'd be obliged if you came with us. If you refuse to come, then we have a new situation, of course . . . and that might require us to act in a different way. But if you haven't done anything, then obviously you haven't anything to fear— right?" He looked to Mosby for support.

"Well..." Shirley allowed doubt to weaken her obstinacy, "...I don't like it at all."

Mosby turned back to Audley. "You think we should go along with them, David—you really think that?"

Audley shrugged. "I don't really think you've got much choice, Sheldon. There's probably been some sort of misunderstanding—if there has been then they'll apologise and bring you back."

"*If*—?" Mosby decided it was time to let a small light of suspicion shine through. "What d'you mean 'if'?"

"I think you had better wait and see."

Mosby gave Audley a hard look. "You sound like you know what's going on."

Audley regarded him with dull eyes, as though they were strangers playing in a boring charade. "Let's just say I can't help what's going on."

Shirley stared at Mosby, wide-eyed. "I don't like it. I don't understand what's happening, but I don't like it. And I think maybe we should phone the embassy."

"That won't be necessary, madam," said the second SB man smoothly. "Not at this stage."

"Uh-huh? Well, maybe this stage is the stage to phone before there's another stage." She nodded to Mosby. "I think you better go phone, honey—just in case."

It was perfectly obvious that they weren't going to be allowed to phone anyone, and Shirley knew it, Mosby realised. But she was playing the innocent game because it was the only game there was to play, at least until they knew better what had gone wrong. And probably even after that, right to the bitter end. But the immediate problem was whether—or how far—to call the Special Branch's polite bluff.

He scratched his head doubtfully. "I don't know...If this is just some sort of foul-up, then we're going to look pretty damn silly...And it has to be a foul-up, because we haven't done anything."

She looked at him pityingly. "Mose, this is a foreign country. We don't know what they may do to us."

"But it isn't a police state," said Audley.

Mosby stared at him. What was also perfectly obvious was that Audley didn't want any trouble that would make the situation irrevocable. Something had gone wrong somewhere, and badly wrong, but if Schreiner's confidence in their cover wasn't misplaced they still had a fighting chance. Even the fact that these were Special Branch agents was a comfort, because it ruled out what had happened in St Swithun's Churchyard as the source of the trouble: if anyone had witnessed that, then it would have been the local police here now, not the executive arm of British counter-intelligence.

"I'll see you get to a phone when you want to," said Audley.

"You will?" Mosby mixed relief and gratitude with doubt. "But if we go with them you're not going to know what happens to us, David."

For a moment earlier on it had looked as though Audley had been ready to take the wraps off himself, but now he seemed content to play along again. It was almost as if he wasn't really sure yet what to believe.

Audley caught the second SB man's eye for a fraction of a second before answering. "Not if I come along for the ride." He gave Mosby a lop-sided smile. "You didn't think I was intending to abandon you just when things were becoming interesting, did you, Captain Sheldon?"

The clatter of the mower began to diminish.

Mosby walked across the room to the French windows and looked out. It was a big lawn, perhaps nearly a hundred yards of smooth, well-tended grass—the sort of lawn that could only be achieved after a century or two of cutting and rolling and weeding. A slender iron railing divided it from the open parkland beyond, with its self-conscious clumps of beech trees. On the most distant slope, as if deliberately placed to complete an old world landscape, a flock of sheep was scattered across the pasture. Only the man with the guard dog patrolling the railing spoiled the view.

Presumably this was one of the minor stately homes which the British had taxed out of private hands and now maintained for a variety of official and semi-official purposes, publicised and unpublicised. But exactly where it was he had no idea since the glass of the rear windows and partition of the SB car had been artfully distorted so that it was impossible to read the road signs. But as they had travelled at a moderate speed for little more than an hour, and by no means always on busy roads, it could hardly be more than thirty miles in a direct line from the Handforth-Jones house. And the position of the sun indicated that the line lay more or less to the south, which meant they must be on or near Salisbury Plain and not far from where Mosby had actually intended to be this afternoon. Which, in turn, might or might not be significant.

He sighed and turned away from the window. The fine mahogany writing desk in the middle of the panelled room suggested that it was (or had once been) the master's private study, with the double doors to his left leading off into the library. A smart look in that desk would very probably reveal the location of the house, but if it did then they weren't really concerned to keep the secret. Besides, a dumb American Air Force dentist in shock from being picked up by the British FBI ought not to act like an old pro on the look-out for information.

But then, the dumb dentist act was starting to feel uncomfortably like the real thing. Because if something or someone had slipped he had not one single idea what or who.

The sound of the returning mower again began to fog his thoughts. He wondered uneasily where Shirley was. They had put her into the second car, but they had not thereafter driven in convoy. The odds were that she was also in this same house by now, but the damn mower effectively drowned out any sound there might have been of her arrival—

Maybe not quite no ideas. If what Sir Thomas and Tony Handforth-Jones had said was true about Audley keeping his wife out of his professional affairs then he hadn't spotted them as American agents straight off. Indeed, it was even possible that he hadn't suspected anything was wrong until the Special Branch men had appeared.

Everything depended on how good Howard Morris's security was. If it *was* good . . . then perhaps it wasn't the fact that they were Americans that was bugging the British, but simply their interest in the time-fused Billy Bullitt.

But either way, the show had to go on. Because whatever happened the CIA was never going to admit that they'd ever heard of Captain and Mrs Sheldon, that was for sure after what Schreiner had said. They were absolutely on their own.

The door opened behind him.

"Captain Sheldon—hullo there."

Tall, dark-haired, good-looking, mid-thirties.

"I'm sorry we've kept you waiting like this, Captain."

Plus a slight limp and a decidedly upper-class English accent: a very different type from the two Special Branch men and their drivers, unless British police recruitment had changed radically.

"My name's Roskill—Hugh Roskill."

Mosby ignored the outstretched hand. "Where's my wife?"

Roskill looked suitably apologetic. "Quite safe and sound, I assure you, Captain. In fact, they're just rustling her up some lunch at the moment—I gather you both missed out on it. We're sorry about that, too. Can I order you something to keep the wolf from the door?"

The man was different, but the idiom was the same: the British were *devilish* sorry about the whole beastly business. But one way or another that business was going to be transacted all the same.

"When can I see her?"

"Very soon. Just one or two questions first." Roskill grinned. "How about that lunch?"

Mosby shook his head. "Being arrested has taken my appetite away, Mr Roskill."

"Good lord—you haven't been arrested, Captain! We simply want to know what you're up to."

"Who's 'we'?"

"The powers-that-be." Roskill waved a hand vaguely. "The authorities. A rose by any other name . . . Does it matter?"

Mosby studied the Englishman. This soft approach could be a carefully calculated phase of the breaking-down process, or it could be that they still genuinely weren't sure about him.

"To me it does. I'm a serving officer with the United States Air Force, attached to NATO—but I guess you must know that already, huh?"

Roskill nodded. "Of course."

"Uh-huh. Well, being—picked up, shall we say?—being picked up by your Special Branch isn't going to make me Man of the Year with my commanding officer."

"Yes, I can imagine that." Roskill smiled sympathetically. "Commanding officers are notoriously—narrow-minded."

"That's right. No matter I haven't done one goddamn thing, I'm going to do the rest of my time on a weather station on Greenland. And up until this afternoon I've enjoyed it over here—so has my wife."

"I'm gratified to hear it. But—"

Mosby held up his hand. "Let me finish, sir. My wife wanted me to phone the embassy when we were back at Dr Handforth-Jones's house. And if I was going by the book now I ought to be demanding you let me phone the base. But I have the impression that somehow I've got into something way over my head—I don't know what, but it's sure as hell not parking on a double yellow line." He looked around him. "All this . . . and now you, Mr Roskill."

"Me?"

"You don't look like a cop to me."

"What do I look like?"

"I don't know. . ." Mosby paused. "But maybe someone I can make a deal with, I'm hoping."

"Well, well . . . now you *are* beginning to interest me, Captain. What sort of deal?"

Mosby shrugged. "You name it. You want me to answer questions—ask the questions. You want me to do something—within reason I'll do it."

"In exchange for what?"

"In exchange for I don't make any trouble, phoning the embassy—and you don't make any trouble calling General Ellsworth if I've accidentally stepped out of line somehow."

Roskill looked at him quizzically. "You think you may have stepped out of line?"

Mosby grimaced. "I don't know all your laws. I guess I'll know when you start asking the questions."

"But you can't guess what?"

"I can't, no . . . Unless the Special Branch is interested in illegal archaeology—if there is such a crime."

"And you've done that?" Roskill raised an eyebrow. "Gone treasure hunting, you mean?"

"No." Mosby shook his head. "But someone might think I had, that's all."

"I see." Roskill considered Mosby thoughtfully for a moment or two. "Well now . . . I'm not exactly empowered to make deals, but it seems reasonable enough. So let's just try it for size and see how it looks—right?"

"You mean a gentleman's agreement?"

"If you like—a gentleman's agreement."

Mosby swallowed ostentatiously. "Okay."

"Fine. You're with the 7438th Bombardment Wing—F-111s with an attached Phantom Squadron?"

"Correct."

"Stationed at RAF Wodden. Does the wind still blow up there six days out of seven?"

"You know it?"

"I knew it years ago. Built during the war as a basic training field—for Tiger Moths. But when I was there it was Jet Provosts."

"You RAF, then?"

"Once upon a time." Roskill's lip twisted as if the memory was painful to him. "You must have done a lot of work on it since my day."

"They haven't stopped since they moved in four years back. When the new runway's ready they'll be ready to take anything that flies now."

" 'They'? But of course you're not a career officer, are you. A three-year volunteer?"

"That's right."

"Which gives you a choice of foreign postings. And you chose England."

"We all make mistakes."

Roskill smiled. "And you're a dentist. Which makes you the very man I want to see, actually."

"Don't tell me you've got toothache," Mosby started to smile back, then noticed that Roskill's smile had gone. "You have to be joking."

"I wish I was." Roskill sighed. "Truth is, if I hadn't had to come down here I should have seen my own dentist by now."

Mosby blinked with surprise. "Well, there's nothing I can do about it—I didn't bring my chair with me."

"Ah, but you can put my mind at rest—that's the least you can do. And knowing what's wrong will take some of the pain away."

It had to be some sort of test, thought Mosby. But why should they want to test him? The Special Branch man had already examined his ID card.

Then professional curiosity welled up inside him. This was one thing he could do, anyway. "You've got a problem?"

"Not at the moment. But last night after dinner—I'd just finished eating as a matter of fact—it was excruciating.

Knocked me sideways for a few minutes, but then it went away. And then this morning, just as I was finishing breakfast—same thing: fearful pain." He looked at Mosby expectantly.

"And at lunchtime?"

"Well, nothing really. But I only had a salad—I didn't want a third go of it, I tell you."

"You had coffee?"

"Coffee?" Roskill frowned. "Yes, I did."

"But it was lukewarm, I guess."

"That's right." Roskill stared at him. "How did you know?"

"And the other two times it was hot, eh? When you had the pain, that is?" Mosby nodded. "Come on over to the window and I'll just have a look."

He led the way to the French windows. The man on the mower was still hard at work. So was the man with the dog.

"Now, just open wide."

"Don't you want me to tell you where it hurt?"

"If it's what I think it is I'll find it. Just open wide."

He peered into the Englishman's mouth. Someone had worked hard on it over the years, but then that figured: the English dentists were paid for what they did, not what they prevented. He worked his way around the jaw, for one happy minute far from reality.

"Okay . . . Well, you've got a semi-erupted wisdom tooth at the back there, with a large gum flap. But that's not your problem just at this moment."

"So what is my problem?"

"Posterior left six—the first molar. You're starting an abscess. There's a swelling on the gum, the inflammation's plain to see. Your dentist'll deal with it in no time."

"How?"

"He'll extract the tooth, and then you'll be okay. No problem."

"No problem. I see." Roskill grimaced. "And that was what the coffee grounds told you?"

"Sure, because I've come across it before. People like to drink their coffee when it's hot. And with an abscess you get small amounts of gas formed, so the heat from the coffee causes the gas to expand and you get terrible pressure on the inflamed nerves. Like you said, it'll knock you sideways until it cools down again." He looked at Roskill candidly. "So now you know I'm a dentist."

"You're cold-blooded enough for one, I'll say that."

"But there must be easier ways of checking up on me than finding a—a whatever you are—with tooth-ache to diagnose."

"Of course. We could have gone straight through to your commanding officer at Wodden. 'We have this man who says he's one of your officers, General. Height five foot ten, brown hair, born in Richmond, Virginia—' "

"You've made your point." Mosby raised a hand in surrender. "Except I never told you where I was born."

"Oh, we've done a little checking here and there."

I'll bet, thought Mosby. But that sort of checking must have started earlier than this morning, and possibly even earlier than yesterday, allowing for the Atlantic time difference. In fact it could only mean that they'd started running the check almost as soon as he'd made contact with Audley.

"And did you turn up anything interesting?"

Roskill shook his head slowly. "I'm bound to admit we didn't. Your life is an open book, Captain Sheldon, and a remarkably easy one to read."

"I'm sorry to disappoint you, Mr Roskill."

"But you didn't disappoint us—we don't disappoint so easily. It merely made us wonder whether you were who you said you were."

"Whether—who?" Mosby screwed up his face in bewilderment. "Now you *really* have to be joking."

"Stranger things have happened, believe me."

"You're telling me! They're happening right at this moment. Only—I was thinking—maybe you should check up with my wife. She just might be able to help you make your minds up."

"Unless she was part of the act, of course."

"Shirley?" Mosby packed scorn into his voice. "Oh, come on! I know I'm kind of ordinary-looking, but you'd have to look some to get a ringer for her. And anyway, why the heck should anyone want to claim to be me—or us— for God's sake? What have we got that anyone else could possibly want?"

Roskill shook his head. "It isn't quite like that, Captain Sheldon. As I told you, we've done a little checking up on you already. And on your wife."

"And we're a couple of open books."

"So it would seem. All except the last page."

Mosby frowned. "The last page? I don't get you?"

"You don't?" Roskill gazed at him in silence for a second or two. "But you're interested in King Arthur, aren't you?"

"In—" Mosby matched silence for silence. "Yes, I am ... in a way. But what's that got to do with you?"

Roskill grinned. "For a man who's promised to give all the answers you ask a lot of questions."

Mosby lifted his hand helplessly. "Sorry. You're absolutely right, it's just—hell—okay, ask the questions, then. Yes, I'm interested in Arthurian history."

"And Badon Hill in particular?"

Mosby drew a deep breath. "You've been talking to Audley—and that isn't a question. Because if you've been talking to Audley we can cut the double-talk."

"What double-talk?"

"He's one of your civil servants. A Special Branch man —or whatever you are—asks him a question, he's not going to tell you to get lost. Or make deals. He's going to talk, right?"

The corner of Roskill's mouth twitched, but he merely nodded.

"Right. Then I guess you know everything I told him— right?" Mosby nodded back. "So I'm a dentist I don't have to be stupid into the bargain. And I'm not going to ask what's so terrible about looking for Badon Hill, but I'm sure as hell going to think about it until you tell me."

"My dear man—think away by all means. But we're just rather surprised that your friend Major Davies didn't bother to tell you, that's all," said Roskill airily.

"He didn't have the chance, is why," said Mosby. "He—"

"Yes? He—what?"

Mosby stared at him. "You sound as though you know."

"Know what?"

"What Davies was going to tell me—about Badon. The way you spoke."

"But of course we know. What I'm trying to ascertain now is what *you* know. Or, to put it rather more charitably, I'm trying hard to believe that you're half as innocent as you seem."

Mosby's panic button was jammed in the 'on' position and the red lights in his brain flickered like a firework display. The British knew what Davies had been up to. Just like that: they knew, and it looked as though they had known for some time.

He scrabbled desperately in his memory. But only the old bookseller's taped voice came back to him: *I told him if it was true it was a great discovery. And he said 'And a great load of trouble, too'*. And then Schreiner's voice, leaving no room for misunderstanding: *If there's trouble you are strictly on your own . . . what matters is the CIA remains uninvolved*.

Roskill looked at him hopefully. "Well, do any answers occur to you now, Captain?"

"Answers?" All the possible avenues of action opened up before Mosby briefly, and then the gates closed on all but one. "For God's sake, you must have the answers. All I've got now is questions."

Roskill shrugged. "Very well. If that's the way you want to play it . . ."

"I'm not playing anything any way. I just—"

"Of course you're not." Roskill lifted the phone at his elbow and dialled a single number. "You're just—hullo, sir... Yes, I'm ready now... No, he hasn't... No, I don't..." He smiled at Mosby. "Yes, he is—and I've got an abscess starting under my first molar to prove it... Quite so, sir—yes. I think he's a good dentist. And I also think he's a good liar."

– X –

AN IMMENSE MARBLE fireplace, surmounted by an equally huge carved coat-of-arms, dominated the drawing room. But neither of the two men who stood in front of it were dwarfed by their setting: Audley, exuding his Ozymandias aura, looked as though he owned the place, and the man beside him, though half a head shorter, looked as though he owned Audley.

Mosby's eyes strayed back for a second to the coat-of-arms, which was held aloft by two winged dragons breathing heraldic fire. So that made four dragons all told, he reckoned dispassionately. Four dragons versus one dentist.

Roskill appeared at his shoulder.

Five dragons. Even Sir Lancelot might have baulked at those odds. And on an empty stomach too.

"Good afternoon, Captain Sheldon," said Audley's owner politely. "My name's Clinton . . ."

The empty stomach caved in on itself: the Number One Dragon himself.

"Mr Clinton," Mosby was aware that he sounded ner-

171

vous, but this was one time when the dentist and the CIA man were in perfect accord. "Hullo, David."

"Sir Frederick Clinton," murmured Roskill in his ear.

"Sir Frederick . . ." Mosby repeated the name mechanically.

"Sit down, Captain." Sir Frederick waved towards the settee. "Make yourself comfortable. Then we can discuss what we're going to do with you."

Mosby sank on to the cushions. The softness caught him by surprise: he sank and sank until he felt he was being engulfed, while the three Englishmen settled themselves into wing-chairs from which they could look down on him. If this was an example of British psychological warfare it was plain that they were dirty fighters.

"Good . . ." Sir Frederick interlaced his fingers across his stomach. "Now tell me, Captain—just for the record—are you or are you not an employee of the Central Intelligence Agency?"

"Am I—*what*?" Mosby struggled to raise himself from the settee's embrace.

"Are you CIA?" asked Audley in a tone only a little less mild than Sir Frederick's.

With an effort Mosby levered himself to the edge of the cushion. Even though this had the effect of bringing his knees up awkwardly under his chin it was a slightly less demoralising posture nevertheless. "You have to be crazy. Why the hell should I be CIA?"

"Meaning, I take it, that you're not?" Sir Frederick nodded. "Which is in accord with what the CIA itself says."

"The CIA?" Mosby blinked with bewilderment.

"Which is what they would say under the circumstances, of course," said Roskill in his bored voice.

"You called the CIA—about me?" Mosby said in a strangled voice. "Just like that? Oh, brother!"

"Don't distress yourself, Captain—at least, not on their account," said Sir Frederick. "They gave you a clean bill of health."

"Oh, sure. I'll be clean all the way back to the States

when my commanding officer hears about this." Mosby gave Roskill a bitter look. "Some gentleman's agreement."

Sir Frederick looked at Roskill questioningly. "What gentleman's agreement?"

"He seems more worried about his C.O. than about us, sir," explained Roskill. "He likes it here, apparently."

"Correction—*liked*," said Mosby. "And I'm beginning to get tired of being pushed around for no reason."

"When you haven't done anything wrong?"

"That's dead right." Mosby looked from one to the other. "Look, so I was searching for the site of Badon Hill—I admit it. But it isn't any crime. You can't hold me for just looking."

"I wouldn't bet on that," said Roskill. "We've a lot of old laws you never heard of, not to mention the new anti-terrorist regulations."

"Anti-terrorist? I'm not a goddamn terrorist."

"Of course you aren't," said Sir Frederick soothingly. "You were simply looking for Badon and your search led you to Billy Bullitt."

"That's . . . right," Mosby's suspicion that Bullitt was the cause of his difficulties hardened. He pointed towards Audley. "It was David found him though. Until yesterday afternoon I'd never even heard of him."

"Indeed?"

"Sure. Though now I come to think of it, it was Sir Thomas Gracey told us about him. Wasn't that so, David?"

Audley regarded him impassively.

"Strange you'd never heard of him, when you were both looking for Mons Badonicus," said Sir Frederick. "Did Major Davies never mention him, then?"

Mosby frowned. "Huh?"

"Obviously not. And by the same token I presume he never mentioned the Novgorod Bede?"

Jesus! Was there anything they didn't know? thought Mosby despairingly. The common sense cancelled despair: there had to be more in this than mere cat-and-mouse cruelty. Sir Frederick Clinton was too important to waste his time merely putting the boot into the CIA, no matter it was a recognised international sport.

"The Novgorod Bede? I never heard of it."

"He never mentioned it?"

"No, he didn't."

"He doesn't seem to have told you very much, your friend."

"Well . . . not about what he was doing." This was treacherous ground. "We just talked about Arthurian history in general. I never knew for sure he was really on to something until after he was killed."

"So you didn't know he'd discovered the site of Mons Badonicus?"

Mosby shook his head cautiously. "I still don't know that for sure. It was—well, it was just an inference from what he told my wife . . . plus the stuff he left behind with us."

"The evidence—yes. We'd very much like to examine that, Captain."

"Help yourself. It's in the trunk of my car." Mosby raised a mental prayer that Howard Morris's ground-bait—lifted from a dozen obscure museum collections—was as authentic—and as untraceable—as he had claimed it was.

"Ah, I don't mean what you showed David. You mentioned some other material . . . bones, and so forth. Could we send someone to collect that?"

Even more treacherous ground: the other material existed strictly in Howard Morris's ingenious imagination. So they had to be stalled—

"Sure. Only I'd have to go with them—I've stored it next to my surgery on the base. I'd only just started examining it."

It was the best he could do, but it was pretty thin. The truth was, however good his own cover, the Davies part of his story had never been designed to be tested to destruction by the British themselves. Already the hairline cracks in it were beginning to show.

But the man Roskill's words on the phone to Sir Frederick—*I think he's a good liar*—meant that those cracks were still suspicions, not certainties; and there were limits to how far the British could go with a serving officer in the USAF, no matter what they suspected he might be, particularly if they really had checked up with the Station Chief in London. In fact, the worst they could do was to ship him home as an undesirable, and that still gave him a margin of time to play with.

Except that margin was a wasting asset, he sensed that as he felt their eyes on him. And the only thing to do with a wasting asset was play it to the limit; attack was not just his last line of defence left, but his plain duty.

He stared back at Sir Frederick. "Now come on, Mr— Sir Frederick—it's time someone answered some of my questions. Like why I'm supposed to be a liar—and a CIA man—for for a start. And what the hell I'm supposed to have done that's so awful."

The Number One Dragon smiled thinly at him. "And where Mons Badonicus is?"

"And that too, yes. Did he really find it?"

"Is that all?"

Mosby thought for a moment. "I'd like to see my wife."

The Dragon nodded. "Well, that I can certainly do." He extended the nod to Roskill. "Hugh, would you ask Mrs Fitzgibbon to bring Mrs Sheldon along here as soon as she's through. And you might see if they can manage a cup of tea for us at the same time."

And cucumber sandwiches, Mosby thought irrelevantly, looking at his watch. It was already past five; he wondered if anyone had bothered to tell Billy Bullitt that his American guests, like Miss Otis, wouldn't be keeping their engagement with him.

"Well, David?" Sir Frederick switched to Audley. "What do you think now?"

Audley's pale eyes flicked over Mosby, giving no hint of what was behind them. "I haven't changed. What doesn't make sense can't be right."

"As your old Latin master used to say . . . I know—

'*Est summum nefas fallere,*
Deceit is gross impiety.'

David sets great store by the observations of his long-defunct Latin master, Captain Sheldon . . . Do you know where we are now?"

"I beg your pardon?"

"Do you know the name of this place?"

"No, I don't. Your men forgot to tell me."

"Weren't you curious about it?"

Mosby shrugged. "I guess I was relieved—just so it wasn't a police station. So what's special about it?"

"If I tell you it could delay your departure somewhat. Would that bother you?"

"Depends how long the delay could be." Mosby looked around the room. "I can think of worse places to be . . . delayed in."

Again that thin smile. "It's where you wanted to be."

"Where I wanted to be? I don't get you."

"Camelot."

"Cam—" Mosby frowned. "There's no such place."

"There *was* no such place." Sir Frederick shook his head. "So one place is as good as another, and this place is as good as any. If King Arthur is alive anywhere he lives here, you might say."

"You're still not getting through to me."

"I'm not?"

"*Est summum nefas fallere,*" murmured Audley.

Sir Frederick laughed. "There—now David doesn't believe you!"

Mosby gave Audley an angry glance. "Frankly, I don't give a damn. I'm not interested in Camelot and I wasn't looking for it. Camelot and Badon Hill are two plain different things—which David knows damn well."

"Of course," agreed Sir Frederick soothingly. "But Billy Bullitt and Badon are not two plain different things, you would agree I'm sure."

"Billy Bullitt?" Involuntarily Mosby found himself looking up at the coat-of-arms. "You mean this is—"

"Red dragon of the Britons, white dragon of the Saxons," Sir Frederick nodded. "The College of Heralds let old Professor Bullitt have them as—ah—'supporters', I think is the correct term, in 1928 when he quartered the Imberham arms of his mother's family. And you can see what they let him have in the bottom left quarter, eh?"

Mosby examined what looked like a shaggy dog, but was obviously a heraldic bear.

"Up until 1924 this was Imberham Manor. But that was the year he published his famous 'Britain in the Dark Ages', and he renamed the manor in honour of his obsession. So you might say that Billy Bullitt grew up in Camelot."

"And he's been looking for the Holy Grail ever since," murmured Audley. "Or his own version of it."

"Following in grandfather's footsteps, naturally. Right down to grandfather's motto, which you will observe just below the shield—'What I seek, I know'. Apparently a line from Matthew Arnold's 'Memorial Verses': *All this I bear, for what I seek, I know.* The College of Heralds enjoyed the 'bear' pun, heraldic sense of humour being what it is."

"Is that a fact?" Mosby overlaid his unease with feigned interest. The last time someone had taken for granted his ability to equate bears with King Arthur had been in the hall at St Veryan's, and the someone had been Howard Morris. It made him wonder, if the British knew so much about what was going on, whether they were not also well aware of Operation Bear. "And does this mean I'm going to get to talk to Group Captain Bullitt after all?"

"If you still want to talk to him. And always supposing he wants to talk to you."

Mosby cocked his head on one side. "Why shouldn't he want to talk to me? Is Badon Hill some kind of top secret, maybe?"

"That's the general idea—you're catching on at last,

Captain." Sir Frederick nodded. "Plus the fact that he's taken rather strongly against the CIA—doesn't care for you at all at the moment."

Mosby stiffened. "But I'm not CIA, for God's sake—I thought we'd got that straight."

"We only have your word for that."

"And *their* word too," Mosby played his deuce with all the confidence of a man convinced he had an ace. "Isn't that worth anything? I thought your security people worked hand in hand with ours—?" He broke off lamely as he saw the expression on Sir Frederick's face. "Uh-huh—I get it . . . Blood isn't thicker than water any more . . ." He spread his hands helplessly. "Well, then there's no way I can prove I'm not what I'm not, I guess. Except if I was I suppose I'd have some smart way of proving that I wasn't."

Sir Frederick turned towards Audley. "Well David. Over to you."

Audley considered Mosby silently for five seconds before speaking. "I told you: I'd need time. And you say we haven't any."

"Today's Thursday. The deadline is midday Friday for Sunday—and that was a personal favour to me."

Whose deadline?

"Not even with a D-Notice?" Audley shook his head, rejecting his own question before it had been answered. "No, that wouldn't hold them this time. You couldn't make it stick."

"I wouldn't even try. The Government wouldn't wear it if I did—we'd be tarred with the same brush, and so would they. They wouldn't wear it, and they'd be right: we'd just be trying to hold the lid down, and it would blow us to kingdom come. If not in our own press, then for sure in the foreign press—including the American. They'd make a meal of it."

The two Englishmen gazed at each other, oblivious of Mosby.

Finally Sir Frederick nodded. "So it's your way or no way at all."

"I get whatever I need?"

"Just ask. If anyone talks back to you refer them to me. I shall be on the end of a phone."

"And they're both mine?" Audley pointed to Mosby.

"Hey! What is this?" exclaimed Mosby.

"They are yours until midday tomorrow." Sir Frederick turned to Mosby. "As of this moment, Captain Sheldon, you and your wife are in the absolute charge of Dr Audley. What he says, you will listen to. What he orders, you will do."

"Like hell I will!"

"I agree, though I would place the emphasis differently: like hell you *will*." Sir Frederick's tone was still conversational, as though he was clarifying a minor point of semantics. but that figured easily enough, because big dragons like Sir Frederick Clinton didn't have to breathe fire to get their own way; with them a glance was as good as a roasting.

"That sounds like a threat."

"A threat? My dear Sheldon, I don't need to threaten you. The situation you are in threatens you. You maintain that you don't know what is happening, that you are innocent . . . and as it happens I do not believe you—I believe you are a most absolute and accomplished liar . . . but your innocence or guilt are now completely irrelevant—"

"Well, it damn well isn't to me! You can't—"

Sir Frederick raised his hand. "Please hear me out, Captain. It is for your own good, I do assure you . . . You see, if you are a CIA operative you are in very great trouble at this moment—the biggest you are ever likely to be in this side of the Iron Curtain. But if you are what you claim to be you are almost certainly in even greater trouble, both you and your wife."

Mosby stared at him. "Greater—? I don't understand."

"David will explain to you. And then he will require your co-operation." Sir Frederick paused to let the words sink in. "And I want you to give him that co-operation as though your life and your liberty depended on it. Because they do, Captain—yours and your wife's."

"Our *lives*?"

"If you are innocent." Sir Frederick nodded. "And your liberty if you are guilty."

"Guilty of what, for God's sake?"

"That again David will tell you. But look at it this way, if you like, Captain: you approached him two days ago and asked him to help you. And that's just what he's going to do . . . And a few minutes ago you offered Squadron Leader Roskill a deal—a gentleman's agreement. So now if David offers you another deal . . . my advice to you is *take it*. Because you'll never get a better offer."

Mosby felt his cheek muscles tighten uncontrollably. Maybe that passage between the two of them a few moments before had been for his sole benefit—*the Government wouldn't wear it . . . it would blow us to kingdom come*—as part of the psychological process of scaring the bejasus out of him. But now he had a gut feeling that it hadn't been at all, and that Clinton was here not so much to see him as for an emergency briefing with Audley, his Number Four top trouble-shooter. Which meant that beneath the Ivy League urbanity the British were running even more shit-scared and desperate than the Americans.

Jesus! And what made that worse was that the British knew why they were running—

Sir Frederick's eyes were on him—the Big Dragon's eyes that burned little dragons into crisps.

"Well, Sheldon?"

He could almost feel the heat.

"Okay. Whatever you want. Just so you protect my wife."

"We shall try to protect you both . . . By that I take it you still deny any connection with your CIA people?"

No choice. Even with Shirley at risk, no choice.

"It's the truth. But since you all think I'm a liar I guess there's not much point saying so."

"Not all of us." Sir Frederick stood up. "David over there believes you, for one."

"David?" Mosby looked at Audley in surprise. "Well— that's great."

Great like a gift-wrapped time-bomb.

"Convenient, certainly." Sir Frederick nodded to Audley before turning finally back to Mosby as he began to move towards the door. "Make the most of it, Sheldon, that's all. Good afternoon to you."

Mosby watched the door close. For the second time in one day he'd been badly frightened, but each time he'd been too busy—or too stupid—to realise the extent of the danger until it had passed.

"Phew!" he breathed out gratefully. There was nothing to be gained from trying to hide what must be pretty damn obvious.

Audley settled himself more comfortably in his chair. "He had you rattled, then?"

"You can say that again." Mosby studied the big Englishman. It was almost like he too was relieved to see Clinton's back, though that could hardly be due to fear—more likely he just had no taste for playing second fiddle. "Top brass always makes me rattle . . . And he's your boss, eh?"

"You could say so."

"And that makes you—" Mosby clamped his mouth shut as though he'd thought better of what he'd been about to say.

"Makes me what?"

Mosby shook his head. "Just . . . I was remembering your wife said you worked for the Government, that's all."

"Does it worry you?"

"Not so you believe I'm telling the truth. Was that on the level?"

"I chose not to believe you work for the CIA, if that's what you mean."

"It'll sure do for a start. But do I get to ask why?" Mosby grinned nervously. "Or you could tell me why everyone else thinks the opposite, I don't mind which, so I get some sort of answer."

"But of course." Audley sounded positively amiable now, almost friendly. "To take the uncharitable view first, quite simply—they were expecting you."

"Me?"

"You meaning the CIA . . . Let me put it another way: if you were a policeman and a rich man came to you and said he thought he was about to be burgled, what would you do?"

"Well, if I was a cop . . . I guess I'd stake out his place —is that what you want me to say?"

"Exactly. And then when a stranger turns up—a stranger with the wrong sort of accent, carrying a sack and set of house-breaking tools—you'd be inclined to take that uncharitable view, I rather think. Wouldn't you?"

Mosby frowned. "Sure. But—"

Audley cut him off. "I know what you're going to say: if the burglar arrived in company with a detective superintendent—and if he could prove the detective himself had suggested they should visit the rich man's house in the first place? Is that it?"

"Something like, I guess."

"Then you could have a bent copper, or a stupid one. So it was fortunate for me that I checked up with my police station first, otherwise I might be in quite a spot now." This time there was no amusement in Audley's smile, and some of the friendliness had drained from his voice. "But I did check. And so the official view is that the CIA was perhaps trying to be a little too clever for its own good."

Mosby cursed Howard Morris and Schreiner both for so grossly miscalculating Audley's reaction. How could they have been so hopelessly off beam, though?

"The official view? But not yours?"

"No, not mine. I knew the CIA has its little moments of weakness, but I can't see my old friend Howard Morris dropping a clanger like that. He knows me much too well."

It was macabre, the way Audley's mind had travelled

along the same line, to the same destination. And the wrong one, too.

"Howard—?"

"Morris. CIA Field Control, UK. Quite a sharp fellow. He'd never have sent his burglar to me—unless he wanted me to know about the burglary..."

Unless? The word pumped Mosby's heart painfully. It wasn't possible, it surely wasn't possible, that Shirley and he had been deliberately sacrificed to stir up the British. That had been a contingency, but not the objective. And yet *unless* was there now, squeezing his chest—

"...which is just about the last thing in the world that he'd be wanting at this moment," Audley continued reflectively. "Which means you aren't his burglar."

"But I'm still a burglar?" It was no sweat to sound puzzled.

"Oh, yes—you are a burglar. I've no doubt about that."

Mosby nodded. "Uh-huh? And just what am I supposed to be stealing?"

"Why, Mons Badonicus, of course, Captain Sheldon— or may I call you Mosby? It fits your character better."

"It does? Well, be my guest. You can call me William Clarke Quantrill or John Wilkes Booth for all I care, just so you tell me how I can steal a battlefield, that's all."

"By finding it."

"That's no crime."

Audley pursed his lips. "Now there you're wrong. In most civilised countries 'stealing by finding' is a crime. If your Confederate ancestor had made away with that Yankee payroll he happened to find behind the lines..."

"But a battlefield isn't a payroll."

"This isn't just any battlefield. This is an extra special one—King Arthur's greatest victory, no less. Knowledge like that could be worth more than a Yankee payroll. Not only could be—but is."

Audley's sudden conversion to King Arthur was curious, to say the least, thought Mosby. But if he really believed that money was the objective then it was time to let a little honest avarice show through.

"You really think so?" He looked at the Englishman sidelong.

"I know so. In fact one of the ironies of your position, Mosby, is that you don't seem to know just how valuable it is. It's so valuable it's already killed four men, and maybe as many as seven."

"Killed—?" Mosby's mind reeled at the arithmetic: Davies and his navigator—the airman Sergeant Gallagher had phoned him about . . . that made three. And if the British knew about Thickset and Tall and Thin . . . *Jesus*! But even that only made five.

"And destroyed a four million dollar aircraft," added Audley. "Or whatever the going price of a Phantom is these days."

"You can't mean it!" Mosby whispered.

"But I do mean it." Audley focussed on a point midway between them. "It's rather like an old Richard Widmark film I saw years ago, when I was still going to the cinema . . . What was it—'Panic in the Streets' its title was, I think. All the police in this seaport—New Orleans, somewhere like that—were hunting this petty thief, so the other criminals thought he had pulled off a big job of some sort and they hunted him too. Only the truth was he had the plague—the Black Death. Which is what Mons Badonicus would have been for you, Mosby . . . If you'd found it on your own it would have killed you, almost certainly."

There was a clatter of tea-cups beyond the door to the hall.

"That's the second irony," said Audley. "And the third one is that you never really needed to look for Mons Badonicus at all: it was right under your feet all the time."

Mosby looked at his feet.

"Not here, man, not here—Wodden."

Wodden?

"Wodden equals Mons Badonicus," said Audley.

"You've got our battle under the new runway extension, so far as we can make out."

The door opened behind Mosby.

"Tea up," said Roskill. "And one American wife, un- damaged, as per specification."

– XI –

THE AMERICAN WIFE certainly appeared undamaged; indeed, with every hair in place right down to the two artfully arranged tendrils curling on her cheeks, she looked as though she'd just stepped out of a beauty salon. Which could mean that the female of the British dragon species was less daunting than the male, even allowing for the fact that Shirley would have seemed just as edible to him on the tilting boat-deck of the *Titanic*.

Which, when he thought about it, was how the floor of Camelot House felt now.

She stared at him from the doorway. "You okay, honey?"

"I'm fine."

Fine meaning unsinkable.

"You look a bit peaky. I guess you know they think you're some kind of spy, huh?" She moved to one side to let a diminutive grey-uniformed maid push in the tea-trolley, fixing Audley with a hostile frown which remained on target like a gyroscopically-controlled cannon.

"David doesn't think so," said Mosby.

"He doesn't?" She assimilated the information without

blinking. "Well, I should think not . . . Some spy!" Hostility for Audley was replaced by derision for absent idiots.

"He thinks I'm a burglar."

"A—what?" The frown came back on target. "What has he burgled? The plans of the Round Table and the formula for getting the Sword out of the Stone?" Mosby winced at the Arthurian reminder—*under the new runway extension at Wodden*—but before he could react the little maid came towards him with a tray.

"With milk?"

Small upturned nose, frizzy blonde hair and that famous sensual gap between the large upper incisors reinforced by a trim little body in the well-cut grey uniform. Only the candid brown eyes belied the general impression of childish sexiness.

"Thank you."

What the hell was he doing, fancying the hired help when the ship was sinking under him?

"And sugar, Captain Sheldon?"

He did a double-take. The voice was wrong and the manner was wrong and the uniform was too well cut to be a uniform. Plus, above all, no mere maid would know his name . . . But she still looked no more than eighteen.

She smiled into his confusion. "My name's Fitzgibbon, Captain. I'm the 'they' your wife was talking about."

He added ten years to his estimate, thought still against the visual evidence. Perhaps the British were recruiting them straight from High School now.

"Pleased to meet you all, Mrs Fitzgibbon—and no sugar, thank you," he heard himself drawl in his best Virginian. "I'm sorry to disappoint you . . . by not being a CIA man, that is."

"That's quite all right, Captain. I was only asking a routine question."

"Routine fiddlesticks," said Shirley. "And she wanted to know more about Di Davies than about you, honey."

"And were you able to satisfy her, Mrs Sheldon?" asked Audley.

"Seeing as how I hardly knew the man, the whole thing was a waste of time. He was my husband's friend, not mine."

Audley looked towards Mrs Fitzgibbon. "Well, Frances?"

"I agree . . . Except I'd go further: I very much doubt that Mrs Sheldon ever met Major Davies, beyond perhaps saying 'good morning' to him."

"That's ridiculous!" snapped Shirley.

"She knows her cover story perfectly," continued Frances Fitzgibbon. "She is extremely resourceful in blocking questions beyond it. I would think it unlikely that anything she has told me will conflict seriously with what her husband may have told you. Not so far, anyway . . . But I don't think the story would stand up to separate in-depth interrogation. Either they didn't have time to put it together in total detail, or they never expected it to be professionally tested."

"Or they are amateurs," said Audley.

Frances Fitzgibbon considered Shirley for a moment. "If she is, she's a natural."

Mosby could feel the water-tight bulkheads beneath him giving way one after another. If he was going to save anything from this disaster, never mind Shirley's skin and his own, it would be from a lifeboat. It was time to abandon the ship.

"Is everyone going crazy?" said Shirley. "I just don't understand what's—"

"Shut up, honey," said Mosby in a flat voice.

"What?" she rounded on him. "Are you going to stand there and—"

"I said 'shut up'. So shut up." Mosby stared round him with what he hoped was the air of a defiant trapped rat. His eyes met Hugh Roskill's over a steaming teacup. "And don't drink that tea, Squadron Leader—it'll blow your abscess through your jaw."

Roskill lowered his cup as hurriedly as if he had smelt

bitter almonds in it. "Damnation! I'd clean forgotten." He grinned at Mosby. "Thanks, Sheldon."

"Think nothing of it. I guess I'm a better dentist than I am a burglar." He shrugged at Audley. "I should have stuck to teeth."

Audley nodded slowly. "You didn't really know Davies, did you? Not as a friend."

"Not really. I just fixed his teeth."

Shirley drew in a sharp breath. "Mose—what are you saying?"

"I'm letting it go, honey. It's gotten too rich for us—and too dangerous."

"Too dangerous?"

"David says it's already killed a bunch of guys."

"Killed?" Shirley's voice cracked. "I don't understand."

"Neither do I. But he's not kidding. And it wouldn't be any use to us if he was. Because he already knows where Badon is: it's under the goddamn runway at Wodden, that's where it is. Right—under—the—goddamn—runway."

"Runway extension," corrected Audley.

"The runway extension." Mosby loaded the words with bitterness and kept his eyes on Shirley. "Davies must have talked to someone else after all."

Shirley licked her lips. "It can't be—you said it was a hill. Badon Hill."

"But it is a hill," said Roskill. "The whole of RAF Wodden is high ground: it's a plateau. And the western spur slopes up to the highest point, where the old windmill used to be—Windmill Knob, they used to call it. They demolished it in 1940, when the RAF moved in, but the foundations were still there in the grass when I was training there twelve years ago."

But not there any more, thought Mosby with growing dismay. The whole of the western end had been thoroughly levelled, bulldozed and landscaped like a pool table, and the spoil spread far and wide into every undulation of the main ridge.

If Badon had been there—

"And you never suspected it was on the base?" Roskill sounded almost sympathetic. "You didn't—"

"Let it be, Hugh," said Audley. "There's no need to probe the wound now."

It took every bit of Mosby's self-restraint not to look at Audley in surprise. This was the exact moment to probe the wound, while it was raw and painful; and ever since the drift of Audley's new scenario had become clear he had been feverishly constructing his role in it as a greedy little interloper who had planned to cash in on accidental knowledge of the dead pilot's discovery. Yet now Audley was deliberately passing up his best chance of quizzing him.

"The only thing I would like to know," said Audley casually, as though it was an afterthought, "is how you acquired the Badon artefacts—just for the record."

Mosby felt almost relieved at getting one of the key questions after all, no matter how awkward; it reassured him that Audley was still running to form.

"Yeah . . . well, what I told you wasn't so far off the real thing . . ." He shrugged. *If you have to make up a story quickly, keep it simple and don't bother about the loose ends. Let the other guy try and tie them up for you—he knows that the truth is untidy.* "He asked me to look after them for him. I got this storeroom behind my surgery—"

"Although he hardly knew you?" cut in Frances Fitzgibbon.

"Not 'although', but 'because'," said Audley. "Davies chose Mosby *because* he didn't know him. And because there's nothing suspicious about visiting a dentist. If there had been we'd have one very dead dentist by now."

"What do you mean—dead dentist?" Shirley had entirely abandoned her Scarlett O'Hara characterisation for a more classical one: this was Lady Macbeth frightened and beginning to crack under the pressure of unforeseen disasters.

"Exactly what I say, I'm afraid, Mrs Sheldon. The fact is, you've both had a very narrow escape. If Davies had really confided in you—or if you had started looking for

Badon in the right place, then the odds against your survival would have been very high. But he didn't, and you didn't . . . which is why you are here safe and sound now."

"But—but we haven't done anything wrong!" Shirley wailed. "Not really."

"So your husband keeps telling me. But then neither had Major Davies—really. Nor that young navigator of his—Captain—what was his name?"

"Collier," said Roskill.

"Collier. He hadn't done anything at all, poor fellow. He certainly didn't deserve to be eliminated."

"That was an accident—they crashed in the sea."

"And very conveniently, too. You've no idea how many convenient deaths have occurred just recently. Deaths and disappearances . . . Let me have the photographs, Hugh. It's time for a bit of positive co-operation."

Roskill snapped open a black briefcase and withdrew a square buff-coloured envelope from it.

"Thank you." Audley in turn slipped out a collection of photographs of different sizes from the envelope, shuffling them like cards into what was presumably the desired sequence. "Now I want you both to have a look at these . . . Mosby first, then Mrs Sheldon . . . and I'd like you to try to identify them. I'm afraid one or two of them aren't awfully clear, and a couple aren't very nice to look at, either, but I'll warn you about them in advance. Just do your best."

He handed Mosby a photograph.

It was a typical USAF mug-shot of a typical American service face, right down to the stern, Defender of Liberty expression, even if the crew-cut and the uniform hadn't placed identification beyond doubt. Four days ago he would hardly have been able to tell this one from a hundred others whose jaws he knew better than their features.

"This is Di Davies," said Mosby.

Audley put his finger to his lips. "Let your wife see them first, if you don't mind. Pass it on."

Mosby handed the mug-shot to Shirley.

Another picture. This one for sure he wouldn't have known until four days ago, mug-shot though it was.

"This one's Di Davies," agreed Shirley. "But this other one . . . I've seen him around, but I don't know his name."

"Captain Collier," said Mosby. "He'd only been over here a few weeks."

"Now a nasty one," said Audley gently. "Be prepared, Mrs Sheldon."

A dead face, slack and blankly staring nowhere. Someone had attempted to arrange it into a more or less life-like appearance, but there was obviously something very wrong with the left side of the head.

Shirley shuddered and drew in a quick breath. "I've never seen him before in my life."

"Nor me," Mosby shook his head.

"I think possibly you have, but maybe not," said Audley. "His name is—or was—Pennebaker. He was an airman on the base at Wodden. Shot himself a couple of days ago."

"He shot himself?"

"Well, that's what we're required to believe. But our forensic people have their doubts . . . They think he was helped, you might say. And I'm very much inclined to believe them." He paused. "Now here's an intersting one."

The photograph was bigger, but not nearly so well focussed—a blown-up fragment of a larger unposed snapshot, maybe—

Hell and damnation!

"Ah! I see that one rings a bell," said Audley happily. "Let your wife have a look, there's a good chap."

Shirley stared. "Why, isn't that Harry what's-his-name —the Public Relations guy?"

"Finsterwald," said Mosby. "Is he—dead?"

"Why, I saw him only three-four days back in the BX," said Shirley. She looked from Mosby to Audley. "Do you mean to say he's dead too?"

Audley raised a hand. "Just look at the pictures, Mrs Sheldon. We'll get to the captions in due time."

Another picture. This time Mosby was ready for anything, but the black face staring over his shoulder was totally new to him.

There followed more black faces, snapped at a variety of angles, and judging from the background detail with a telescopic lens. By the time they reached Calvin Merriwether's portrayal of sullen emptiness the fact was pretty well established that to Captain and Mrs Mosby Sheldon, of the Commonwealth of Virginia, all coloured men looked alike; which the British could hardly quarrel with, since they obviously had had the same difficulty.

The hopeful sign about all the pictures—and about Harry's too—was that they were taken from life, unlike the Pennebaker shot. But the deduction from that was that the British were on to the pair of them, even if they hadn't yet established any connection with their captives.

Audley offered him another picture. "Another nasty one."

It was of another dead face—not so horrible as that of the airman, but with the same lifeless stare . . . yet quite unlike anything he had so far been shown: the wrinkled features of old age beneath an untidy halo of white hair—

Oh, God! Mosby thought with sickening certainty, recalling Merriwether's admiration. *'He's a great old guy'.*

James Barkham, old-fashioned bookseller.

"I'm sure I never met him," said Shirley firmly.

Mosby shook his head. "He's new to me too."

Audley nodded. "Only two more."

The permutations of what he had said earlier raced through Mosby's brain. *Four killed*—they had seen four dead men already. *Maybe seven*—but they had already seen two possibles, and another two would make eight. So it didn't add up.

He gazed into the face of Tall and Thin. Sickeningly, it bore the same smile as it had done in its last minute of life in St Swithun's Churchyard a few hours earlier.

"No," he said.

Shirley looked. "Same here—no."

And then Thickset, his own victim.

He was calm now. The stakes were altogether too high for panic.

"No. Never seen him before either. Sorry." He watched Audley as he passed the photo to Shirley. "I guess we've not helped very much."

"I didn't expect miracles."

"Were they all—have they all been killed?"

Audley shook his head. "Not all. You've seen four dead men—you'll have worked out which they were, of course. Plus two missing and two killers."

"Killers?" Mosby set his teeth. "Murderers?"

"The presumption is overwhelming, yes."

Mosby pointed to the picture in Shirley's hand. "You mean—that guy and the other one?"

"No. Those are two of our men who haven't reported in. The killers are your comrade Captain Finsterwald and his coloured associate, whom we haven't yet identified."

Mosby gaped at him. "Harry Finsterwald? You can't be serious!"

"Why not, Captain Sheldon?" asked Frances Fitzgibbon.

Mosby stared at her. "Harry Finsterwald? Hell—he's in Base Public Relations, not Murder Incorporated. He's just a dumb son-of-a-bitch with an expensive smile."

"That's right." Shirley nodded. "He maybe fancies himself as a lady-killer—at the Cobra Squadron Fourth of July party I had to fight him off in the parking lot—"

"You never told me that," said Mosby hotly.

"Honey, I don't tell you every time someone gets fresh with me. You'd only get your teeth knocked in."

"Harry Finsterwald—" Audley broke in "—is not Harry Finsterwald."

"Huh?" Mosby and Shirley turned towards him simultaneously.

"His name is Harry Feiner," said Frances Fitzgibbon. "And he's a veteran CIA operative—Vietnam, Cambodia, Thailand, all the way down to Singapore. Counter-insurgency expert, Special Operations Unit commander, counter-intelligence strongarm man—you name it, he's been it. We know him from Singapore, no mistake."

"Though we didn't know he was here in Britain until yesterday, apparently," said Audley, looking at Roskill.

"Well, he's not on the embassy list, for heaven's sake," said Roskill defensively. "And they've got nearly ninety on it already, it's one of the biggest single overseas posts. We just can't keep track of all the extras they've brought in outside London, we just don't have the manpower—at least, not to watch our own bloody allies."

"Bloody allies is right," murmured Frances Fitzgibbon.

"He's a CIA man?" said Mosby. "Harry Finsterwald?"

"Harry Feiner, Captain." Frances Fitzgibbon corrected him with the air of a little schoolmarm trying to straighten out a big stupid pupil. "We caught up with him yesterday when we were inquiring into the death of the man who supplied Major Davies with his books, an old man named Barkham."

"You mean he was murdered—that old man?" said Shirley.

"It looked like natural causes, Mrs Sheldon. But now we're not so sure . . . What we are sure of, from what his assistant says, is that Mr Barkham was visited by Harry Feiner and a coloured man several days ago. And they were checking up to find out how much Major Davies told him."

"And whatever it was, it was too much," said Roskill.

"So we put two men on to Feiner this morning, and those two men are now missing," said Frances Fitzgibbon.

The late afternoon sun slanted in through the tall windows, blazing on the legs of a suit of armour which stood sentinel on one side of the door—

> *And flamed upon the brazen greaves*
> *Of bold Sir Lancelot*

—reminding Mosby of the lines he had learnt so recently in his role of Arthurian enthusiast. And reminding him also, more terrifyingly, that it was the same sun which had shone so brightly on the bodies of the two British security men in the churchyard.

Nightmares in daylight were bad; and nightmares in sunlight were worse. But worst of all were nightmares that weren't nightmares at all, but reality.

"You know, I do think he's beginning to catch on," said Roskill. "He looks quite sick."

"Well, I'm still lost," said Shirley huskily. "Because you just can't mean that the CIA's going round murdering people—innocent people."

"Why not, Mrs Sheldon?" asked Frances.

"Why, we simply don't do that sort of thing."

"Not in Vietnam?"

"In Vietnam?" Shirley floundered beautifully. "But this isn't Vietnam—this is England." She looked around her as though for confirmation. "This is England."

And it could hardly be more England than right here, thought Mosby bitterly: Camelot House, in the midst of its green parkland. The heart and capital of King Arthur's Avalon.

"It's England," Frances nodded. "And it's a foreign country, just like Vietnam. Where Harry Feiner cut his teeth, among other things."

"I don't believe it," said Shirley obstinately. "And I won't believe it. We're on the same side—we're allies. And I don't mean like in Vietnam, either. That was different."

"It certainly was—for the Vietnamese."

"Your politics are beginning to show, Olga dear," said Roskill lightly.

"Olga?" Shirley frowned. "I thought it was Frances?"

"Ah, but haven't you noticed the striking resemblance to Olga Korbut? The shape and size—the delicate sense of balance? The swift kárate chop?"

"Children—children!" Audley intervened. "What Mrs Fitzgibbon means, Mrs Sheldon, is simply that the CIA is concerned with the welfare of the United States. There's nothing in their so-called 1947 Charter about being kind to foreigners—and nor should there be. National security won't run in tandem with international relations—they trip each other up."

"Doesn't run awfully well with the Ten Commandments either, and that's a fact," said Roskill. "Whatever Olga thinks."

"Don't paraphrase Lenin at me," Frances snapped back.

"Wasn't thinking of Lenin—it was Allen Dulles, who ran the CIA when you were playing with your dolls. 'Obedience to a higher loyalty' was what he called it." Roskill nodded amiably to Shirley. "Meaning, you can fight as dirty as you like if it's for your country."

" 'My country, right or wrong'," murmured Mosby.

"That's what it used to amount to, you're right. Nice convenient double standards all round—Germans bomb Coventry, that's terror bombing, we bomb Hamburg, that's *area* bombing. They have wicked U-boats, we have brave submarines—life was a great deal simpler in the old days. But not any more, because now it works the other way round."

"How d'you mean?"

"Because we have the U-boats now, and they have the submarines, my dear fellow."

Mosby looked suitably puzzled.

"What he means," said Audley, "is that if the Russians—the KGB, that is—play dirty, no one takes much notice. But if the CIA plays dirty and gets caught, then there's likely to be a major scandal. You only have to look at the headlines over here, never mind in the United States. And exactly the same applies to . . . us . . . if we play dirty."

"Which leaves us both with the Eleventh Commandment—'Thou shalt not be found out—or else'," added Roskill. "Which the CIA has jolly well transgressed with a vengeance over Badon Hill, unfortunately."

Mosby fought to keep his puzzled expression steady. For beyond the fear for himself and Shirley, and the helplessness and loneliness of their position, there was forming a terrible doubt. It was no longer a question of how the British could have gotten everything ass-about-face, *but supposing they hadn't?*

"Let me get you straight—" Shirley spoke more harshly now, as though the same doubt had proved too strong for the Lady Macbeth interpretation "—you are really asking us to believe that our own Secret Service would not only kill—murder—some old man, some innocent old man . . . and maybe two of your people . . . but Americans too? Our own servicemen? You're asking us to believe *that*?"

"The evidence is circumstantial." Audley stared at her silently for a moment. "But that's the way it looks."

"In the cause of a higher loyalty," said Frances.

"Higher loyalty my fanny!" snapped Shirley.

Roskill started to laugh.

"You think that's funny?" Shirley rounded on him fiercely. "It's all a big joke—killing people? You have to be sick."

"I'm sorry, really I am." Roskill looked contrite. "But I wasn't laughing at you, and it isn't funny. It was just the look on Olga's face when you said 'fanny'."

"Huh?"

Mosby cleared his throat. "It isn't the same part of the body in English as it is in American, honey."

"It isn't? Well, what is—?" She stopped suddenly and blushed to the roots of her hair. It was the first time Mosby had ever seen her blush.

"You were saying, Mrs Sheldon?" said Audley gently.

"I think I know what my wife was going to say—" began Mosby.

"It's okay, Mose," said Shirley. "If that's playing dirty I can take it. I guess they won't take any notice of what I say anyway, but I'm still going to say it. And it's this: if you think we're the sort of people who'd kill a dog just to hush up that we've maybe accidentally messed up a piece of ground where somebody fought a battle a million years ago, then you aren't only crazy—you really do have to be sick. And you can laugh at that if you like."

Atta girl, thought Mosby fondly. Not a Stephen Decatur patriot, nor even a Sam Smith one, but a pure John Paul Jones—*I have not yet begun to fight*—even with the ship sinking under her.

"I agree with you, Mrs Sheldon," said Audley. "But, alas, it doesn't happen that way. With the KGB certainly, but not with you Americans, nor with us British. With us both it happens by slow degree, not by wicked intention."

"I don't get you."

"I don't expect you to. Take Vietnam, for instance, about which Mrs Fitzgibbon is so very sure . . . No, Frances. Your view is far too simplistic . . . I happen to believe that Kennedy and Johnson were both great presidents. And what's more, fundamentally honest men too, both of them. But by degrees they got into—Vietnam. And My Lai, and all the rest of it.

"And Watergate too, to make a more practical example . . . It wasn't the original crime—the stupid little break-in —that wasn't even necessary. Somebody simply had a higher loyalty on a much lower level, that's all—somebody took a bad decision on a lower level, and somebody else took another bad decision on a slightly less lower level. And after that one thing led straight to another, and brought the whole house down."

"But the rottenness at the top was the measure of the rottenness at the bottom, David," said Frances Fitzgibbon.

"Simplistic again. Your rottenness at the top brought the boys back home from Vietnam, Frances. Your rottenness gave Henry Kissinger his chance . . . But that's all a matter of opinion, and ours is a problem of fact. We have a much more important crisis here and now to resolve—which matters to Britain as well as America."

"Which is?" said Mosby.

"Which is that the CIA in Britain is in jeopardy, and with it the whole of the American presence here. And that means in Europe. And that means the North Atlantic Treaty Organisation. And *that* means the Strategic Arms Limitation Talks." Audley pointed at Shirley. "All because of your little piece of ground where somebody maybe once fought a battle—are the stakes high enough for you now, Mrs Sheldon? Are they enough to kill a dog for?"

Mosby was astonished at the Englishman's vehemence: it was like discovering that in reality the game of cricket was played not for the sake of the game, but to the death.

"I don't understand," said Shirley.

"No?" Audley's tone was brutal now. "Well, I'll tell you. Destroying the site of Mons Badonicus would have been a bit of damn bad publicity for you—for the United States. People care about things like that nowadays, and some of them care passionately even. In fact even *I* care, and I'm one of your dirty trick players. Because a country's past is the sum of its present, or should be, and I happen to love my country—even enough to have some of those higher loyalties of Allen Dulles's. Not for England, or Wales, or Scotland, but for Britain."

"But we don't—" Shirley began.

"No, honey," said Mosby, "let him have his say."

Audley looked at them for a moment. "Every year thousands of ancient sites are destroyed—half the time without anyone even knowing. We've even got an organisation called 'Rescue' which tries to save them, or at least to record them, before the damned motorways cut through them—or the runway extensions. This year the Government's given Rescue over a million pounds, when we're flat broke—that's the measure of it. People care.

"And Badon isn't just another Roman villa, another mediaeval pottery. Badon's King Arthur—the lost battle. Nine-tenths of the people have never heard of it, but they've all heard of Arthur. So for a start, it isn't just a piece of ground, do you understand *that*, Mrs Sheldon?"

Mosby stuck his jaw out. "Okay, Audley. We both understand what it is."

"Good. But your General Ellsworth didn't understand."

"General Ellsworth?"

"That's right. 'Build the runway' he says. And that was the first bad decision, because at that point you could have saved the whole thing. Wodden isn't the only base surplus to RAF requirements by any means, if you want longer runways."

"General Ellsworth said that?"

"He said it. And then when they'd bulldozed Windmill Knob flat and the thing started to blow up in his face, the CIA made another bad decision. They said *cover up*."

He looked at Mosby expectantly, but this time Mosby had nothing to say. General Ellsworth?

Audley shook his head. "If they'd come to us instead, we couldn't have stopped the bad publicity. Not by then, anyway. But we could have taken Ellsworth's head on a plate, and we could have just about survived it one way or another. Only someone in the State Department must have realised how bad the publicity would be—someone who knew his Arthurian history, for all I know. Someone who could see the headlines and thought he couldn't handle them. So Davies had to have his big mouth shut for good."

"And *bingo*!" murmured Roskill. "Watergate!"

"Only the name will be 'Wodden' in future," said Frances.

"Or 'Badon', more likely," said Roskill.

Audley silenced them with a look. "And that was the dirty job the CIA had given to them: cover it all up. Bury it."

For five seconds—ten seconds—nobody spoke. It was as though the last two words had told the whole story.

Then Shirley spoke: "How can you be so sure that's the way it was? You said it was—circumstantial?"

"It's more than that. I wish to God it wasn't, otherwise we'd still have a chance of smothering it. And don't think I wouldn't if I could, Mrs Sheldon."

She stared at him. "But—but Badon's been destroyed.

And Davies is dead. I know it's—horrible. But he is dead."

"But Billy Bullitt isn't," said Audley.

"And we can't shut his mouth, Mrs Sheldon," said Frances. "Because he's already opened it."

– XII –

MOSBY SQUINTED AT the villainous typescript. If British Intelligence couldn't rise to anything better than this for its top secret documents then it was small wonder that they were about to preside over the biggest Anglo-American debacle since the Boston Tea Party.

"I am sorry about the typing," said Frances Fitzgibbon. "It's absolutely accurate—my shorthand's one hundred per cent. But I don't get much typing practise, and it was a rackety old machine—I had to put in all the g's by hand, as you can see."

"Excuses, excuses—and qui s'excuse, s'accuse," said Roskill. "There you are, Mrs Sheldon—I've given you a slightly better copy than your lord and master . . . If that typewriter was good enough for Billy Bullitt's grandfather, little Olga, it ought to be good enough for you. And his thrifty use of old worn-out carbon-paper matches our thrifty use of you as a tape-recorder. If the Civil Estimates chaps knew how we operate, they'd sleep a lot sounder after lunch."

There were nine or ten closely typed pages, Mosby estimated, but no indication of what they contained by way of title—

"This country has lost nothing but its honour, and having lost that has lost everything—"

What the hell?

He looked up to find Audley's eyes on him.

"I want you to read just the first page, to show you what we're up against," said Audley. "Then you can skip the next few pages and go straight to the meaty part. But that first page to start with, please."

"What is it?" asked Shirley.

"It's Billy Bullitt's *credo*," said Frances. "And it also explains why he's going to evict the CIA from Britain—and how he intends to do it. That's all."

Mosby bent over Page One—

"This country has lost nothing but its honour, and having lost that has lost everything. Fifty million people, the people who stood alone against Hitler. The people who broke the German Army in the '14-'18 War, Napoleon, Louis XIV, Philip of Spain, who produced Shakespeare, Newton, Penicillin, Radar—"

He looked up at Audley again.

"You must go on reading," said Audley flatly.

"Radar, the Hovercraft. Not that we are a super-race, far from it. We are a mongrel race. Nor because we have coal and oil if we had the courage to win it. A mongrel race, as I said: an amalgam of Celts, Anglo-Saxons, Vikings and Normans—imagination, staying power, restlessness, pragmatism—and the waves of refugees and immigrants, French Protestants, German Jews—and Africans and Asiatics too. I am no racist, as some foolish young people want to think—I'd as soon see a daughter of mine, if I had one, married to the best of my Arab levies than to the worst of the young fools I saw at Oxford. But we have no honour

left. No honour. Perhaps it comes from losing the best
in the two wars. And the loss of empire. But we won
the wars, perhaps that is the trouble, for it has happened before—Gildas told the same story, of course.
And I have watched this happening for thirty years,
but for most of the time without understanding. That
it's not the winning that matters, but the fighting for
something. Strange that I fought for so many causes
—other people's causes—and never understood that
until quite recently, in Arabia. It was there I began to
understand, and I remembered my childhood, here in
Camelot. My grandfather understood, he glimpsed it
—Rex quondam rexque futurus—what it has always
meant. It is no accident that the British have endlessly
pursued Rex quondam rexque futurus, the Present and
Future King. However vague the understanding, the
instinct was true. And the Grail legend is never truer
than now: the Fisher-king lies wounded unto death in
the magic castle in the wasteland. The Grail-knight
reaches the castle and asks a certain question. The
king is healed and the wasteland blossoms . . ."

"The Fisher-king and the Grail-knight—for God's sake!"
Mosby scowled at Audley. "Does it really go on like that?"

"For five or six pages."

"More than that," said Frances. "There's a page on what
he calls 'the historicity of Arthur', and another on the influ-
ence of Arthur on British history—plus why Henry II had
a grandson named Arthur and Henry VII's eldest son was
named Arthur. And the Korean War and the TSR-2 get
mixed up in it too at one point. And it all adds up to how
finding Mons Badonicus and proving Arthur won it will
give Britain back her honour."

"Well then . . ." Mosby looked to Audley for confirmation. ". . . He's crazy."

"Of course. Not certifiable—but crazy." Audley nodded. "But up until a few days ago he was also harmless,

and now he's most definitely not. Thanks to the CIA . . . So what page do we turn to, Frances?"

"Halfway down page eight. It's marked with a pencil cross."

A pencil cross—

"I first met Major David 'Dai' Davies at Woodhenge, which I was visiting in connection with other studies I was making at the time. He was measuring a burial mound. I asked him what he was doing, and he explained he was looking for Mons Badonicus. I told him that he was almost certainly far to the south of the most promising search area, that I myself had explored the Chilterns and the general line of the Icknield Way north-eastwards of the Thames as being a strong possibility, and that I had only recently returned to the belief that the western end of the Berkshire Downs was the likeliest site. To my surprise he disagreed firmly, though courteously. It soon became clear to me not only that he believed Badon to be in the Salisbury region, but that he was as in possession of some information or evidence to confirm this belief—"

Mosby looked up at Frances. "Either this is not verbatim, or he's taken a turn for the better."

"It's word for word, Captain."

"Well, it reads like an official statement."

"There's a reason for that," said Audley. "This wasn't the first time he dictated this part of the statement. Go on and you'll find out."

"confirm this belief. This intrigued me a great deal, the more so after I had discovered that he was extremely well-informed about all aspects of Arthurian studies. I accordingly invited him to Camelot for dinner."

"Not so crazy after all, maybe," said Mosby.

"Being crazy doesn't mean not being shrewd," agreed Audley. "He's all of that, Billy Bullitt is."

"It was during this first evening that I learnt he was a USAF pilot, flying PR Phantoms in the NATO Order of Battle. In fact, our combat experience overlapped, and although of different front-line generations we had much in common. And not only as concerned flying, for although a third generation American, he was also the grandson of a Welsh coal miner who had emigrated over 50 years earlier. Hence his christian name and its Welsh diminutive 'Dai'—"

"So it's 'Dai' with an 'a', not D-I," said Mosby.

"Of course. 'Dai Davies' is as Welsh as 'Paddy O'Reilly' is Irish. Which could account for his interest in Arthur, of course."

"—and his interest in Arthurian Britain. I pressed him on the subject of the battle's location, but he was reticent about it. Also, while promising to keep in touch with me he insisted that I should never contact him at the base. Before he left I supplied him with one of my blank physical relief maps of the district, having first ringed all potential Badon sites for him. He stated his intention of viewing these from the air. He visited me on three subsequent occasions. It was on the first of these that he asked me about the Novgorod manuscript of Bede's 'Historia Ecclesiastica' and I was able to show him my grandfather's copy of Bishop Harper's 'Russian Missionary Letters', from which he made notes. Shortly after the third visit he phoned me in a state of great excitement. He said he had found Badon, but that he would not be able to see me until he had completed his exchange duty with the RAF in Germany. I awaited his return also in a state of excitement. On the 5th of this month he phoned me again.

This time he was in a state of extreme agitation and
rage. He informed me that promises made to him by a
certain USAF general officer, by name Ellsworth, had
been broken, as a result of which the site of Badon, or at
least its cenotaph and grave pits, had been totally dese-
crated. He explained to me in detail the circumstances
leading to his identification of Mons Badonicus as
Windmill Knob at Wodden. He further informed me
that he had been 'grilled' and cautioned by a CIA
officer, and that he was now confined to base pending
transfer to South-East Asia. He had told this officer that
he intended nevertheless to 'blow this thing wide open'.
Although he had not revealed my involvement he said
he relied on me to support him in this, and that his
navigator, Captain Collier, who was a witness to many
of these events, would be bringing me evidence of his
discovery after the next day's training mission had been
completed. In the event Captain Collier did not visit me,
and I learnt from Press reports of the loss of a Phantom
aircraft on a routine training flight. I made further inquiries in connection with the information Major Davies
had given me, and these confirmed certain suspicions of
mine that a monstrous crime, or series of crimes, had
been committed by, or with the connivance of, the
American CIA. Full details of this are now with the
editor of a certain newspaper. Two further copies are in
places of safety with my instructions as to their publica-
tion in the event of my death or unexplained disappear-
ance."

The final lines swam before Mosby's eyes.
A certain newspaper.
Their deadline is midday Friday for Sunday.
Two further copies in places of safety.

"And what does the CIA say to this?" Shirley's voice
was absolutely steady. "And our State Department?"
"We haven't approached them."

"You haven't approached them?" Incredulity now. "Don't they have a say?"

"What can they say?"

"Well, they can deny it for a start."

"Of course they'll deny it. They'll say there's not one single word of truth in it. Major Davies never found Badon Hill and Badon Hill isn't Windmill Knob. So General Ellsworth never promised him the bulldozers wouldn't move in until the archaeologists had excavated it thoroughly. And Davies wasn't being posted to South-East Asia. He just crashed by accident—and took Captain Collier with him. Why would the CIA want to grill him? No reason at all— just a pack of lies made up by Group Captain William Lancelot Bullitt, DSO, DFC."

Audley paused. "And James Barkham died in his sleep, like an old man should—or if he didn't, then it was some wicked relative who wanted to inherit his bookshop. And our two men who followed Feiner haven't come to any harm—they've just lost their way and they haven't got tuppence between them for a phone call, that's all. And Airman Pennebaker was just playing with this pistol of his, and it just went off by accident—"

Where the hell did Airman Pennebaker fit in? thought Mosby desperately. Where the hell did any of them fit in?

"And Asher Klaverinsky never went for a swim. He just dropped out of circulation. Or maybe he didn't like it in Tel Aviv as much as Gorky. He was homesick, perhaps."

"Who on earth is—Asher Klaverinsky?" said Mosby.

"He's the man who stole the Novgorod Bede, Captain— Mosby. But then he never met Major Davies anyway, did he? There's not one single piece of evidence that he did— except in Billy Bullitt's fevered imagination. He just imagined the deal they made. Or perhaps it was Major Davies's fevered imagination. Or they cooked it up between them, just to cause trouble."

"What d'you mean—he stole the Novgorod Bede?"

"Just exactly that. He was working on its restoration when he finally got his emigration permit, and he reckoned the Russians owed him something for taking all his possessions and his money in exchange for letting him go. So he pretended he'd sent it on to Moscow for further specialist work, but in fact he smuggled it out with him. They probably don't even know they've lost it yet, the way they do things."

"But—" Mosby stopped, realising that he wasn't supposed to know that there was nothing of interest about Badon in the Novgorod Bede. And that nobody had stolen it.

"But what is there in it? In the Bede text—absolutely nothing. Just a straightforward early eighth century Bede, just like the Leningrad one. Only when Asher Klaverinsky got down to looking at it carefully he noticed that the Preface started about four inches down the page—that's four inches of wasted sheepskin before the dedication to 'the Most Glorious King Ceolwulf'. And he then noticed that those four inches were rougher than the rest of the page, which meant that they'd probably been scraped clean and re-chalked. Which in turn meant that the page had been written on before, and then cleaned and re-used, because parchment was enormously expensive—it was a common practice in those days. So he popped the page under ultra-violet light, and you'll never guess what he got instead." Audley nodded to Roskill. "Give him the first sheet, Hugh."

Roskill handed Mosby a typed sheet of paper—

. . . usque ad a??um obse??io?s Bad????? montis qui p??pe Sord'n?? host?um ex D?r??v??a ?r?ur? habetur novi???ma????? ????? de furci???ris . . .

"Which may not be very clear to you and me, but seems clear enough to the experts. Sheet Two, if you please, Hugh—"

. . . usque ad annum obsessionis Badonici montis qui prope Sord'num hostium ex Durnovaria Arturo habetur nossissimaeque ferme de furciferis . . .

Mosby stared hypnotically at the word *Arturo*.

"The free translation of which, more or less," continued Audley, taking the third sheet into his own hands, "reads as follows: . . . *until the year of the siege of the enemy hosts from Dorchester-on-Thames by Arthur at Badon Hill, which is near Salisbury* . . . They aren't absolutely sure about Dorchester-on-Thames, because they only know its Saxon name. So they've worked on a comparison with Roman Dorchester in Dorset. And technically 'Sord'num' is the monkish abbreviation for Sorviodunum, which is Sarum, just outside Salisbury. But historically and militarily the whole thing fits rather well then, with the Saxon army coming down the Icknield Way right from Cambridgeshire, picking up men as they moved along from one stronghold after another right to Dorchester, their big base on the Thames—and then striking at the main British army in the south and biting off more than they could chew." He looked at Mosby. "Can you identify the passage—the original passage, that is?"

He was deliberately ignoring the real dynamite, thought Mosby. The dynamite which blew the thing far higher than Badon by itself could ever do.

"I guess it has to be Gildas the Wise."

"Good man! Gildas it is—the end of Chapter XXV, only with seven new words. And of course, that fits too: the monks of Jarrow obviously had a copy of Gildas to make their own copies from, because Bede used it. And their copy had something like that Cambridge gloss in it—the one everybody ignores as corrupt. And so it was. But not quite."

"Plus Arthur," said Mosby.

Audley drew a deep breath. "Plus Arthur. You've put your finger on what really matters. And what ties our hands completely."

"What d'you mean?" said Shirley. "I thought it was Badon that was driving everyone crazy."

"Uh-huh." Mosby shook his head wearily. "Badon's a big thing—just knowing where it was will change a lot of history books. But they always knew it existed. Arthur is the real blockbuster: the first absolutely conclusive historical proof that puts him squarely on the historical map. Not somebody everyone wants to believe in, but a real person. Right there in—"

He stopped as the full significance hit him. He stared at Audley with the beginning of panic stirring in him. "You have got the Novgorod Bede—or the Israelis have?"

"No."

The question dried up in Mosby's mouth.

"Klaverinsky apparently went for a swim, and never came back," said Audley. "His rooms were ransacked— Billy Bullitt checked with an Israeli air force general he knows, who checked with the police. Nothing was stolen. Except what they didn't know was there."

That was the final pay-off: suddenly everything clicked into place in Mosby's brain, like the tumblers of a time-lock which no one had been able to pick until too late.

It was all a con. The KGB hadn't been planning any action against the USAF in Britain. That had just been the come-on to get them stirred up. The thing had been planned against the CIA itself from the start—the ultimate dirty trick. And everything they'd done had only helped to make it dirtier—and deadlier.

Operation Bear had already been completed.

"So there's no evidence?" said Shirley.

"No evidence at all," agreed Audley.

"Then it's just Billy Bullitt's word against the CIA's?" Her voice started strongly, but the confidence began to fade from it as she spoke.

"That's right, honey," said Mosby. "Just the word of a man who'll be believed—and who's telling the whole goddamn truth—against a bunch of people who'll never be believed in a million years. And no proof."

"What d'you mean, he's telling the truth?"

"Telling the truth—telling the truth, that's what I mean. Bullitt is telling the truth: every damn thing that's been fed to him he's telling truthfully. And there's nothing on earth we can do to prove otherwise. In fact every bit of circumstantial evidence—every death, every *fact*—says we've got to be lying in our teeth."

"My God!" said Audley in an appalled voice. *"My God!"*

"What's the matter, David?" said Frances Fitzgibbon.

Audley stared at Mosby. "You are the CIA, aren't you?"

"What the hell did you think we were?"

"Mose!" Shirley cried. "Are you crazy?"

"Crazy? I'm not crazy—I've become sane, honey. We've been suckered—led right up the garden. *Framed*." He swung back towards Audley. "Who the hell did you think we were? You never bought that cock-eyed story I told you this afternoon? Not in a pig's eye!"

Audley blinked at him, every bit as embarrassed as Shirley had been earlier. "I have to admit it, Captain Sheldon. Until nearly midday today I thought you were just a dentist interested in Arthurian history. I didn't know anything else —I've been on leave for four months."

"And after you'd talked to your boss?"

Audley shrugged helplessly. "Maybe CIA . . . but maybe KGB."

"What?" Mosby felt an insane urge to laugh. "How could I be KGB?"

"We knew they were sniffing around—one of their better-known London men met Airman Pennebaker in London on Saturday. Only we didn't know where Pennebaker came from until his body turned up two days ago."

"And then you thought we'd killed him? Oh, brother! I'll bet you just thought that—another home run for the CIA! And he was the guy that knocked out Davies, too. Man! They really fed it to you, just like they fed it to us . . . so you thought my function was to make sure the British got in on the act, whether they liked it or not. So you'd get tarred with the same brush—wasn't that the phrase?"

"What's that?" Shirley said cautiously.

"The British just don't want to be involved, honey," said Mosby. "If the CIA is playing dirty tricks and cover-ups in

Britain, and the M15 was thought to be helping them—that really would be curtains for them too, as well as us. Once their Parliamentary left-wing got hold of that, it'd be Watergate for them too. And even the Conservatives would never forgive them for helping to re-bury King Arthur into the bargain."

"Why the blazes didn't you tell us what you were doing?" said Roskill suddenly.

"Why the blazes didn't *you* tell *us*?" said Mosby.

"Because we weren't doing anything, for heaven's sakes. We were just trying to find out what was going on."

"And so were we. I tell you—we've both been suckered. It was all laid on before we knew what was happening. They just had one or two witnesses to remove after they'd played their part—like the poor old man Barkham. So now we can never disprove anything."

"And our two men," said Frances harshly. "The cold-blooded bastards."

Mosby swallowed. "Yeah, I guess them too."

"Plus one of their own people. And Asher Klaverinsky," said Roskill. "No one can say they're not thorough bastards."

"I have my doubts about Klaverinsky now. I rather think he may have lived to fight another day. We only have Major Davies's word for what he had to say, and we can hardly rely on that."

"And . . . that?" Frances Fitzgibbon pointed to the sheet of paper Mosby still clutched.

"The Novgorod Bede?" Audley shook his head. "I don't think we're ever going to know the truth about that now—whether it really did contain those extra words, or whether some clever devil thought the whole thing up. They just can't afford to tell us, so it will have to stay stolen."

"Probably never left Comrade Panin's bookshelf," said Mosby.

"Panin?" Audley frowned at him. "You don't mean Nikolai Andrievich Panin?"

"That's the comrade. D'you know him?"

"Panin!" Audley closed his eyes and struck his forehead. "Of course I know him—Panin . . . Well, there's our clever devil, anyway. An archaeologist and a historian—this would be right up his street . . . How long have you known he was in on it?"

"We had word months ago he was dreaming up something against us. That's why we've been watching out for trouble."

"I see . . ." Audley seemed almost relieved. "And of course he calculated you would—yes, of course he would. It's exactly the way he works: starting something, and then letting the other side do all the work for him. And we did it for him."

"We?" said Shirley sharply. "You mean you're still on our side?" She looked at Frances. "I thought we were the foreigners?"

"Oh, you are, Mrs Sheldon." Audley smiled lopsidedly. "But we still need you to defend us—in your own interest, maybe, but we still need you. And so does Western Europe, however badly it may treat you. We need each other, and so long as we do there isn't really a 'your' side and a 'my' side, but only an 'our' side—not when it comes to standing up to Soviet Russia. Not so long as people like me remember Hungary and Czechoslovakia, anyway. Or Warsaw in 1944."

For a moment Shirley seemed tongue-tied. Then she shook her head. "Well, what are you going to do about it?"

"I'm very much afraid that there isn't much we can do now—except tell your version and hope someone will believe you."

"But that isn't going to be good enough, you think?"

"I'm pretty certain it won't be."

Mosby frowned. "But Sir Frederick said 'your way was the only way left'. What way was that?"

"I was going to expose you to Billy Bullitt as a possible KGB agent. I was going to pull your story to pieces—right from the unbelievable coincidence of meeting me on that beach. That's why I took the trouble to tell you so much—

I didn't want you to be able to show too much surprise at anything, I wanted you to know too much, just in case you were innocent."

"And what did you hope to achieve by that?"

"Just enough doubt in his mind to delay him releasing the story. I wasn't trying for an acquittal, just a stay of execution."

"You mean you were playing for time?" said Shirley.

"That's right. Time to dig a lot deeper."

"So you can still play for time, you can still dig—we'll help you. We'll play KGB agents for you, and the UK station will do whatever you want."

Audley shook his head. "But I don't want to dig any-more, Mrs Sheldon. I'm afraid of what I'll find, frankly."

Mosby thought again of St Swithun's churchyard.

"What do you mean—afraid?" said Shirley.

"I mean we don't even know that we've found all of Panin's traps yet. Knowing him, I think it's possible there are a lot more of them still, and they may be designed to catch us—us meaning the British." He gazed at Shirley sadly. "Because, you see, we're not quite caught yet. You are—the CIA is—but we can still survive by throwing you to the wolves. And the fact that we haven't done so yet is the greatest proof I can give you that blood is still thicker than water."

"But—it wouldn't be true."

"Truth is what we can prove—and in this case what we dare to try and prove. But as it is you don't even have to be proved guilty—you just have to be thought guilty, and that'll be enough."

Shirley looked at Mosby. "There has to be another way —there has to be a weakness in their operation."

"There is," said Frances Fitzgibbon. "There's still one weakness left."

"What is it?" said Shirley.

"Billy Bullitt."

They stared at her.

"Why is he a weakness?" said Mosby.

"Because he can still change his mind. He can still withdraw the article—and everything they've done hinges on that. If he says 'publish' they've got everything. But if he says 'don't publish' they've got nothing."

Shirley looked around her. "Why, then you've got to make him change his mind."

"Do you think we haven't tried?" said Roskill. "Do you think we haven't begged him—just to hold off for a week? Sir Frederick practically went down on his knees. And all the old blighter said was he was sorry to see that MI5 was working hand in glove with the CIA, against the national interest."

"But it isn't against the national interest. Why—David said—"

"That's just David," said Frances. "Billy Bullitt says he understands if the Americans were thrown out of Britain things would be rough."

"More than rough, by God!"

"And more than rough," the little face lifted. "But he says it could be the making of us, having to stand on our own feet. Even being forced to lead Western Europe, which he thinks we can. He says we've been alone before —and not just in 1940. He says we were alone long before that, when the Romans left us to the Anglo-Saxons in King Arthur's time. And then we damn nearly won—we would have won if we hadn't thrown away Badon Hill."

Gildas.

And more than Gildas—Arthur himself. Both lined up in an obstinate old fighter's imagination against giving in to reason.

Bullitt would never believe them, no matter what evidence they brought him, because he didn't want to believe them. It was a question of forcing his countrymen to regain their honour by standing alone, as they had once stood, in the hope that this time they wouldn't fail.

Not Gildas. Just Arthur.

Rex quondam rexque futurus—that wasn't a dream to Billy Bullitt, it was a promise.

"How is he a weakness, then?" Mosby couldn't keep the despair out of his voice. "He'll never give in—not even if we threatened to kill him if he didn't."

"But the Russians can't be sure of that," said Frances. "They're reckoning on it, but they can't be sure."

"Well, they'd be better off if he was dead, then," said Mosby. "That way, with how he's got it fixed, nothing could stop the story breaking—'fact, it's a wonder they haven't knocked him off already."

"Perhaps they don't know he's given the story to the Press," said Shirley.

"Oh, they know all right." Audley shook his head as he spoke. "Our information is that Fleet Street is already buzzing with the big scandal one of the Sundays has got itself. They even know it has something to do with archaeology."

"How's that?"

"Because the word is that the fee is going to Rescue—£20,000 the rumour is. Which with Fleet Street the way it is, is big money. So—big scandal . . . Oh, they know sure enough."

"Does he realise he's in danger?"

Audley smiled grimly. "Of course he does. He doesn't underrate the ability of the CIA to trace Major Davies back to him—I told you, he was just waiting for you to turn up on his doorstep. That's why he made his mini-statement to us: he wanted to get the record straight before it happened."

"Before—" Mosby frowned, "—before what happened?"

"Before he gave you the opportunity to complete your wicked crime. Part of the deal he's made with the newspaper is that he gives them a filmed interview they can sell to television—a joint BBC-ITV offer, they have to make. They've filmed him in his library already and he's taping a commentary for the location shots at this very moment."

"Location shots?"

"That's right. At 10.00 a.m. tomorrow morning Billy Bullitt will be striding up Liddington Hill in Wiltshire—in his famous red shirt and combat hat—to tell the world where he thought King Arthur's greatest battle was fought, and why. And why he now knows he was wrong. And at 3.00 p.m.—supposing he's still alive—he'll stride up to Windmill Knob, or as near as your barbed wire will let him—"

"You're joking!"

"I wish to God I was, but I'm not. And what's more he doesn't want us around under any circumstances. Protection here he'll accept, but no protection tomorrow morning at Liddington Hill."

"But it'll be—suicidal. That'll be open country there."

"True. But then he has a strong sense of the dramatic, and people have been shooting at him off and on for the last thirty-six years without hitting him."

"Not these sort of people. Doesn't he realise that?"

"Actually, he does. He pretends he doesn't, but I do believe he thinks tomorrow is the day."

"Then he's absolutely insane. He doesn't even need to do it—he doesn't have to prove anything."

Audley was silent for a moment. "Now there . . . I think you're wrong. Prove something is exactly what he needs to do. He knows that if he is killed that really will prove his case—particularly if they get his death on film. But I don't think even that is the deciding factor with him, not now. It's much more a matter of honour . . . he's going to prove honour is worth dying for. This is his version of the old Ordeal by Battle, the great Arthurian ideal."

"Insane," echoed Shirley. "It's insane."

"Of course it is. Honour doesn't make anything true—it's a mere convention. One of the very best Arthurian tales is about a knight who came to realise that—not Sir Lancelot or Sir Galahad, but a *bad* knight named Sir Aglovale, who learnt the hard way. But Billy Bullitt is so steeped in conventional Arthurian morality that Ordeal by Battle comes quite naturally to him."

"I just don't understand you," said Shirley. "You're talking double-dutch."

"No, Mrs Sheldon, you wouldn't understand. Because

it's one of the better sides of women that they respect life more than men do . . . But let me put it this way: you remember what the New Testament says— 'All they that take the sword shall perish with the sword'. Now does that sound like a threat to you?"

"Of course. If you kill you must expect to be killed."

"Exactly. But to a chivalrous knight it wasn't a threat at all—it was a marvellous promise. In fact, it was the one thing that made Christianity worth having: no horrible toothless old age, no long-drawn-out agony in a smelly bed—just a good, clean death in the prime of life, and then straight to Heaven, or Valhalla, or wherever.

"Which is exactly the way Bullitt sees it now. He knows he's had the best of his life—there's even a possibility it's running out on him, because it's rumoured he saw a heart specialist last year sometime, though we don't yet know which one. But in any case he appears to be ready to collect on that promise, so the risk simply doesn't worry him. If anything it makes the whole business more attractive: it's as though he's challenging us—his life to prove his case. And that makes it a matter of honour."

Roskill heaved a sigh. "And that's why we're beaten."

Mosby stared at the great coat-of-arms, with its fiery dragon supporters. He wondered whether there had ever been a Sheldon coat-of-arms. It was a pity William Lancelot Bullitt couldn't wear full armour on Liddington—

The Sheldon coat-of-arms?

Everybody had a coat-of-arms if you went back far enough.

"No."

"What d'you mean 'no'?" said Roskill.

"I meant—" Mosby swung towards Audley, "—screw Billy Bullitt's honour. What about *my* honour?"

"Your honour?"

"Sure. My honour—and the honour of the CIA."

"The honour of the CIA?" Frances Fitzgibbon laughed.

Mosby looked at them. "Sure. Do you have to be British to have honour? Is it something lesser mortals can't have?"

"But—"

"Hush!" said Audley. "Go on, Captain Sheldon."

"Okay. You said it was a straight challenge. He thinks we're a bunch of assassins and murderers. Okay—then I accept the challenge. I say we're not."

"But how do you accept it?" said Frances. "Do you want to fight him?"

"No. I accept it the way he accepted it. And if he's a man of honour then he can't refuse me first go."

"First go at what?"

"At Liddington Hill. I'll wear the red shirt—I'll wear the combat hat. And I'll prove the truth." Mosby pointed at Audley. "And you catch the guy that pulls the trigger."

"Mose—"

"Shut up, honey. I'm challenging Billy Bullitt to his Ordeal by Battle. And he can't refuse me."

"What d'you mean—he can't refuse you? Why not?"

"Because that's the way the game is played. And once I accept his way of playing it then I take precedence over him because it's my honour that's at stake more than his. So if David's right about the way he thinks he has no choice in the matter."

Shirley stared at him unbelievingly. "But Mose—if David's also right about the KGB—" She stopped.

"Then you get shot." Frances Fitzgibbon had no scruples about completing the sentence. "And if Bullitt's right about the CIA you also get shot."

"But he isn't right. So then David can scoop up their hit man—in that open country it shouldn't be too difficult." Mosby nodded at Audley. "He was probably fixing to try that anyway, and I can make it nice and easy for him by being just where he wants me to be. And then Billy Bullitt can see for himself who's really gunning for him, which is going to make him think twice about blowing the whistle on us."

"But you'll still be shot," Frances was frowning now, as perplexed as Shirley.

Mosby continued to look at Audley. "Well—do I get my challenge delivered or not?"

For a moment Audley said nothing. Then he nodded slowly. "You realise that he won't be bluffed? That he'll take you at your face value?"

"Of course. It won't work any other way."

Again Audley was silent for a second or two. "And you realise I can't guarantee to cover you? If I keep my men away from the hill so as not to scare them off they'll be bound to get a clear shot—you realise that?"

"Sure." Mosby nodded. "I'm counting on it."

"Very well. You've got yourself a deal, Captain Sheldon." Audley's voice was almost non-committal, but he watched Mosby shrewdly. "What else do you want?"

"He wants his head examining," said Shirley sharply. She squared up to Mosby. "Mosby Sheldon, have you gone entirely out of your mind? What in hell's name are you playing at?"

It was nice to be noticed at last, thought Mosby—even when being noticed didn't matter any more.

"I'm not playing, honey. Or maybe I am at that: it's an old Arthurian game, carrying someone else's shield in to battle. Malory's full of knights doing that in good causes, on the level."

She shook her head helplessly. "Mosby—you can't. You just can't." She put her hand on his arm.

"I can." He smiled at her happily. "Don't fret, honey. Good knights aren't allowed to get killed in good causes. The book says so. Leastways, not if they remember to put on their magic armour."

– XIII –

BUT OF COURSE they did get killed, Mosby thought for the hundredth time as he opened the car door. Good causes, bad causes, they were all the same to bullets.

And Bullitts?

That was one symptom: irritatingly inconsequential thoughts and an even more annoying inability to concentrate on those important matters which still concerned him.

Not that there were many of them now—that was another of the mental symptoms. What had once seemed important was now no longer important. Or perhaps just in abeyance. What was still in the future mattered little when the future was a matter of very considerable doubt.

Matters, mattered, matter. All ugly words.

"Are you all right?" asked the camera man.

If he was a camera man. He certainly had a camera, so that made him a camera man whether he was or not. Making a movie entitled *Le Morte de Mosby.*

They that take the sword . . . Except that wasn't strictly correct. They that take the Mothers' Union banner, that was correct.

"Sure. It's just this goddamn bullet-proof vest. I just can't bend so good."

The best vest money could buy, as recommended by the British Army in Northern Ireland. And not really a patrol vest, either, but a custom-built job for look-outs in exposed positions favoured by IRA snipers. The last word in safety first, but with disadvantages, the man said—

"It's made for a direct hit. Anything short of an anti-tank shell, and you've got a chance—a very good chance. Though we can never be sure, naturally—"

Great!

"And, of course, we're only protecting your chest plus the upper abdomen. We could do more, but you'd hardly be able to move, and I gather you've got to do some walking."

Mosby looked up the hillside. Walking was right.

"What you've got to pray for is a professional—a natural marksman who's prepared to take that extra second if he needs to. Sometimes the amateurs try for the head-shot. Or they squeeze off in a panic and miss altogether—"

Can a miss altogether be bad?

"Which can be very serious with some of these very high velocity weapons. Tear your bloody arm off without even hitting you, they can. Just a near miss is enough."

Yes, a miss altogether can be bad.

"But you'll probably have a professional—"

Trying to cheer me up now.

"—so my advice to you is move nice and slowly. Let him hit you where he's been taught to hit you. Then you'll just have a sore chest next morning, take my word for it."

What—no dissatisfied clients? Obviously not.

As he stepped out on to the side of the road Mosby realised that nice and slowly was the only way he was going to be able to move. Under his red shirt the bullet-proof vest weighed a ton, or seemed to, and he was already sweating . . . Though maybe that was just good honest fear.

But Billy Bullitt was no youngster, so that didn't matter too much. With his combat hat pulled well down and his tinted glasses—and the target shirt—he would do well enough at a distance.

He was already used to the two physical symptoms he had noticed, the dry mouth and the tightness of his calf muscles. He had experienced them from the moment of getting up. The cup of hot tea had hardly moistened his mouth and the exercise of behaving normally, of walking to the bathroom and then down to breakfast as though it was any other morning of his life, hadn't eased the muscles.

Nothing wrong with his stomach, though. It was true that condemned men could eat a hearty breakfast, going to their deaths with a bacon-and-egg cliché inside them.

It was Shirley who hadn't eaten.

Strange that Shirley didn't matter any more either. Or perhaps it was simply the recognition that he didn't matter to Shirley.

But that wasn't quite true any more, to be honest—and honesty was one of the real luxuries still left.

"Come to bed, honey."

No doubt about the invitation, the first ever of its kind: big soft Camelot bed and little soft Shirley, both inviting him to enjoy the present and forget the future.

"Just got to clean my teeth, that's all."

Shirley fulfilling—ready to fulfil—the ancient night-before-the-battle-rôle, so that even if the good guys lost there'd be another generation of good guys to take up the quarrel in the future.

Future was another ugly word.

This would be the first time, and there always had to be a first time for everything. Even dying. Mark up another cliché.

And that made this first time unlucky, as though nothing would more surely ready him for death than the taking of this opportunity which the possibility of death was giving him.

"I think I'd better get all the sleep I can."

The gentlest way he could think of saying it.

"You don't have to, Mose."

Logical answer. He didn't have to do anything difficult next morning, just walk a little way up a hill, nice and slow. And either way, he could have all the sleep he wanted after that.

"I know. And the thought is very much appreciated. Is there any chance of being given a rain-check?"

She smiled at that: Mosby Sheldon III running true to form to the last.

"Of course. One rain-check issued."

"I won't forget—I warn you."

"Neither will I."

But now he was already forgetting the softness and the perfume. They were part of the past and the future. Now there was only the present, and the hill in front of him, rising up steeply.

Foot by foot he went up. The camera man was trudging on his left and the two other men a couple of yards to his right. Not a very big crew, three.

The turf under his feet was soft and springy now. Further back it had been trampled by cows and was sprinkled with big, round crusted pats of dung. There were flowers growing in it, yellow buttercups and white ox-eye daisies. He reached down and picked a daisy for luck, realising as he did so that he had moved too quickly. For an instant his back tingled with fear.

And there were birds sweeping over the hillside, skimming and diving like fighter-planes searching for targets over a battlefield. Major Davies would have known what sort of birds they were—or would he?

Davies was the odd man out who had been bugging him. Even in the middle of the night, when he had woken up to find Shirley breathing softly beside him, the unsettled question of Davies had come between them, like a ghost.

They had checked out Davies so thoroughly before he had flown to Israel, and he had been clean. And they had checked him out thoroughly after his death, and but for that one letter from old James Barkham, the bookseller, he had been clean again. Indeed, if that letter hadn't popped through the letterbox slit, then the thing would never have been started. Without that there had been nothing left to connect Major Davies, the bird-watcher, with Major Davies, the expert on Arthurian history, the Badon-hunter.

So it had been deliberate . . . He heard a car on the road below him, and turned slowly and deliberately to face it.

Distance; a little over three hundred yards maybe.

He closed his eyes behind the tinted glasses and waited.

The car began to decelerate, presumably as it came towards where they had parked their vehicle half on the grass verge. Then he heard it accelerate.

Nothing.

He opened his eyes. Already the countryside was flattening out beneath him, with the chequer-board of tiny English fields becoming visible and the sweep of the new freeway which cut through them less than a mile from where he stood.

Somewhere out there, carefully hidden, was all the paraphernalia of David Audley's department, men, cars, helicopters—all waiting for the camera man's first assistant to fire his flare gun. Perhaps even the men loading the bales of straw in the newly-cut wheatfield away to his left . . . and for sure those repairmen blocking one of the freeway lanes so conveniently.

He turned back to the hillside. So the planting of that letter had to be part of the KGB's trap, the first clue designed to direct their attention first to Davies, then to Billy Bullitt. Nothing too easy, nothing too obvious . . . They had to work their way to disaster by their own efforts.

He could hear another car. So let this one be in the back —that would be more appropriate, anyway.

He stared down at the daisy in his hand. How had they been so sure that the Americans wouldn't catch up with Davies? And more, how had they managed to place Davies in the exact spot where he had been needed, to feed Billy

Bullitt with the great lies so very carefully constructed that it took this walk in the sun to cast doubt on them?

The second car had passed as peacefully as the first.

"I think we could get some shots here," said the camera man.

"Okay," said Mosby.

"Fine. Well, the original script is for you to point up towards the hill-fort on the top. Then down towards the Ridgeway, where the road is . . . and across over the line of the railway—over there on the far left—which is towards the line of the Roman road from the south-west."

Billy Bullitt's original script. This had been where he had thought it must have happened, at this vital strategic crossroads of Dark Age Britain, where the ancient down-land trackway from the north-east crossed the Roman roads from the east and the south.

Mosby looked up obediently towards the line of the ramparts on the hilltop.

You are assigned to locate the map reference of Badon Hill, England. Just that.

Well, this was as close as he'd ever get to fulfilling that assignment, because with Wodden out of the running they were never going to know for sure if this was the place. The old arguments would go on and on, and round and round, as they'd always done.

They wouldn't even know who had besieged who— whether there'd been Saxon horse-tail standards waving up there or the banner of Our Lady. Whether the Saxons had been trapped and starved into the open to be caught by one great scything charge of Arthur's fabled horsemen, or whether the Britons had been trapped and saved at the last by an epic Arthurian ride-to-the-rescue.

They'd never know, and it didn't matter a damn because that was how it ought to be: a matter of faith, not fact. Because the enduring value of Arthur existed not in the elusive truth of his historical victory and defeat, but in the vision each generation had of him. Even in Billy Bullitt's crazy vision.

For the first time Mosby was utterly sure of himself. This was the place, not Wodden. And this was where they would come for him.

He wondered, strangely without rancour, whether Schreiner and Morris had envisaged anything remotely like this—whether the strict assignment to hunt Badon Hill, and not the agents of the *Komitet Gosudarstvennoi Bezopasnosti* as he had been trained to do, had been carefully calculated to achieve the same result.

But that was another thing which was no longer important.

"That's great," said the photographer. "Now look back the way you've come. Admire the view."

Mosby turned to the huge open landscape.

This was the place. But not the place which fitted in with the KGB's plans, so they had invented a whole new piece of history—

. . . usque ad annum obsessionis Badonici montis qui prope Sord'num hostium ex Durnovaria Arturo habetur . . .

—which enabled them to work at their leisure on their false Badon, free from the worry that anyone might disturb them.

"Now look down towards the road," commanded the photographer.

Mosby didn't want to look down. The horizon was so close he could almost reach out and touch it, as though it was a painting. A bird swooped past him, banking away at the last moment.

Davies the bird-watcher.

Davies the Arthur-hunter, the Badon-hunter.

The sun came out from behind a big, fleecy cloud, blinding him even through his dark glasses.

The only person we can trace he ever spoke to was the bookseller.

That was Merriwether.

He insisted I should never contact him at the base.

Billy Bullitt's statement.

But there was something else in the back of his mind—something the Englishman Roskill had said, but about Mosby himself.

It made us wonder whether you were who you said you were.

Simple.

Liddington Hill—the real Badon?

Wodden—the false Badon.

Davies—the bird-watcher.

Davies—the Badon-hunter.

Just as there had been a false Badon, so there had been a false Davies. Any loner among the pilots would have done. Davies just happened to fit best. But so long as there was a general resemblance it didn't matter, because there weren't going to be any witnesses left around long enough to argue the difference. Once the real Davies was dead, the false one automatically ceased to exist, leaving only his lies behind him.

It was as gloriously simple as the sun in his face was blinding.

He never even heard the car.

EPILOGUE:

*Captain Finsterwald
and
AIC Merriwether*

CAPTAIN FINSTERWALD WALKED across the tarmac to where Airman First Class Merriwether stood watching the heavily-laden transport preparing for take-off.

Merriwether sketched a salute. "Everything okay, Harry?"

"It'll do. They'll never love us again, but they don't hate us any more."

"And those two Russians they picked up?"

"What Russians?" Finsterwald shaded his eyes.

The transport's engines roared.

"That Sheldon's a lucky son-of-a-bitch," shouted Finsterwald.

"Because he's going home and we're still here?" Merriweather shouted back. "Don't fret, man. We're going to be on one of those big birds ourselves pretty soon. I got the feeling we are now surplus to Air Force requirements . . . If not pos-it-ively unwanted."

"That's not what I meant."

"No? Well, you can't mean his state of health, with

233

those ribs cracked like he's been kicked by a Georgia mule."

The transport jerked forward.

"I was thinking of that woman of his."

"Uh-huh? Well, he's not going to enjoy any of that, the way he's strapped up . . . not for a while anyway." Merriwether watched the transport with a professional eye. "That guy's going to need a lot of runway, the way he's taking his time."

Finsterwald showed no sign of having heard the last sentence. "The way she was fussing him, I wouldn't bet on that," he said, finally.

Merriwether considered the proposition. "Could be you're right at that . . . Funny thing, though . . ."

"What?" Finsterwald cupped his ear.

"Nothing really. But he always used to look at her like he was a dog hoping to get scratched behind his ears, and she never took one damn bit of notice of him."

The roar of the engines was fading.

"So what?"

"So when I saw them just now it was right the other way round, that's all."

Finsterwald shook his head. "So he's learnt to play it cool. I never said he wasn't a smart son-of-a-bitch as well as a lucky one." He turned back towards the car.

Merriwether watched the transport eat up the last yards of old runway and lift into the air, up and out over the site of Windmill Knob towards distant America.

MORE MYSTERIOUS PLEASURES

HAROLD ADAMS
MURDER
Carl Wilcox debuts in a story of triple murder which exposes the underbelly of corruption in the town of Corden, shattering the respectability of its most dignified citizens.   #501 $3.50

THE NAKED LIAR
When a sexy young widow is framed for the murder of her husband, Carl Wilcox comes through to help her fight off cops and big-city goons.
                                                                                                #420 $3.95

THE FOURTH WIDOW
Ex-con/private eye Carl Wilcox is back, investigating the death of a "popular" widow in the Depression-era town of Corden, S.D.
                                                                                                #502 $3.50

EARL DERR BIGGERS
THE HOUSE WITHOUT A KEY
Charlie Chan debuts in the Honolulu investigation of an expatriate Bostonian's murder.   #421 $3.95

THE CHINESE PARROT
Charlie Chan works to find the key to murders seemingly without victims—but which have left a multitude of clues.   #503 $3.95

BEHIND THAT CURTAIN
Two murders sixteen years apart, one in London, one in San Francisco, each share a major clue in a pair of velvet Chinese slippers. Chan seeks the connection.   #504 $3.95

THE BLACK CAMEL
When movie goddess Sheila Fane is murdered in her Hawaiian pavilion, Chan discovers an interrelated crime in a murky Hollywood mystery from the past.   #505 $3.95

CHARLIE CHAN CARRIES ON
An elusive transcontinental killer dogs the heels of the Lofton Round the World Cruise. When the touring party reaches Honolulu, the murderer finally meets his match.   #506 $3.95

JAMES M. CAIN
THE ENCHANTED ISLE
A beautiful runaway is involved in a deadly bank robbery in this posthumously published novel.   #415 $3.95

CLOUD NINE
Two brothers—one good, one evil—battle over a million-dollar land deal and a luscious 16-year-old in this posthumously published novel.
#507 $3.95

ROBERT CAMPBELL
IN LA-LA LAND WE TRUST
Child porn, snuff films, and drunken TV stars in fast cars—that's what makes the L.A. world go 'round. Whistler, a luckless P.I., finds that it's not good to know too much about the porn trade in the City of Angels.
#508 $3.95

GEORGE C. CHESBRO
VEIL
Clairvoyant artist Veil Kendry volunteers to be tested at the Institute for Human Studies and finds that his life is in deadly peril; is he threatened by the Institute, the Army, or the CIA?   #509 $3.95

WILLIAM L. DeANDREA
THE LUNATIC FRINGE
Police Commissioner Teddy Roosevelt and Officer Dennis Muldoon comb 1896 New York for a missing exotic dancer who holds the key to the murder of a prominent political cartoonist.   #306 $3.95.

SNARK
Espionage agent Bellman must locate the missing director of British Intelligence—and elude a master terrorist who has sworn to kill him.
#510 $3.50

KILLED IN THE ACT
Brash, witty Matt Cobb, TV network troubleshooter, must contend with bizarre crimes connected with a TV spectacular—one of which is a murder committed before 40 million witnesses.   #511 $3.50

KILLED WITH A PASSION
In seeking to clear an old college friend of murder, Matt Cobb must deal with the Mad Karate Killer and the Organic Hit Man, among other eccentric criminals.   #512 $3.50

KILLED ON THE ICE
When a famous psychiatrist is stabbed in a Manhattan skating rink, Matt Cobb finds it necessary to protect a beautiful Olympic skater who appears to be the next victim.   #513 $3.50

JAMES ELLROY
SUICIDE HILL
Brilliant L.A. Police sergeant Lloyd Hopkins teams up with the FBI to solve a series of inside bank robberies—but is he working with or against them?   #514 $3.95

PAUL ENGLEMAN
CATCH A FALLEN ANGEL
Private eye Mark Renzler becomes involved in publishing mayhem and murder when two slick mens' magazines battle for control of the lucrative market.   #515 $3.50

LOREN D. ESTLEMAN
ROSES ARE DEAD
Someone's put a contract out on freelance hit man Peter Macklin. Is he as good as the killers on his trail?   #516 $3.95

ANY MAN'S DEATH
Hit man Peter Macklin is engaged to keep a famous television evangelist *alive*—quite a switch from his normal line.   #517 $3.95

DICK FRANCIS
THE SPORT OF QUEENS
The autobiography of the celebrated race jockey/crime novelist.
                                                                  #410 $3.95

JOHN GARDNER
THE GARDEN OF WEAPONS
Big Herbie Kruger returns to East Berlin to uncover a double agent. He confronts his own past and life's only certainty—death.
                                                                  #103 $4.50

BRIAN GARFIELD
DEATH WISH
Paul Benjamin is a modern-day New York vigilante, stalking the rapist-killers who victimized his wife and daughter. The basis for the Charles Bronson movie.   #301 $3.95

DEATH SENTENCE
A riveting sequel to *Death Wish*. The action moves to Chicago as Paul Benjamin continues his heroic (or is it psychotic?) mission to make city streets safe.   #302 $3.95

TRIPWIRE
A crime novel set in the American West of the late 1800s. Boag, a black outlaw, seeks revenge on the white cohorts who left him for dead. "One of the most compelling characters in recent fiction."—Robert Ludlum.   #303 $3.95

FEAR IN A HANDFUL OF DUST
Four psychiatrists, three men and a woman, struggle across the blazing Arizona desert—pursued by a fanatic killer they themselves have judged insane. "Unique and disturbing."—Alfred Coppel.   #304 $3.95

JOE GORES
A TIME OF PREDATORS
When Paula Halstead kills herself after witnessing a horrid crime, her husband vows to avenge her death. Winner of the Edgar Allan Poe Award. #215 $3.95

COME MORNING
Two million in diamonds are at stake, and the ex-con who knows their whereabouts may have trouble staying alive if he turns them up at the wrong moment. #518 $3.95

NAT HENTOFF
BLUES FOR CHARLIE DARWIN
Gritty, colorful Greenwich Village sets the scene for Noah Green and Sam McKibbon, two street-wise New York cops who are as at home in jazz clubs as they are at a homicide scene. #208 $3.95

THE MAN FROM INTERNAL AFFAIRS
Detective Noah Green wants to know who's stuffing corpses into East Village garbage cans . . . and who's lying about him to the Internal Affairs Division. #409 $3.95

PATRICIA HIGHSMITH
THE BLUNDERER
An unhappy husband attempts to kill his wife by applying the murderous methods of another man. When things go wrong, he pays a visit to the more successful killer—a dreadful error. #305 $3.95

DOUG HORNIG
THE DARK SIDE
Insurance detective Loren Swift is called to a rural commune to investigate a carbon-monoxide murder. Are the commune inhabitants as gentle as they seem? #519 $3.95

P.D. JAMES/T.A. CRITCHLEY
THE MAUL AND THE PEAR TREE
The noted mystery novelist teams up with a police historian to create a fascinating factual account of the 1811 Ratcliffe Highway murders. #520 $3.95

STUART KAMINSKY'S "TOBY PETERS" SERIES
NEVER CROSS A VAMPIRE
When Bela Lugosi receives a dead bat in the mail, Toby tries to catch the prankster. But Toby's time is at a premium because he's also trying to clear William Faulkner of a murder charge! #107 $3.95

HIGH MIDNIGHT
When Gary Cooper and Ernest Hemingway come to Toby for protection, he tries to save them from vicious blackmailers.   #106 $3.95

HE DONE HER WRONG
Someone has stolen Mae West's autobiography, and when she asks Toby to come up and see her sometime, he doesn't know how deadly a visit it could be.   #105 $3.95

BULLET FOR A STAR
Warner Brothers hires Toby Peters to clear the name of Errol Flynn, a blackmail victim with a penchant for young girls. The first novel in the acclaimed Hollywood-based private eye series.   #308 $3.95

THE FALA FACTOR
Toby comes to the rescue of lady-in-distress Eleanor Roosevelt, and must match wits with a right-wing fanatic who is scheming to overthrow the U.S. Government.   #309 $3.95

JOSEPH KOENIG
FLOATER
Florida Everglades sheriff Buck White matches wits with a Miami murder-and-larceny team who just may have hidden his ex-wife's corpse in a remote bayou.   #521 $3.50

ELMORE LEONARD
THE HUNTED
Long out of print, this 1974 novel by the author of *Glitz* details the attempts of a man to escape killers from his past.   #401 $3.95

MR. MAJESTYK
Sometimes bad guys can push a good man too far, and when that good guy is a Special Forces veteran, everyone had better duck.   #402 $3.95

THE BIG BOUNCE
Suspense and black comedy are cleverly combined in this tale of a dangerous drifter's affair with a beautiful woman out for kicks.   #403 $3.95

ELSA LEWIN
I, ANNA
A recently divorced woman commits murder to avenge her degradation at the hands of a sleazy lothario.   #522 $3.50

THOMAS MAXWELL
KISS ME ONCE
An epic *roman noir* which explores the romantic but seamy underworld of New York during the WWII years. When the good guys are off fighting in Europe, the bad guys run amok in America.
        #523 $3.95

THE CURSE OF THE PHAROAHS
Amelia and Radcliffe Emerson head for Egypt to excavate a cursed tomb but must confront the burial ground's evil history before it claims them both.   #210 $3.95

THE SEVENTH SINNER
Murder in an ancient subterranean Roman temple sparks Jacqueline Kirby's first recorded case.   #411 $3.95

THE MURDERS OF RICHARD III
Death by archaic means haunts the costumed weekend get-together of a group of eccentric Ricardians.   #412 $3.95

ANTHONY PRICE
THE LABYRINTH MAKERS
Dr. David Audley does his job too well in his first documented case, embarrassing British Intelligence, the CIA, and the KGB in one swoop.
#404 $3.95

THE ALAMUT AMBUSH
Alamut, in Northern Persia, is considered by many to be the original home of terrorism. Audley moves to the Mideast to put the cap on an explosive threat.   #405 $3.95

COLONEL BUTLER'S WOLF
The Soviets are recruiting spies from among Oxford's best and brightest; it's up to Dr. Audley to identify the Russian wolf in don's clothing.
#527 $3.95

OCTOBER MEN
Dr. Audley's "holiday" in Rome stirs up old Intelligence feuds and echoes of partisan warfare during World War II—and leads him into new danger.   #529 $3.95

OTHER PATHS TO GLORY
What can a World War I battlefield in France have in common with a deadly secret of the present? A modern assault on Bouillet Wood leads to the answers.   #530 $3.95

SION CROSSING
What does the chairman of a new NATO-like committee have to do with the American Civil War? Audley travels to Georgia in this espionage thriller.   #406 $3.95

HERE BE MONSTERS
The assassination of an American veteran forces Dr. David Audley into a confrontation with undercover KGB agents.   #528 $3.95

BILL PRONZINI AND JOHN LUTZ
THE EYE
A lunatic watches over the residents of West 98th Street with a powerful telescope. When his "children" displease him, he is swift to mete out deadly punishment.   #408 $3.95

PATRICK RUELL
RED CHRISTMAS
Murderers and political terrorists come down the chimney during an old-fashioned Dickensian Christmas at a British country inn.

#531　$3.50

DEATH TAKES THE LOW ROAD
William Hazlitt, a universtiy administrator who moonlights as a Soviet mole, is on the run from both Russian and British agents who want him to assassinate an African general.　　　　　#532　$3.50

DELL SHANNON
CASE PENDING
In the first novel in the best-selling series, Lt. Luis Mendoza must solve a series of horrifying Los Angeles mutilation murders.　#211　$3.95

THE ACE OF SPADES
When the police find an overdosed junkie, they're ready to write off the case—until the autopsy reveals that this junkie *wasn't* a junkie.　　　　　　　　　　　　　　#212　$3.95

EXTRA KILL
In "The Temple of Mystic Truth," Mendoza discovers idol worship, pornography, murder, and the clue to the death of a Los Angeles patrolman.　　　　　　　　　　　　#213　$3.95

KNAVE OF HEARTS
Mendoza must clear the name of the L.A.P.D. when it's discovered that an innocent man has been executed and the real killer is still on the loose.　　　　　　　　　　　　#214　$3.95

DEATH OF A BUSYBODY
When the West Coast's most industrious gossip and meddler turns up dead in a freight yard, Mendoza must work without clues to find the killer of a woman who had offended nearly everyone in Los Angeles.　　　　　　　　　　#315　$3.95

DOUBLE BLUFF
Mendoza goes against the evidence to dissect what looks like an air-tight case against suspected wife-killer Francis Ingram—a man the lieutenant insists is too nice to be a murderer.　　　　#316　$3.95

MARK OF MURDER
Mendoza investigates the near-fatal attack on an old friend as well as trying to track down an insane serial killer.　#417　$3.95

ROOT OF ALL EVIL
The murder of a "nice" girl leads Mendoza to team up with the FBI in the search for her not-so-nice boyfriend—a Soviet agent.　#418　$3.95

JULIE SMITH
TRUE-LIFE ADVENTURE
Paul McDonald earned a meager living ghosting reports for a San Francisco private eye until the gumshoe turned up dead . . . now the killers are after him.   #407 $3.95

TOURIST TRAP
A lunatic is out to destroy San Francisco's tourism industry; can feisty lawyer/sleuth Rebecca Schwartz stop him while clearing an innocent man of a murder charge?   #533 $3.95

ROSS H. SPENCER
THE MISSING BISHOP
Chicago P.I. Buzz Deckard has a missing person to find. Unfortunately his client has disappeared as well, and no one else seems to be who or what they claim.   #416 $3.50

MONASTERY NIGHTMARE
Chicago P.I. Luke Lassiter tries his hand at writing novels, and encounters murder in an abandoned monastery.   #534 $3.50

REX STOUT
UNDER THE ANDES
A long-lost 1914 fantasy novel from the creator of the immortal Nero Wolfe series. "The most exciting yarn we have read since *Tarzan of the Apes.*"—*All-Story Magazine*.   #419 $3.50

ROSS THOMAS
CAST A YELLOW SHADOW
McCorkle's wife is kidnapped by agents of the South African government. The ransom—his cohort Padillo must assassinate their prime minister.   #535 $3.95

THE SINGAPORE WINK
Ex-Hollywood stunt man Ed Cauthorne is offered $25,000 to search for colleague Angelo Sacchetti—a man he thought he'd killed in Singapore two years earlier.   #536 $3.95

THE FOOLS IN TOWN ARE ON OUR SIDE
Lucifer Dye, just resigned from a top secret U.S. Intelligence post, accepts a princely fee to undertake the corruption of an entire American city.   #537 $3.95

JIM THOMPSON
THE KILL-OFF
Luanne Devore was loathed by everyone in her small New England town. Her plots and designs threatened to destroy them—unless they destroyed her first.   #538 $3.95

DONALD E. WESTLAKE
THE HOT ROCK
The unlucky master thief John Dortmunder debuts in this spectacular caper novel. How many times do you have to steal an emerald to make sure it *stays* stolen?   #539 $3.95

BANK SHOT
Dortmunder and company return. A bank is temporarily housed in a trailer, so why not just hook it up and make off with the whole shebang? Too bad nothing is ever that simple.   #540 $3.95

THE BUSY BODY
Aloysius Engel is a gangster, the Big Man's right hand. So when he's ordered to dig a suit loaded with drugs out of a fresh grave, how come the corpse it's wrapped around won't lie still?   #541 $3.95

THE SPY IN THE OINTMENT
Pacifist agitator J. Eugene Raxford is mistakenly listed as a terrorist by the FBI, which leads to his enforced recruitment to a group bent on world domination. Will very good Good triumph over absolutely villainous Evil?   #542 $3.95

GOD SAVE THE MARK
Fred Fitch is the sucker's sucker—con men line up to bilk him. But when he inherits $300,000 from a murdered uncle, he finds it necessary to dodge killers as well as hustlers.   #543 $3.95

TERI WHITE
TIGHTROPE
This second novel featuring L.A. cops Blue Maguire and Spaceman Kowalski takes them into the nooks and crannies of the city's Little Saigon.   #544 $3.95

COLLIN WILCOX
VICTIMS
Lt. Frank Hastings investigates the murder of a police colleague in the home of a powerful—and nasty—San Francisco attorney.
                                                        #413 $3.95

NIGHT GAMES
Lt. Frank Hastings of the San Francisco Police returns to investigate the at-home death of an unfaithful husband—whose affairs have led to his murder.   #545 $3.95

DAVID WILLIAMS' "MARK TREASURE" SERIES
UNHOLY WRIT
London financier Mark Treasure helps a friend reaquire some property. He stays to unravel the mystery when a Shakespeare manuscript is discovered and foul murder done.   #112 $3.95

TREASURE BY DEGREES
Mark Treasure discovers there's nothing funny about a board game called "Funny Farms." When he becomes involved in the takeover struggle for a small university, he also finds there's nothing funny about murder.   #113 $3.95

■ ■

AVAILABLE AT YOUR BOOKSTORE OR DIRECT FROM THE PUBLISHER

Mysterious Press Mail Order
129 West 56th Street
New York, NY 10019

Please send me the MYSTERIOUS PRESS titles I have circled below:

103 105 106 107 112 113 208 209 210 211 212 213
214 215 216 217 218 219 220 301 302 303 304 305
306 308 309 315 316 401 402 403 404 405 406 407
408 409 410 411 412 413 414 415 416 417 418 419
420 421 501 502 503 504 505 506 507 508 509 510
511 512 513 514 515 516 517 518 519 520 521 522
523 524 525 526 527 528 529 530 531 532 533 534
535 536 537 538 539 540 541 542 543 544 545

I am enclosing $ _____ (please add $2.00 postage and handling for the first book, and 25¢ for each additional book). Send check or money order only—no cash or C.O.D.'s please. Allow at least 4 weeks for delivery.

NAME _____

ADDRESS _____

CITY _____ STATE _____ ZIP CODE _____
New York State residents please add appropriate sales tax.